I'm Here

a novel

by Christy Chafe

ISBN-9781791837365

Dedication

To my wonderful family for so many reasons. Adam, thank you for building me an office with a beautiful view and for being my biggest cheerleader. Jono, you are a gifted writer and I love reading every nugget you create. Sam, we've been best pals for seventeen years. I started my journey back to writing when you went to first grade, so this feels very connected to you. Abbygirl, this is dedicated to you as a long overdue birthday gift. Thanks for the push. Happy Birthday. I love you. I love each of you.

Meg
November 4, 2013

The night of her husband's funeral was not like she'd imagined, and she had imagined it more than she cared to admit. After all of the family, friends, colleagues, acquaintances, and well-meaning neighbors had finally left, and Meg was alone downstairs, she did not feel lonely, exactly. She wandered through the empty rooms, turning off lights. As usual, she paused in the front entryway by the base of the stairs before turning off the hallway chandelier. Meg had always liked standing in this particular spot in the evening, looking back into her home, so quiet and still. Pale blue walls and natural tones, peaceful beach colors that could easily get lost in the chaos of an average day, seemed highlighted in the calm of night. It was strange to see her plump, overstuffed couches, her cozy throws, her pictures on the shelves looking so…normal. Typically, she would pick up toss pillows from the floor and put them back where they belonged; she would gather stray dishes and hang sweatshirts on hooks as she headed toward bed.

But today was not an ordinary day. Her blankets had been neatly folded and every pillow was in place. Meg fought the urge to grab them all and hurl them to the ground. She sucked in a deep breath and forced herself to turn off the last table lamps. On the round table in the corner of the family room, she found one clear, plastic plate and a plastic cup, overlooked. The cup appeared to have been half-full of red wine, but someone had stuffed a crumpled napkin into it, and now it was a soggy pink mess. The cup was balanced on the plate, which was covered in cookie crumbs, the remains of a sandwich, and a fork, smeared with traces of coral lipstick. Meg reached for the dishes, then shuddered. The vignette of the partially eaten food, abandoned on her table on this particular night, left her stomach sour. She turned the light off; she could toss it all in the garbage in the morning.

Heading toward their bedroom in the back corner of the house, Meg trailed her fingers along the painted windowsills. The large windows that allowed perfect views of the lake seemed dark and bottomless. She had never once considered window coverings of any kind, always happy to enjoy the changing view. Rain on the lake was her favorite, especially when she had time to sit on the covered back porch, snuggled in a blanket, reading or watching the drops fall onto the water. In the summer, there were geese and ducks, bright sunshine reflecting off the water and glinting on the dining room windows. The sunlight caught the dust specks floating in the family room, but Meg never cared. The lake was why she and Ben had bought the lot, built the house.

She remembered standing with him next to the "For Sale" sign, knee-deep in grass and thorny brush. Ben had been staring at the water, and her own feet had been planted in a way that felt different from any other time, in any other empty lot or beautifully staged home they had explored. Meg had stood, rooted, hearing the water, seeing the trees, feeling the expanse of sky. It had been their space from the beginning. The view had been the reason for the house, and tonight she didn't want to be afraid of the windows that she had loved for so long. She hurried past, ignoring the darkness.

In the bedroom, she kicked off her new black heels (Ben had always liked high heels, she hated them) and sank onto their bed. A wave of something she couldn't name crept over her, tinged with both familiarity and guilt. She was used to Ben being gone; he traveled all the time. The two of them had a running joke about forgetting which city he would wake in on any given morning. Now Meg felt a deep ache as she glanced out the bedroom window, knowing there was no other city, no morning wake-up call.

She pulled the bedroom drapes against the night, the beautiful pale aqua velvet she had finally found at Macy's, and glanced out of habit at her cell phone charging on her nightstand. Now was the time she would check for texts or wait for the phone to ring, when Ben would call to say that he'd arrived in Chicago, New York, Atlanta, London. It wasn't the empty bed that felt unusual; she'd grown accustomed to sleeping alone, sometimes even looked forward to it, to stretching out in the king bed and using every pillow. Her friends would say, "I don't know how you do it!" when they discussed Ben's business travel that left Meg at home with the children. Meg would smile and say it was nothing, nothing at all. Really, this was the truth. Though she rarely admitted it to herself and never out loud, often she preferred it this way. She always missed Ben, but this was their routine, and aspects of it quite appealed to her.

Sometimes, Meg wanted to return the question, asking, "I don't know how *you* do it" to the women with husbands who arrived home every night for a five-thirty dinner, husbands who never traveled, or, God help them, husbands who worked from home. Meg's comfort with Ben's work was no secret to her husband, who knew that while he was dining in hotels and having meetings in conference rooms, Meg was often feeding the children pancakes for dinner, and she herself was quite content to munch on Lucky Charms in bed while flipping between HGTV and the Food Network. Nights when Ben was entertaining clients at a swanky golf course or fancy hotel, Meg might be relaxing in the bath after the kids were settled, reading late into the night, or catching up with an old friend on the phone. She could just as easily be paying bills or cleaning out the kitchen junk drawer, but this was the beauty of it; a couple of nights a week, Meg did whatever she wanted.

"It's not a glamorous life I lead, you know," he would sometimes say, smirking.

"I'm sure not," she would say. Meg didn't equate his business travel to a life of luxury (though other women did), and he, in turn, did not begrudge her the opportunity to stay home and raise their children. This balance, created by the choices they made together, was one of the qualities about their marriage that Meg most cherished.

Early on, she worried every time he boarded a plane. "Be safe," she would say. "Call me when you get to the airport, before you leave. And then when you land. And remind the pilot, you know? To fly safely." He would laugh, kiss her head, promise to have a safe trip. Early on, Meg always had a copy of the itinerary, and she knew where Ben was, where he was supposed to be, and when. If there was breaking news on television, she would drop everything to make sure a plane hadn't crashed.

It wasn't that now, years later, she cared any less about his location or his well-being; it was just that time, life, and the addition of two children had softened the edges of this particular anxiety. She no longer had room in her brain for his day-to-day travel schedule and often depended on an evening phone call from the Dallas Marriott or the Orlando Hyatt to remind her of where her husband was sleeping. There were so many other worries in the world, and Ben was always safe. Meg had subconsciously chosen to accept it as a given. Now and again, Meg realized that Ben never had to worry about her own everyday safety. He always knew where she was resting her head, and no world news alert would likely affect her well-being. Meg was home to meet the kids after school, schedule the appointments for dental cleanings, write the Boy Scouts a check for the flower sale, and attend the school conferences if Ben was away. She was always … there. It was part of their unspoken de, and sometimes Meg wondered if Ben appreciated not having to worry about the little things. Perhaps those were the moments that Meg allowed herself to worry less.

Earlier, Meg had tucked her children in bed upstairs, as she had done hundreds of nights before, but tonight was not any other night. Tonight, Ben was not landing at an airport or checking into a hotel. Tonight, she had not given one kiss from Mommy and one from Daddy. Tonight, she had not been barraged with the expected questions. "When will Daddy be home? Can we go for Mexican? Can we Face Time? What time is it where Dad is?" Tonight, she had lain with Annabelle, who at seventeen, prone to mood swings and the occasional teenage outburst, had been the perfect girl all day. She stood solidly by her mother, helping her little brother with whatever he needed, grasping his hand during the service. In her bed tonight, covered in white eyelet pillows and pale pink sheets, Annie had finally turned into Meg and clung to her like a toddler, sobbing until she exhausted herself. Meg had smoothed her daughter's long, beautiful brown hair away from her damp forehead and let her cry herself to sleep; there was nothing left to say today that had not already been said by far too many friends and family. They were both worn out by the words buzzing in their brains. When her daughter was breathing evenly, she eased herself off the bed, and closed the bedroom door only part-way, in case her daughter needed the hallway light this evening.

Across the hall, Willie was only half asleep, surrounded by his Pillow Pets and Legos.

"Are you okay, buddy?" Meg asked him, petting his soft hair.

"I guess," he said. "Do you have Fred?"

"I think he's downstairs. I'll go find him."

"And some water, Mommy, please?"

"You got it."

Fred the Panda had been a favorite since Willie was small; now, for the first time since Willie was five or six, Fred was appearing downstairs, and had even traveled as far as the funeral home and the church, where Willie had left him in the car. But even so, it was the resumption of an old habit, and not only did Meg understand, she herself was weirdly happy to see Fred. She ventured back downstairs to find the bear, noticing for the first time that someone had also tidied the kitchen after the somber gathering. The sink was empty, and the dishwasher was humming softly, Meg reached to open the cabinet for a plastic cup, and then pulled her hand back in shock. Looking down at her fingers, then looking at the cabinet, she saw that both were covered in a smear of chocolate frosting.

"Oh," she said, on her exhale, "oh."

She almost laughed, wondering how frosting could have ended up on the cabinet, and worse, how all the kind cleaning fairies could have missed it in their very thorough tidy. She washed her hands, then used the carefully folded dishtowel to dry her hands and wipe the cabinet knob. She paused for a moment, afterward—holding the towel, now covered in dark stains, suddenly unsure of what to do next. What would she have done with the towel last week? Tossed it in the laundry room? The sink? Rinsed it out?.

"It doesn't matter," Meg said aloud, dropping the towel into the sink.

She spotted the worn, soft bear on the couch where Willie had watched a little TV before bed. By the time she snuggled the panda next to Willie, he was sleeping. Meg studied her nine-year-old, grateful that he was asleep, at least for now. What was left for them to endure? Losing her, she supposed, but Meg said a silent prayer for that day to be so far in the future that both her children would be surrounded by family. She could only hope that neither would ever feel the grief of losing a spouse too early, or God forbid, a child. The only sadness more unbearable than what she was feeling, she imagined, was the grief that must accompany the loss of a child. The very thought filled her with an uncomfortable mix of sorrow and thankfulness, and she shook off the extra sadness and gently traced the dimples on Willie's cheeks. If there was something bigger in the universe that she could reach to for the strength to lead her children through whatever was yet to come, Meg was reaching now.

The house was completely quiet.

Still, lonely was not what she felt.

It was so easy to convince herself that Ben was traveling or at a late meeting, she thought, as she carefully removed her new black dress and hung it in the closet. A dress worn once, perhaps never again. What was the protocol for re-wearing the dress you wore to your husband's funeral? As she tossed her bra into the hamper and peeled off her new pantyhose and threw them directly into the garbage, she could almost believe she would hear Ben's car pulling into the garage. She found her comfiest pair of fleece pajama bottoms and her favorite long sleeved tee shirt, and while she dressed for bed, she waited to hear his shoes on the kitchen floor, his voice calling her name. "I'm home! Who's coming to give me a hug?" She wondered how long she could play make-believe.

It was true that circumstances had forced her to imagine Ben's funeral before, including what it would be like to stand in front of friends and family and deliver a eulogy, and today was not at all the worst-case scenario she had concocted. It always had been her nightmare; Meg would challenge anyone who had a partner who traveled to deny having thought the possibility through to its tragic end. Receiving the phone call, hearing the news, telling the children, trying to move on with some semblance of a life that had been created first for two, then for a family, and now...what? If she had ever thought she could prepare herself, she'd been mistaken. In those times when she had allowed herself to drift into the scary imaginary--while on endless stretches of highway driving, sitting at stoplights, waiting in lines at preschool--when she had really allowed herself to consider the "what if?" she had been entirely wrong. She had stood this morning and spoken, but was she the eloquent voice she'd always thought she might be if ever called upon? Yes, she thought she was being strong for her children, but at the same time, the day had gone by in such a blur, so much had felt out of her control, even here, in her own home, that she wasn't entirely sure. At this moment, all she felt was spent. The memories of the day had drained from her, for she couldn't remember one moment with any clarity. She wondered whom she could thank for this tiny miracle.

Business trip, business trip, business trip. The mantra ran through her brain while she brushed her teeth and washed the make-up from her face. It would be so convenient, she thought, to continue this game forever. "My husband is at a conference," she could say. "Ben? He's meeting clients in San Francisco." She could pull it off, and it would feel almost real. For Christ's sake, she thought, angrily, it was real every other week of her life. Why not now? She slammed her hand down onto the marble vanity.

Why was it so simple to convince her brain of one thing when the pit in her stomach knew otherwise? Why, when her heart was broken, was she standing in the bathroom getting ready to go to bed as if it were any other evening, and finding it relatively easy to do so? She splashed cold water on her face and stared at herself in the oval mirror over the sink. Her first thought was that she really didn't look like a widow. Except for the large bags under her puffy eyes, remnants of the day, she still looked like herself, which was both mildly comforting and seemingly impossible. Her blue eyes were red-rimmed and tired. Her shoulder-length blonde hair looked, she thought, actually better than usual, which felt like a tiny, yet entirely unexpected silver lining on the greyest cloud in the sky. She reached for a make-up wipe to rub off the bit of blush that remained on her cheeks. First the right, then the left. Normal to dry, as she always told the aesthetician, same as usual. She wiped her eyes and her forehead, letting her neck sink deep into her shoulders for a moment. She looked into the glass again. The pieces fit together to create a vision that looked like her, but she couldn't be the same person, because this woman had a dead husband. Meg had no memory of doing her hair or applying her make-up before the funeral, but she must have--bits of mascara and tiny flecks of eye shadow wiped clean on the cloth.

Meg's second thought as she stood and stared was that she really, really loved her bathroom mirror. The frame was a whitewashed wood oval, intricately carved, an antique in the midst of the bathroom that she and Ben had recently redone, with new marble subway tile and chrome fixtures. She and Ben had bought the mirror at an antique show in Perry Pike the first year they were married. Meg had loved it, Ben had bargained for it, and for years it had hung in the foyer, where it had been a bit small for the space, but at the time, had sufficed. Now, the front hall held a grander piece, but neither Ben nor Meg had been willing to part with their first antique. Meg found herself lost in thought, remembering how Ben had re-hung the mirror for her, knowing how much she had loved its graceful curves and its imper-fections.

"Ben," she whispered to herself, tracing the frame with her finger.

She shivered and shook herself out of her reverie. She glanced down at the prescription bottle on the bathroom counter, and before she could talk herself out of it, she popped the lid and poured two pills into her hand. The CVS bag that her best friend Elise had brought to the house had been marked "URGENT." She flipped the bathroom light off and headed toward her bed. Some kind soul had turned down her bed for her and left her a glass of ice water ("God," Meg thought, "People have been everywhere in this house") which she now used to swallow the sleeping aid her doctor had called in for her. She pulled back the duvet and tucked herself under the familiar bedding. Why did it feel the same?

She had been trying all day to name what she felt, even at this moment when she crawled into bed, Meg did not feel lonely. Heartbroken because the love of her life was never coming home. Normal, because she was used to Ben not being home. Bad, because she still felt normal. Guilty, because she was a woman who had never minded being alone. Worried, because she wasn't sure if lonely would happen. Sad, because her children were devastated. Scared, because she had never faced life without Ben having a return flight.

Meg turned off the light, and in that instant the emptiness slammed into her as if the darkness itself was made of a thousand tons of stone and had been waiting for just this moment to tumble. Grief that was composed of only sadness, fear and heartbreak, worry and guilt, flooded over the stone and threatened to drown Meg with its strength. Her husband was dead and suddenly Meg understood the power of loneliness.

Quickly, she turned and reached for the television remote on her nightstand and pressed the power button. CNN brightened the room with light, but the world news was too unsettling. Meg desperately scrolled to find the first home, garden, or food channel on her list, feeling weirdly comforted when she recognized Guy Fieri touting a diner or a dive in Baltimore. Or Boston. She didn't care, as long as any sound other than silence filled the sudden expanse of emptiness. Even with the volume level barely audible, Meg found comfort in the low buzz and the light from the television, finally drifting into a restless sleep, which was more than she had expected.

In the middle of the night, she woke to a noise. She rolled over slowly, wondering what she had heard. The wind? The TV? She powered the set off and rolled over, hopeful for just a bit more sleep. After a few moments, her eyes began to close but she was again startled awake. It was the chime of her phone, indicating a text message.

She reached out in the dark, struggling to find her iPhone on the nightstand, to check both the time and the message. Who would be sending her a text at this hour? Annie was sound asleep upstairs, and everyone else in her world would certainly know that Meg shouldn't be disturbed, tonight of all nights.

Meg found the phone and rolled onto her back, pressing the button on the home screen to bring the cell phone screen to life in the dark room. The brightness made her squint, but the first thing she saw was "2:16 AM. " The second thing she saw was a text. Two words.

I'm here.

The phone clattered on the hardwood floor as it fell from Meg's hand. The text was from Ben.

Ben
September 16, 1988

He'd always remember the day he fell in love with Meg. He'd met her several weeks before, by chance, at the student union, at the start of the school year. Ben had been alone at a small table struggling through some Econ homework, and she and Sophie were at a nearby booth, laughing loudly, talking about anything but the books and notes spread before them. He'd known Sophie since their Freshman Western Civ class, and he noticed she'd cut her hair differently. It was late and the two girls were stretched out, tanned legs up on the seats, sipping their sodas. A pile of nachos oozed cheese off the paper plate in the center of their mess. They seemed relaxed, throwing their heads back, tossing their hair, two friends, happy to see each other after a long summer.

Even from a distance, Ben couldn't help but notice how pretty Sophie's friend was, sitting casually in the booth, elbow on the table, her her chin in her hand. Her contagious giggle kept floating across the room, as if reminding him to look again. Her blond hair was pulled into a loose ponytail, and her heart-shaped face was glowing as she laughed with her friend. It felt like a natural move for Ben to stop by the booth to say hi to Sophie, and as he got closer, he saw Meg's blue-grey eyes. She wasn't laughing anymore, and her mouth had settled into a soft smile.

"How was your summer?" he asked Sophie, glancing at Meg.

"Um, it was fine, dude. Yours?" she replied, nudging Meg with her foot.   "What?" Meg said. She looked surprised and vaguely annoyed.

Ben glanced at Sophie knowingly and reached across the table to grab a nacho.

"Hey!" Sophie said.

"What?" Ben feigned innocence. "I'm just a starving college boy."

Meg smiled and glanced at Sophie, who was rolling her eyes and nodding her head in an exaggerated fashion toward Ben, as if to say, "Are you getting this?"

"I'm Ben," he said. He extended his hand toward Meg.

Her palm was warm and smooth. "Meg," she said.

"So," he said. "Are you girls getting some serious work done here?" He helped himself to another chip.

Meg giggled.

"Well," Sophie said, "it comes easier to some of us." She gave Ben a jab in the arm.

"That Econ is killing me already, Soph. I miss having you next to me in class!"

"You'll be okay. It's early days, Bennie."

"If you say so. On that note, I'm off to tackle these books in the library. Too many distractions here," Ben said, winking at the girls. "It was nice meeting you, Meg."

"You too, Ben," she said, looking him in the eye. He was not oblivious to the whispers from their booth as he walked away.

The next morning, when Ben called to get Meg's number, Sophie gave it with one stipulation:

"You be sweet to her, Ben. She's a good girl. She's special."

Their official first date was a movie uptown followed by Skipper's cheese fries on High Street. Ben was pleasantly surprised by her quick and witty sense of humor, and he appreciated both the breadth and ease of their conversation.

"So smart!" he told Sophie later. "And funny! Where have you been hiding her?"   Sophie had simply smiled. "She's a keeper, Ben. Don't break her heart."

The second time he called, they met for coffee and a study date at the library, but talked (whispered) the whole time. They were both shocked to check their watches and see that nearly four hours had passed, for they weren't nearly finished with all their conversation. Gathering her books and backpack, Meg asked if he would mind walking her back to the dorm. With any other girl, he might have suggested that the night go on—and maybe at his fraternity house—but not this night, and not with this girl. They walked in the dark, and when he bent to kiss her goodnight on the front porch of the dorm, he could see Meg smiling beneath the hanging lantern light.

As early as that night, Ben felt it pulling on him, an unexpected connection to this girl, holding him in such a way that made it difficult to walk away from her. Ben shook his head, hard, as if to knock out the craziness inside. He struggled against the urge to run back and knock on her door that night, and during the week that followed, he sorted his attraction to a girl he barely knew. He was in danger of coming on too strong, so he laid a bit low for his own sanity.

Surely it couldn't be love; Ben didn't do love. But on this particular September evening, he was quite certain he didn't want to spend one more minute hanging out around the keg with a bunch of guys, so he slipped out and jogged across campus in the dark. It was a cool, early fall night in Ohio, and he was breathing hard when he got to her hall, just before the doors were locked for the evening. He needed to calm himself before picking up the lobby phone to call her dorm room; his heavy breathing would make him sound like an obscene caller.

When he called her room, the line was busy. Busy! Ben paced the lobby, calling every few minutes with no luck, knowing that any minute the hall monitor was going to send him home for breaking curfew in the girls' dorm.

Finally, it rang.

"It's Ben," he said, when Meg answered. "I'm downstairs in your lobby."

"Here?" she said. "Now?"

"Can you come down?"

"Give me just a minute." It sounded like she was smiling.

Five minutes later, Meg was in the lobby, dressed in a pink sweat-shirt and ripped jeans. Her long hair was pulled back into a messy ponytail, and she had on no make-up.

"Hey," she said, looking at him inquisitively.

"Hey," Ben said. "Want to take a walk?"

"Okay," she said, glancing back at him over her shoulder as she led the way to the front door.

Moonlight washed the campus as they walked and talked. Small talk was already out of the way, and the night sky provided the ideal backdrop for deeper discussions. Ben spoke of his dreams, how he hoped to design and build a golf course, that he wanted three children and hoped to meet his wife in college because he didn't want to wait years to marry. He couldn't imagine, he said, playing the singles' scene after college, and he swore he saw her smile in the darkness. Meg shared with Ben that her parents had married right after college, that she had two younger brothers, she adored kids, and wanted to be a mom and a journalist. At some point Ben grabbed Meg's hand, and they walked on easily, hands linked. When he stopped under the streetlight by the science building, took her face into his hands and kissed her, it was natural. More than natural; it was as if that moment had simply been waiting for them to take their places. Though the path seemed fast, it also seemed real, and both were sensing that the other felt the same. Magical.

Ben walked Meg back to her dorm, knowing it was going to be tough to let her go, even for the evening. They stopped and sat in the dark, on a low brick wall in the courtyard. With Meg leaning against him in the stillness of the night, after a few short dates and one wonderful evening, Ben knew. So he told her.

"I'm falling in love with you," he said, "I think."

He waited in the dark for her to answer, or not answer, or freak out. For a while, Meg did nothing.

Then she finally looked at him with a face he knew he would love forever and said the best thing he had ever heard.

"Well, that's good," she said slowly, "because I know I'm falling in love with you." She kissed him softly and walked inside, leaving him to wonder about the turn this night had taken

Meg
November 5, 2013

Meg could feel her heart racing, but her body lay still. What time was it now, she wondered? 2:18? 2:20? Certainly she had not seen what she thought she had seen. It was dark, she was overtired, she had taken medication. Ben was dead and she was obviously going insane. She was overwhelmed with sadness and grief. There were a thousand explanations for this. Or none. Meg shoved her hands under the comforter to stop them from shaking, but she couldn't keep the blood from pounding at her temples and her heartbeat threatened to wake her children. She could not bring herself to reach for the phone on the floor by the side of the bed; she pictured her iPhone lying there, taunting her. She switched on her bedside lamp, carefully maneuvered herself out of bed, and tiptoed around the phone, which still lay screen-side down on the hardwood floor. In the kitchen she got a glass of water and tried to collect herself, and walked back to the bedroom where she put the glass next to the one that was already there.

"See?" Meg thought to herself, glancing at the two full glasses of water. "I'm exhausted. I'm overtired." From the edge of the bed, she looked down at the phone. Tentatively, she nudged it with her toe, as if it were alive and might jump. Finally, she reached down and retrieved it, turning it over in her hand. What was once such a familiar shape in her palm felt foreign and pulsing with life. She pressed the home button.

I'm here.

Bright, shining on the screen.

The sender simply read "Ben," as if it were perfectly fine to see his name next to the green Message icon, shining in the night. It was 2:27 AM. Ben. Ben?

Meg's contacts were listed casually. Annie, Ben, Elise, Mom, Sophie. Ben's contacts were listed alphabetically by last name, even hers. McAfee, Meg. Everything was always very organized and businesslike, which sometimes used to bother her. "Why do you need my last name?" she would ask. "How many Megs are texting you?" She had no idea why she was thinking of this now. Perhaps Ben's first name, shining on the screen in this particular moment, seemed anything but casual.

Any other time, any other day, this text would have been the very last thing to shake her. *I'm here* could have meant everything or very little.

I've checked in to the Four Seasons.

I've landed in Mexico City. Don't worry; security is tight.

I'm at Willie's game. Can you bring Gatorade?

Or even, *I'm here, I'm home. Where are you?*

That is not what was happening. Was it?

She sat on the edge of the bed, staring at the phone. What was this?

An old text that was never sent.

A prank.

A mistake.

A text from Ben.

A text from Ben.

Please be a text from Ben.

She placed the phone gingerly on Ben's side of the bed, not wanting to disturb the words, and covered it with her hand. It was not unlike the position she had slept in for so many years, on her side with her hand on Ben's chest. Meg lay in the dark and ran her thumb back and forth along the phone's edges. Back and forth, back and forth, wondering what would happen if she texted back.

Meg
September 16, 1988

He loved her! Meg tried to fall asleep that night but sleep wouldn't come. They had only just separated and now she was in her bed, hardly able to contain herself. Meg had shared things with Ben that her closest friends didn't know--her dreams of writing books, her worries about fitting in. She had even recited a poem from her writing class--oh, God, had she really done that? Ben had talked about their possible future together (hadn't he?) by describing his parents' marriage and his own hopes for a relationship. He wanted children, he dreamed of renovating a historic home, of coaching Little League. Meg had shared her desire to be a wife and mother, which she knew (she'd said) sounded old-fashioned. He had earnestly disagreed and they had seemingly exchanged unspoken promises. That's when Ben had turned to her on the corner by Bachelor Hall and kissed her as she had never been kissed. Ben had claimed her then, and if he didn't know it, Meg certainly did.

"I had to find you tonight," he'd said. "I couldn't stand one more minute without you."

Now it was Meg who could hardly stand one more minute, more convinced than ever that she wasn't being swept away by the moonlight and kisses under street lamps. The thoughts keeping her awake were that of her possible future with Ben.

In the morning, before Meg was entirely awake, or maybe before she had ever fallen quite asleep, her phone rang. She jumped from bed and grabbed the receiver from the wall.

"Hello?" She knew she sounded hopeful.

"Hi," he said. He sounded sleepy.

"Where are you?"

"I'm here. In your lobby."

"Again?"

"Is that weird?" Now he sounded worried.

"No!" Alone in her room, Meg smiled, and caught a glance at herself in the mirror. She had slept in sweats and a tee shirt, she was still in a pony-tail and had yet to shower.

"I thought we could have breakfast," he said. "I wanted to see you."

So it began.

Meg
November 5, 2013

Meg woke the next morning with the bedroom light still on, clutching the phone in her hand. It had been a night of fitful bursts of sleep and short, odd dreams. Not a half-hour had gone by without Meg looking at her phone, wanting to see Ben's name, wanting it to disappear, wishing it were all a dream, hoping it wasn't. Time and again, she'd lifted the phone and stared before drifting off, only to wake and wonder again.

Ben.

Ben.

Ben.

At some point, maybe close to dawn, Meg finally swiped the "slide to unlock" feature at the bottom of the screen, fearing the worst. But what would the worst even prove to be? The text would disappear, the phone would explode, she would wake from this crazy dream? Nothing changed, except the text now appeared in her message list with a bright blue dot next to Ben's name. Unread.

Meg hadn't been so grateful for morning for as long as she could remember. Certainly, in the fresh light of a new day, she would think more clearly. She eased herself into a sitting position and inhaled slowly, deeply. This could be any day, Meg thought. The November sun would soon be creeping higher, trying to shine through the cloudy sky. Leaves would rustle under the feet of the dog-walkers on the street. It would be her favorite kind of morning--brisk and quiet, the plum tree outside her window offering the perfect perch for the birds not yet migrated. It was autumn in Ohio. Any other day, she would pull back the drapes, grab some boots and a sweatshirt to meet her friends for a hike after the kiddos left for school. But today, the day after her husband's funeral, Meg had things to take care of, two of whom were still sleeping upstairs, and one of which was the unanswered message. The room was chilly. She wrapped herself in her bathrobe, and tucked the phone safely into her robe pocket. Her fingers curled around the phone, her thumb rubbing the edges back and forth, back and forth.

Meg turned on every lamp and overhead light as she made her way through the family room and into the kitchen, comforted by the brightness. She took her teakettle from the stove and turned to fill it at the faucet, as she did every morning. The dishtowel, messy with chocolate, was crumpled in the sink. Meg picked it up with two fingers and delivered it directly to the trash can.

"That was easy," she said, to no one but herself.

She turned on the gas burner for her tea, and flipped on the small kitchen TV to catch *The Today Show* before anyone woke. The familiar sounds of Matt and Savannah were strangely soothing as she stared out the window at the backyard. Gentle ripples on the lake, the lake that Ben loved. While she had grown accustomed to her breakfasts alone when Ben was out of town, or after he'd run through the kitchen to grab a banana on his way to the airport, Meg couldn't grasp how she'd live in this house without him. With a sigh, she turned to see what was in the fridge for breakfast for the kids. Though it shouldn't have, she was surprised to find the shelves stocked with Tupperware and foil-covered dishes. A huge ham on a platter took up the entire top shelf, where her milk and juice usually sat, and at least five aluminum trays were stacked and labeled: au gratin potatoes, lasagna, green salad, chicken salad, chicken parmesan, chicken bake. On the counter were neatly arranged bakery boxes of cookies and cakes. "No nuts," read one neatly printed tag.

She picked up the landline and dialed the number she had called every morning for the past seventeen years.

"Hey," answered Elise. "I was hoping you were still asleep."

"Touch and go," said Meg. She stuffed a cookie in her mouth. "Mmmffph, this is delish."   "Found the cookies, did you? Good."

"Mmmm-hmmpffh."

Elise laughed. "Have you seen the freezer?"

"No. Oh, my God. The freezer too? I'm a little scared!"

"You're set until Christmas."

"People are good, I mean it," Meg said, opening the foil on another tray. "Holy shit, there's like a three-layer chocolate cake thingie here."

"I saw that. Happy breakfast. So, how are you doing this morning?"

"Okay, I guess. I've always though it was funny that people say food helps, but you know what? People are totally right."

"Good to know. What else do you need?"

"God, I don't even know. The kids aren't awake yet, at least I don't think. I'm going to give them a few more minutes before I check on them, and then maybe we'll just hang here, or go get some air. It's been a lot, you know? People and small-talk and that kind of stuff."

"I *do* know."

"I don't want to sound mean. Everyone meant so well. I'm starving, is that weird?"

"No, it's not weird."

"I so appreciate you taking care of the food and the house while I was doing all that stupid funeral stuff. I really mean it."

"Jesus, Meg. Stupid funeral stuff." Elise giggled.

"What else can I say?" Meg let out a giant sigh. "It was *so* stupid. It's so stupid that Ben died." Meg clasped the phone tightly in her pocket.

"Yes, you're exactly right. So stupid. But you did a great job yesterday, Meggie."

"Thanks."

"How was your night? Did you sleep?" Elise had reminded her several times to take the medication as the doctor prescribed, not to much, not too little. This morning, as Meg continued to find her footing in her strange new reality, she also recognized that this was new space for Elise to navigate as the best friend.

"I took the meds, don't worry. But they didn't knock me out. Willie fell asleep in his own room for the first time since, well...since. I don't even think he meant to. He was just completely exhausted. I don't really know if I ever slept or not. Too many dreams, I think."

Meg reached into her robe pocket again. She always told Elise everything. When she worried about Annie and her friends, when she had a fight with Ben, when she had a suspicious new mole, when she found a good sale at Macy's. They talked several times a day and texted more. But the message on her phone was something that Meg felt unwilling to mention, at least this morning. Elise would try to make sense of something so seemingly nonsensical, but Meg wasn't willing to play the part of the unhinged widow, nor was she willing to place the texts into any category at all —nonsense, misunderstanding, or real communication.   With so many waves of possible answers crashing together, she only needed to keep this secret; Elise would be her first confidant once she was ready.

"Dreams aren't surprising," Elise said.

"No," Meg said. "I suppose they're not."

On the afternoon that Ben died, it was Elise who came first, who had rushed to the house after a barely coherent phone call, who cradled Meg on the bathroom floor after Meg vomited and before Meg told her children. It was Elise who helped Meg to her feet after what felt like hours of dry heaving into the toilet, Elise who coaxed Meg into the shower, where Meg sobbed under the stream of hot water, while Elise sobbed sitting on the toilet outside. Elise made the tea, called the doctor, sat on the floor in the hallway outside Annie's bedroom, tears streaming down her face, while Meg quietly told her children what would likely be the worst news they would ever receive in their young lives. From the first moment of their friendship, it had always been Elise. And although the best friends had never been at a loss for words, and often had never needed words at all, Meg didn't know how to share what had happened in the middle of the night. Just this next morning, there were fleeting moments when Meg could convince herself that it had never happened at all; she might never need to explain the text to anyone. Then, just as quickly, she would realize how badly she wanted entirely the opposite to be true.

Elise
July 1996

Every afternoon, alone with Thomas at the park, Elise thought she might recognize someone from the preschool, or meet some other stroller mom on the walking trail, but so far, she'd been the only one at the park with her toddler. Plenty of older couples strolled by, offering waves and smiles; joggers passed, dog walkers walked, and young professionals strode briskly past, but no mommies.

"Cheerio?" she offered her baby boy, who sat contentedly in his seat, playing with his stroller toys.

Thomas reached out and grasped the cereal in his tiny hand. He was her favorite companion for sure, but Elise was still adjusting to the life of a new mom, or at least a mom in a new town. She had tried a mom-and-tot playgroup but had known instantly that an organized play situation was not in her wheelhouse. The coffee, Danish, and chit-chat seemed a mind-numbing way to pass the time while the six-month old babies lay on the floor for an hour (sometimes two!) and looked around the room. "It's simultaneous play," claimed one mother, as her daughter worked to pick up a rattle while another baby batted a play gym that was hanging above the blanket.

"Is it?" Elise had speculated aloud,. "Or are they just lying there being babies?" Her comment and bored tone inspired raised eyebrows and pursed lips, and certainly gossip about her later. She'd managed to stick it out through that one afternoon, but that was the end of playgroups for Thomas. Elise much preferred strolling with her son in town, or taking to him to the local library for the afternoon story hour. She'd been thrilled when Kyle had accepted this recent transfer, forcing them to move from their hometown where they had been high school sweethearts, and allowing them a fresh start in the very small town of Perry Pike, Ohio.

Elise loved the idea of a smaller town, the promise of good schools, and the proximity to a couple of bigger cities for theater, restaurants, and culture. But mostly she been won over by how she'd felt when they first drove into the town, down the main street, which was actually called Main Street.

"Can you believe it? It's like a story book. 'Main Street!'" she'd turned to Kyle with a wide smile, and then peeked into the back seat at her sleeping baby. Elise smiled.

"Yep, Main Street," he'd answered, seemingly unimpressed with the street sign, trying harder to locate the for-sale house numbers and make correct turns. But Elise was taking it all in with an openness that surprised her. The storefronts were quaint, the windows showcasing what was promised inside. Cupcakes and cookies at Sugars, sweaters and dresses displayed at Mrs. Pommers For Women, the Crooked Nook Bookstore, a coffee shop, a few small restaurants. There was a green space with a gazebo across from the shops on Main; kids were playing in the open grass, and a band was setting up for some sort of concert.

"We should come to the show," she said to Kyle.

"We need to find a house," he chided her.

"But we will, someday. Come to a show, I mean. With Tommy, and he can play on this grass, and dance to the music." She sat back in her seat, determinedly.

Kyle looked over her, and shook his head, smiling.

"Sounds like a plan."

She could picture their life here, easily. That's why the actual move had been easier than she expected.

"We can stay if you want, you know," Kyle had said for what seemed the hundredth time, as they had labeled the last box in the basement. "I'm not trying to force you to leave this place, you know, where he was."

"I don't want to stay," Elise had assured him.

"But the house? His things?"

"Well, all the important things come with us. Memories come with us. All we really leave behind are paint and wallpaper." She tilted her face up to Kyle. "In my head, I'm already moved to our fairytale town."

"I'm so lucky," he said, kissing her.

"Yep. Pack another box."

Kyle and Elise lived in the Baltimore home where she had grown up as a child, the home where her father had died and her son had taken his first steps, where Elise had taken hers. It was a house full of memories, but as Kyle knew, not all of them were cherished. Moving her sweet, young family to a new town, a fresh place to grow, sounded perfect.

Elise threw herself into the task of moving as if it were her job; and for that moment in time, it was. Every spare moment was spent organizing, packing boxes, and tidying the house to sell.

"Hospital bed?" Kyle said. They were down in the basement one afternoon while Thomas slept in his bassinet nearby. The rails of the dissembled plastic bed were stacked and leaning against a wall in the corner. Mattress, bed tray, commode. It was all there.

"Donate," Elise said, not looking over.

"Okay," he said. "What about the…"

"Everything that goes with it. All of it. Donate. I mean, please. Please donate."

Elise's dad had died when she was 16, after his second bout of cancer. Prostate cancer that had metastasized to the lungs. She remembered a few details, like the medicine bottles on the kitchen counters, and the hospital bed in the living room, and that her mother had abandoned them both when the cancer returned. That she remembered clearly.

Most of her memories were of her dad, healthy and vibrant. The stereotypical traveling salesman, always on the road, briefcase in hand. Elise could picture him, even now, always coming in the door with a trinket in hand— homemade caramel from a few towns over, or a promotional calendar he had received at a convention. He was warm and funny and he thought she was the best girl in the world.

"The brightest and most beautiful princess I know!" he would exclaim, picking her up for a big hug.

"What did you bring me?"

"What did I bring you? Is that all you have to say?" But his green eyes were twinkling, and he would glance toward the pocket of his suit coat.

Elise would reach in to find her lollipop, her tiny troll, her Pet Rock with a vendor's phone number inscribed on the bottom.

Memories of her mother, on the other hand, were now tied only to the fact that Elise had been left to care for her dad while still finishing high school.

Her mother had disappeared one evening after piling the dinner dishes in the sink, leaving a phone number and address taped to their olive green refrigerator. "Honey, I just can't! It's too much. I'm sorry. I love you. Call me if anything happens with your dad." Elise called the number exactly once, the day her father died. No one at the other end had ever heard of her mother.

The phone number and address stayed on the fridge, just in case.

Every last piece of hospital equipment could go, as far as she was concerned. It wasn't him, it wasn't them. Her favorite memories of her dad were of parks and swing sets. Not evenings spent feeding him and managing his pain. She hadn't visited that corner of the basement, or her mind, in several years, and she knew that if she started today, she might never get through the job at hand.

"Thank you, Kyle." She said it, still, without glancing over.

"You got it. You might want these, though. " He handed her a metal box on his way up the stairs, his arms full of plastic medical supplies.

Her box. How could she have forgotten? Inside were stacks and stacks of postcards from her dad, from every city and state he visited. Whether he was gone a day or a week, he would write to her religiously.

"Hi, honey, Pittsburgh is pretty neat-o! Love, Daddy."

"Dear Princess, I miss you! Love from Toledo, Daddy."

The notes were short, the stack was thick. Under the postcards Elise found four envelopes, written in her own handwriting, sent to her mother at the refrigerator address. Each envelope was stamped in red, RETURN TO

SENDER. Report card, graduation announcement, obituary, Tommy's birth announcement. Elise felt the openings of a wound deep within her, so she shoved the letters back into the bottom of the box and placed her treasured cards on top. Putting the lid on tightly, she placed the box in the crate marked "Keep" and turned to check on the sleeping baby.

She sat on the bench in the warm sunshine, watching her toddler toss cereal off the stroller tray. The park had a swing set, a sandbox, a slide and a jungle gym. Everything was still a bit out of reach for a two-year old, but there was a trailhead off to the side. A little exercise wasn't going to kill her, Elise thought, so she pushed her rubber-wheeled stroller through the playground and over to the trail, just as a young woman was struggling to unload a stroller from the back of a minivan in the nearby parking lot. The side door was open, and Elise could see the pudgy legs of a baby kicking happily from the car seat while the woman grew more and more frustrated.

"Oh, shit!" the woman said loudly, obviously unaware that she wasn't alone. Elise smiled, and moved a little closer, just as the diaper bag came tumbling out of the back of the van and the baby started to cry.

"Shit shit shit," the woman whispered, and Elise tried not to laugh.

"Can I help?" she asked, approaching slowly so as not to scare this woman, who was already having a rough time.

"Oh my God!" the woman said, jumping in shock, putting her hand on her heart. She blushed.

"I completely understand," Elise said, bending to retrieve the diaper bag and the sippy cup that had rolled out of the bag and under a tire.

"Thanks."

"No problem. I can give you a hand with the stroller, too."

"Awesome."

Elise popped the brake down on her own stroller, and then helped to maneuver the stroller out of the back of the van. The diaper bag fit snugly into the bottom basket, the baby (a girl, about two) was soon easily buckled in, the van locked up, and the woman was able to take a big, deep breath.

"Thank you. Sorry for the language."

"That? I said worse than that before I left the house this morning. I'm Elise, by the way. Are you walking the trail?"

Elise saw the woman give her a quick once-over. She knew that her jeans and fitted aqua tank top were perfectly park- appropriate, Her shoulder-length brown hair was tossed back into a baseball cap, and though she had on no real make-up, she had on some lip-balm, and a bit of natural color in her cheeks, thanks to the summer sun. Elise had been told before that she often looked put-together with an aura of "this old thing?" all at the same time. The woman before her was wearing stretchy black leggings and a long t-shirt. Her blond hair was tossed into a ponytail, and her Keds were dirty. But her face had an easy friendliness, and Elise could sense a camaraderie of spirits. In fact, if she had to venture a guess, she would imagine that the woman was kicking herself for not dressing better, and Elise already wanted to tell her not to worry.

"I am. I'm Meg, and this is Annabelle. Annie. I normally don't look so. . ."

"Stop," Elise said," smiling at her own intuitiveness, bending to peek at Annie, now completely relaxed in her stroller, kicking her feet in tiny pink sparkly gym shoes.

"It's very nice to meet you, Meg and Annie." She turned to her own stroller, patting her baby boy on his blond curls.

"This," she said, "is Thomas." "Thomas, please meet Annie, and her mother, Meg. Now let's take a walk with these shitty strollers."

Annie
November 5, 2013

So what was she supposed to do now? She could hear her mom down in the kitchen on the phone with Aunt Elise, which made sense. That was an everyday kind of thing, so she supposed she should get on with her everyday routine. Annabelle opened her bedroom door and peeked across the hall. Willie's door was open, and he was sitting up in bed, playing on his iPod Touch with Fred the panda on his lap. She crossed the hall to his room.

"Hey," she said quietly, approaching his bed and wiggling his toes.

"Hi," he said.

"What are we doing today?"

"I don't know," he said.

"Are we going to school?" It was a Wednesday, and Annie usually liked Wednesdays. The high school had a late start, and she would meet her friends in the commons for muffins and coffee.

"I don't want to," he said.

"I don't think you have to," she said, "but I might go. Do you think that's okay?"

Willie nodded. "It's okay."

"Will you be all right here?" Annie asked her little brother. "You can text me if you need me."

"I'll be good. You can text me, too."

Annie smiled. "I will. Thanks."

Willie turned back to his iPod. Annie went down the hall to their shared bathroom and turned on the shower. She saw in the mirror that she looked exactly the same as she had last week when her dad was still alive. That seemed weird, especially since she felt so different, but whatever.

While the water heated, she scrolled her iPhone for music, trying to ignore all the notifications popping up on the screen.

She hadn't checked her Facebook or Twitter accounts in the last couple of days, and this morning, these were totally freaking her out. Her friends, and people who weren't her real friends at all, were all trying to do the right thing, post the right comments, but it all seemed so wrong. What's the correct thing to write on social media when someone's dad dies? Going on the Internet to offer virtual condolences had become the new sympathy card. "Hey Annie, I don't really know you that well, but you seem like a great girl and I'm really sorry about your dad." That was a good one. There were lots of "RIP Mr. McAfees" showing up on her Facebook homepage today. RIP sounded like something you would see in a Halloween graveyard, and it was scary and stupid and impersonal. The inexplicable rush of anger Annie felt at the words was almost frightening— her Facebook page used to show funny videos of crazy cats, selfie pictures of her girlfriends. Now it was a wall of sadness, and while she didn't want to delete the messages, she didn't want to look at them, either. Annie didn't know anyone else in her school who had a parent who had died, and she was suddenly one hundred percent pissed off. Actually there had been this one kid, Billy Bruckheiser, whose mom had died from cancer a few years back. Annie remembered that there had been a big fundraiser, a race or something in her honor, after school let out for summer. A 5K maybe? She wondered if someone would try to do something like that for her dad next summer. When your dad has a heart attack on an airplane on a business trip, there aren't any races or ribbons for that.

She turned up the music and stepped into the shower. The water felt good pouring over her hair, her skin, her face. It had been a long few days, and maybe it would be good to get back to school and see her friends. She washed her hair, cleansed her face, and stayed a while in the hot water, just listening to her music and breathing in the steam.

About an hour later, she appeared in the kitchen, hair dried and straightened, dressed for school in skinny jeans and a long pink sweater, make-up perfect. Her mother was at the kitchen table staring at her cell phone, nibbling tiny bites of a biscotti from an unfamiliar tin, lost in thought.

"Hey," her mom said, looking up at Annie. "You look great! Why?"

"Um, school...?"

"School? Today?" Meg stood and walked toward her daughter, reaching out to touch her gently on the arm. "Honey, are you sure? It's so soon."

Annie shrugged off her mother's hand.

"Mom, I want to go be with my friends."

Meg wasn't really sure what the right thing was, or if there was a right thing. So she sighed and kissed Annie on the head. "Okay."

"Okay," replied Annie, heading for the pantry.

"What about Willie?" asked her mom. "Is he up?"

"He's up, but I don't think he's feeling like school."

Her mom nodded. "That's fine."

Annie rummaged in the pantry for a Pop-Tart and a lemonade juice box and stood at the counter to eat. She watched as her mom glanced back down at her phone.

"What's up?" asked Annie.

"Nothing," Meg said, sliding the phone back into her pocket.

"Were you on the phone with Aunt Elise?"

"Earlier, yeah."

"What else is new?" Annie said, showing traces of a wry smile.

"What else is new, indeed," her mother said, wistfully. "Ah, my Anniegirl. We'll be fine, I promise." She followed her daughter to the front hall and grabbed the worn denim jacket off the hook.

"Here, it's chilly."

"Thank you," Annie said, taking the jacket.

Meg hugged her tightly, pulling back to plant a kiss on her daughter's forehead. "Call me if you need me. I'll come. Anytime."

"I know, Mom."

Meg
November 5, 2013

Meg watched as her daughter walked toward her red VW bug, jingling her keys. The cute used car that Ben had searched online to find had been delivered off a flatbed truck right to their house during the previous summer--Willie had loved watching! It seemed a lifetime ago. Dear God, the car was going to make her cry.

"Be careful!" she called from the front step, out of habit.

Annie threw her a look over her shoulder and got into the driver's seat.

Then she was gone.

Not gone. Just at school.

Business trip. Business trip. Business trip.

Meg swallowed a gulp of tea and padded up the back staircase to check on Willie. She loved her back staircase, a secret passage to her children's bedrooms where she could creep in her pajamas early in the morning and late at night. From her bedroom on the first floor, she could use that staircase to get to them without ever passing the front door, so she never felt exposed as she went to wake them for school or to kiss them goodnight. She knew they often came right back down those stairs into the kitchen for midnight snacks, as if she wasn't in tune to every creak and noise in her home, but she didn't care. Meg knew that, all too soon, she would miss the days when there were children sneaking around on the steps, leaving crumbs for her to wipe away in the morning.

"Hey, buddy," she said, peeking around the door of her younger's bedroom. He was on his floor surrounded by Legos. His curly head was bent over the instruction manual, but he looked up and gave her a weak smile. She missed his deep dimples; she wondered when they might come back.

"Hi, Mommy." Mommy. The word had returned with the panda a few days ago, and it equally melted and broke her heart.

"Watcha doin?"

"Building my mini-van." Willie had Lego kits of all shapes and sizes, and unlike some kids, he was not apt to build them and keep them whole on a shelf. He would build them, take them apart, and rebuild them. The mini-van had over a thousand pieces, and it appeared that they were all on the bedroom floor.

"Can I help?"

"Really?" Willie looked at her in surprise.

"Sure."

Meg lowered herself to the floor across from her son and picked up the worn instruction booklet. Willie pushed a pile of pieces toward her. Meg picked up a few small building blocks and began to assemble the front end of the van.

"Wait, Mommy. That's wrong."

"Is it?" Meg looked up from her pile of Legos.

"Yes. You need two reds there and then a yellow long one on top. Not another red."

"Oh, I'm not always so great at Legos," Meg said.

She shifted to lie on her side, propping her head onto her bent elbow.

"Are you tired, Mommy?"

"I am, kiddo."

Willie nodded. "Me too."

Meg felt the all-to-familiar sting behind her eyes. "It's been a tired kind of week. It's a good day to do lie down and play Legos."

At some point in the morning, a light rain began to fall, adding appropriate background music to the morning. Fred was on the floor nearby, and they all stayed sprawled on the carpet until nearly noon. Finally, Meg suggested a break for lunch.

"I'm starving, are you?"

"Yep," Willie said. "Can you make mac-n-cheese?"

"Sure. Let's go down."

Meg, Willie, and Fred made their way downstairs to the warm kitchen, where Meg put a pot of water on the stove to boil, and Willie sat on a stool at the big kitchen island and waited.

"Chocolate milk?" she asked.

"Yes, please."

Meg handed him all the ingredients, so he could make it himself as he liked to do. He began to pour and stir, and as the spoon clinked on the glass, she realized he was silently crying.

"Baby, what is it?"

"I don't know how…"

"How to what?" She began to rub his back in slow circles. "Honey, what?"

"I don't know how to feel good." Willie began to sob. "I don't f-feel good."

As he continued stirring, his elbow knocked the table, and the glass tipped, spilling the milk. Willie slipped down from his tall stool, and tried to sop up the milk from the floor with his one paper napkin, his sobs gaining momentum as he pushed the milk around. Meg crawled under the table next to him and grabbed both of his hands in hers. She grabbed the crumpled, wet, napkin and tossed it aside.

"Stop," she said quietly. "Stop wiping the milk."

Meg took his face in her hands and kissed his cheeks, over and over, shushing him as if he were an infant.

"It's okay to be this sad. It's all right not to know how to feel, do you hear me?" He nodded, just barely.

"Willie, I'm so sad, too. So, so sad."

He looked at her, tears still leaking.

"Okay, Willie?" Meg said.

"Okay," he whispered.

"Okay, then, " Meg whispered back. "So let's just be sad for a little bit."

He lay his head in her lap, and under the table, they both cried over the milk puddling on the floor.

Later, with the floor mopped up and Willie and Fred settled on the sofa watching SpongeBob, Meg retreated to her room. It was late in the afternoon, and she was still wearing her pajamas and robe; it had been that sort of day. In the bathroom, she reached into the shower to turn the hot water on full blast, then leaned against the counter, waiting for the temperature to adjust. As she did, she pulled the phone from the pocket for probably the tenth time that day (or was it the twentieth? or the hundredth?) and opened her message app.

"I'm here." There it was, still untouched, marked as "unread." Her fingers traced the words, over and over, just above the sensitive glass of the phone. Did she dare? She was so afraid to open the message. Would it disappear forever, would it prove to be spam, or a joke, or would it lead her to the real sender? Which of these did she even want? Alone in the bathroom, as the steam started to rise, she gently touched the message, and it blipped to life, the blue dot disappearing, and the message falling into the stream of messages she'd recently exchanged with Ben.

November 5, 2:16 AM
Ben: I'm here.

October 30, 11:37 AM
Meg: LOL Dog in purse. I totally want a purse dog for Christmas. Safe flight. See you soon. XOXO

October 30, 11:30 AM
Ben: Checking out of hotel--headed to airport--crazy woman in front of me with tiny dog in big pink purse. Love you!

October 29, 10:20 PM

Meg: Love you, too. Get some sleep. Talk in the AM :)

October 29, 10:16 PM
Ben: this hotel is nicer than i expected. How are the kids? Kiss them for me.
And you. See you tomorrow:) Love you.

On and on, the messages went back for weeks. Probably years. How long would her iPhone have stored them? She hoped forever. For now, though, she was just interested in the last message.

I'm here.

Her thoughts about what the text implied made her worry about her sanity. Within a few seconds, she vacillated between hoping the text was indeed from Ben and then praying that it wasn't. If she believed Ben was texting her, what did that mean? That there was Wi-Fi in Heaven? That there *was* a heaven and that Ben was saying *I'm here. I'm here with you, Meg, in spirit?* This, of course, made sense if Ben's spirit could text. Or it could mean *I'm someone else, I'm a teenager, I'm a psycho, I have Ben's phone and this is the worst prank anyone has every played on a grieving widow. I'm here. I'm a murderer in your house, watching you, and this is the beginning of a horror movie. I'm here. Meg, the police got it wrong. That wasn't me on the plane. There was a crash and I'm on a deserted island. Meg, come find me, it's Ben and I'm not dead, this has all been a horrible mistake. I'm not dead. It's Ben.*

I'm here.

I'm here.

I'm here.

What was she supposed to do with these two small words that were haunting her? There they were, shining from the screen. The words were real. She suppressed the urge to squeeze the phone or slam it to the ground, and instead, placed it firmly on the counter and turned away from it while she slipped off her robe, hung it on its hook, and took a step toward the shower.

Then she stopped and took a step back toward the counter and picked up the phone.

Was she coming unglued? She was managing to care for her children, feed them, clothe them, build a Lego mini-van, clean up spilled milk, and she was about to take a common, everyday shower. Meg looked at herself in the vanity mirror, standing naked in the bathroom, holding her phone. She was also about to reply to a text from her dead husband. Wasn't she? She was. She looked away from the mirror.

Hello? She typed, and looked at the word as if she had never seen it before. What else could she say? She stared at the word for a long few seconds, and then, almost in slow motion, pressed SEND. This time she placed the phone very carefully back into the pocket of her pink robe, which seemed to be its new home. She took a deep breath and tried to focus on the task ahead, which was simply to take a shower, but nothing felt simple anymore.

Meg
February 1994

"So, Meg, a woman in the elevator could not stop complimenting my fancy new shirt and my good-looking tie," Ben said, dropping his briefcase in the mudroom and coming into the kitchen to kiss her hello.

"Well, hello to you, too, and I suppose you mean the clothes that I picked out," she said, giving him an eye-roll. "Honestly, Ben."

"Can I help it if I'm the snazziest dresser in the building?" Ben strutted around the kitchen" In the first few years his work clothes weren't anything really special, but Ben wore them well. His dark hair was striking against his fair skin; he had a devilish grin and a genuine heart. It was no wonder that the women at the office flirted with her husband, but Meg never worried. She just shook her head, and let him ruffle his new feathers.

"You can't help it, Ben," she said, turning back to her own work. "You really can't."

"Meg, baby. What's the matter?" Ben put his arms around her from behind the chair.

"Nothing, I'm tired. Feeling a little underdressed at the moment."

She was sitting crossed-legged in a kitchen chair in denim shorts and a white t-shirt, her blond hair pulled back into a messy ponytail, not a bit of make-up. Her notebooks and texts were spread all over the kitchen table.

"You really are a mess," he said.

"You'd better watch it," she said, swatting at him with a pile of papers.

"You're my beautiful girl."

"You're going to have to work harder than that," she laughed.

Meg was working at a bookstore in downtown Perry Pike and finishing her Master's degree in English. She loved her job, but was up late most nights, studying and writing at the kitchen table to finish her thesis. May, she kept thinking, February-March-April-May, counting down the months in her head, until she could stop the researching, the footnoting and the typing and turn in her final paper. The Crooked Nook, the bookstore where she worked, was great. She could write and revise, and even use the resources available there during the slow periods of the day, helping customers when the store was busy. No one loved a good book more than Meg, except maybe the owner, Kate.

Kate, beautiful Kate. Meg had loved her since the moment she saw her behind the counter, draped in a pale green sequined tunic, wearing long silver earrings. Kate had owned The Crooked Nook for ten years before Meg walked in; the storefront on Main Street had been a gift from Kate's late husband who had wanted his wife to fulfill her dream. With his help, she had transformed the former shoe store into a warm and inviting book-lover's haven. Kate loved books and she knew books. The Nook was filled with the newest bestsellers, the much-loved classics, and everything in be-tween. Soft chairs were tucked in every corner, string quartets played softly, and the light was perfect for reading. At the register, Kate offered book-marks, tiny trinkets, gift cards, and a local vendor's homemade chocolate creams. Though she had been a widow for several years, Kate still found happiness in her bookstore, but she spent an increasing amount of time trav-eling with friends, collecting beautiful clothes and art from places she'd been; objets d'art from her travels decorated the shelves of the Nook, and she loved talking to her customers about the items she'd found in Singapore, Australia, Alaska. Kate's daughter Piper lived in the apartment above the shop and was able to fill in at the store during Kate's excursions and to pro-vide holiday help, but there was always more to be done! More shelving, more ordering, more inventory--Kate was becoming less enthralled (and perhaps a bit overwhelmed) with the daily tasks—so when Meg applied for the part-time clerk job, Kate hired her immediately. A young, eager girl, working on her degree, well-read and well-spoken--it was as if the book-store gods had dropped Meg into Kate's lap.

"You'll fit right in, won't she, Bookmark?" asked Kate, petting the fat orange cat who lived in the store. Bookmark had purred and rubbed up against Meg's jeans.

After that, Meg never came home in a bad mood. Instead, she came home with stories, her messenger bag full of papers and notebooks, and a few new books that she had bought, or had been lent by Kate to read and review for the "staff picks" shelf in the store. The Nook was a landmark spot in town, just one of the many things that was special about Perry Pike. From the moment Ben and Meg had driven through with a realtor, they had known that this was the perfect place to begin their own adventure. They fell in love with the town as they had fallen in love with each other--they were quick to decide on forever.

One particularly gray day in February, Ben was taking off his suit after work, putting on jeans and a sweater, and chatting about his day. Meg was sitting quietly on the side of the bed, just watching him, her messenger bag nearby. They had decided to grab dinner at a cheap Mexican restaurant, one of their favorite spots. It was Friday, Ben had been paid, Meg had Saturday off, and they'd been planning a night of Margaritas, maybe even a bar or two, and then some fun back at home.

"Let's get ready to go, Amiga!" he said, rubbing his hands together. "I need some steak tacos and a Corona, like, yesterday!"

"Okay."

"Okay? Meg, c'mon, I'm *starving,*" Ben whined.

"All right," she laughed, rolling her eyes.

"You know you're hungry, and you love those Margaritas."

"I do…huh." Meg smiled slowly, realizing.

"Huh, what? What is it?" he asked. "Spit it out, baby, and then let's go eat." He grabbed her hand and tried to pull her up from the side of the bed, playfully.

She pulled him down, instead.

"Nothing's wrong, really," she said, "I mean, maybe a little wrong."

Ben looked at her, suddenly serious.

"Are you okay?"

"I'm okay."

"Meg, please,, what is it?"

She knew he would be shocked, even though she really hadn't been. Maybe she'd been a little surprised when she'd fully realized, but she'd begun to suspect a few weeks ago. Today, when she couldn't stomach the turkey club sandwich from the little cafe she was beginning to frequent at lunch, she knew.

"So, I've been feeling a little weird, so I, uh. . ." Meg was stumbling over her words.

"You don't want Mexican."

"I do."

"We can do Chinese, except I really do want those tacos, you know those—"

She grabbed both of his hands and he stopped speaking.

"I'm pregnant."

Ben stared at her.

She took a deep breath and announced it all at once.

"I was feeling a little weird and so I took a test and I'm pregnant." Meg rushed to finish the sentence and looked her husband in the face, exhaling fully.

Ben sat next to her on the bed, slowly, saying nothing.

So Meg continued to talk, quickly.

"So I brought home all of these books and a couple more tests just in case." She reached for her messenger bag behind them on the bed, turned it upside down and dumped out <u>What to Expect When You're Expecting</u>, <u>Baby's First Year</u>, a few more books, and at least two different early pregnancy tests.

"I can take another test, you know, now that we're both here, but I'm fairly sure. And Ben, I know we weren't planning it, I mean not really. But we weren't really *not* planning it, you know? Everything happens for a reason, right? Or, everyone? It's good news, I know it. We can figure everything out. It's going to be fine." Meg stopped talking, and the quiet around them expanded.

Ben had still said nothing. One by one, he lifted each book from the pile on the bed, and moved it to his bedside table, creating a neat stack.   It was when he saw the copy of <u>What Every New Daddy Needs to Know</u> that Ben started to cry.

"Ben?" Meg leaned her head against his shoulder, looking up at him. He didn't answer her.

"It's going to be wonderful."

He nodded.

"You're going to be the best dad."

He nodded again, through his tears.

"Hey, Ben? I kind of do want Mexican," Meg said softly.

When he'd finally composed himself he turned his head and whispered into her hair, "You can have anything you want."

Annie
November 5, 2013

Everyone stared at her as she walked through Door B. She went straight to her locker and didn't stop in the commons to chat and find her friends as she usually did. Annie had walked past the gathering area and glanced at her regular table but didn't see anyone. Her friends might have already gone to class; they wouldn't have been expecting her today. The hallways were extra quiet, or maybe she was extra sensitive, she couldn't be sure. Some lockers were decorated with blue-and-white streamers and balloons for the home football game on Friday. Annie assumed the lockers were for cheerleaders or football players, or maybe the cheerleaders decorated the lockers for the players? Annie thought she probably knew the answer to this unimportant question but couldn't remember, and she wondered if this was a bad sign for how the rest of her day might go. She twisted open her combination lock and hung her backpack on the hook. She stood and stared at the shelf and the binders, the Vera Bradley lunchbox and the grey cardigan she must have left at school the previous week.

What was she supposed to bring with her to class? She took a deep breath and started grabbing things. Green binder? No, blue. Wait. What class was she headed to? Her eyes started to fill with tears. She had an urge to bolt for the door and go back to the safety of her dark bedroom. Her mom had been right—this was a terrible idea.

"Annabelle?"

She felt a hand on her shoulder and turned to see Mr. Garvin, the Junior guidance counselor standing next to her. She'd only ever had a couple of talks with him--once to turn in her college interest questionnaire and another to have her junior schedule verified.

"Hi," she said. He had emailed her a couple of times, even called her cell, after...after. "I'm sorry I didn't call you back."

"You don't owe me a phone call, Annie. I'm surprised to see you. Don't take that wrong. I'm very glad to see you. Are you doing okay?"

"I think so."

He glanced at her empty hands and took a quick survey of her locker. "What's your first period class?"

"I have…I have Honors English."

Mr. Garvin pulled out his iPad and pressed a few buttons. "Yep," he said. "That's where you're headed. Can I walk with you?"

Annie nodded.

"Do you have your books and binders?"

She pulled out her thick literature text and the binder of notes and papers. "Okay," she thought to herself, with one quiet, deep breath. "I can do this."

"Take your time," he said. Do you need your planner?" They were still at her locker when the first warning bell rang. She startled. "Don't worry about the bell," he said, putting a hand on her shoulder, as if to ground her.

"My planner, oh yeah." Annie turned back to her locker and grabbed the spiral notebook. Then she looked at Mr. Garvin anxiously.

"I haven't finished any assignments that were due last week. Or this week. I haven't even seen them. God, I'll have to get those. I'm gonna be so far behind. Do you think I'll need to stay after? I'm sure I missed that quiz on vocabulary last week, and if there's a test--"

"Annie." Mr. Garvin held up a hand to stop her mid-sentence. "No one expects you to be caught up. Not now and not soon. Come on. Let's walk."

The second bell rang indicating the start of first period, and Annie physically startled.

Mr. Garvin put a gentle hand on her shoulder as they walked. "It's okay, Annie. I already sent a text to Mrs. DeMarco saying that I was walking you to class and you'd be a few minutes late. She's just so happy that she'll see you today."

Annie relaxed a bit; she realized she'd been hunching her shoulders and she let them slump. They walked past the cafeteria, where he stopped at the vending machine and bought a bottle of water and a pack of peanut butter crackers. "Put these in your backpack," he instructed. "Eat and drink right away if you start to feel light headed or if you need something to do with your hands. This could be a long day, and I want you to come see me anytime. If you need anything at all, if it gets to be too much, or if you just need a place to be. Got it?" They were approaching her classroom door.

She took the snacks and the bottle, willing her eyes not to fill.

"Thank you," she said quietly. "I will. Thank you." She smiled a small, grateful smile.

Mr. Garvin knocked lightly on the door and opened it. "Good morning, ladies and gentleman. Sorry for the interruption, but we're going to let Annie take her seat and then you can all get on with class."

Some kids looked up and smiled. Mrs. DeMarco came over and gave her a tiny hug, but not enough to make her feel weird. Her best friend, Lizzy, got up quietly, grabbed Annie's binder and books out of her arms, then took Annie by the hand, and walked her to her desk, which was, thankfully, next to hers. Lizzy opened Annie's book to the correct page as Annie opened her water bottle and took a big gulp. She nodded to Mr. Garvin, as if to say, "I'm good." He gave her a barely noticeable thumbs-up and quietly left.

Annie snuck a quick smile at Lizzy, then settled in to listen to the class discuss Macbeth. With that, she started to feel a little bit more like herself.

Meg
November 5, 2013

She hoped Annie was doing okay. The afternoon dragged as Meg watched the clock, wondering what her girl was doing, who she was talking to, what she was thinking. She had the feeling in the pit of her stomach usually reserved for the first day of each school year, when she couldn't wait for her kids to walk back through the door. Who did you sit with, who was kind, how was your teacher? Did you eat a good lunch, did you make a new friend? Annabelle had ventured into such foreign territory today, and though she had been insistent that she was ready, Meg's heart had been heavy with worry.

She felt better after her shower. Cleaner, certainly. Meg had stayed in the water for a long time, letting the steam open her pores as she leaned against the tiled back wall. Meg had closed her eyes, trying to put the phone, the sleepless night, the texts, the words, all out of her mind, even if just for a moment. Under the water, she felt safe, unreachable. No neighbors greeting her with awkward stares, no cell phones beeping with unexplained messages.

"Mommy?" There was a sudden banging on the bathroom door. Meg was startled at first, and then smiled at the irony of it. Back to the reality of being naked, wet, and needed.

"What, buddy? I'm in the shower."

"Oh," Willie said. "I just didn't know where you were."

"Don't worry. I'll be right there."

She dressed quickly in leggings and a comfy, gray sweater. She towel-dried her hair and pulled on some thick socks, the kind usually reserved for hiking. Out of the corner of her eye, she spied her robe hanging on the bathroom hook, but decided to ignore the thoughts beginning to race. From the bathroom window, she could see Annie's car in the driveway. It was after three, then, if Annie was home. Her daughter was still in the driver's seat, head down, typing furiously on the phone. Well, at least that hadn't changed.

Meg closed the bathroom door behind her in a weak attempt to shut out whatever it was that might or might not be happening on her own cell phone, and she went to find her son in the family room. Willie was curled up on the couch, and she sank down beside him, curling one arm around his slim shoulders.

"You missed me, did you?" she asked.

"No," he said. "I was just checking."

"I'm glad you're checking on me."

They both turned as they heard the back door open.

"She's home!" Willie said, smiling.

"Let's get her," said Meg.

Together, they met her in the mudroom, a welcoming committee.

"My girl!" Meg cried, scooping Annie into a bear hug. Annie tensed and began to sink into her hug.

"So," said Meg, pulling back and smoothing her daughter's hair. "How was it?"

Annie stiffened. "Weird," she said. "Totally weird, and you're wet." She disengaged from Meg's arms and wandered over to the pantry.

"I built a Lego mini-van," piped up Willie, from the kitchen table, where he was now sitting with Fred next to him on his chair.

"Ah-em…" said Meg, with an exaggerated stare toward her son.

"I mean, *we* built a mini-van," said Willie, smiling. Meg smiled back.

"Cool," said his sister.

"I'll make you guys a snack," said Meg. "I want to hear about your day. Sit."

Annie sat, a bit reluctantly, and Meg brought over a jug of apple juice, three glasses, and yet another tray of cookies.

"Are we going to only eat stuff that comes on trays now?" said Annie, looking skeptically at the platter.

"Probably," said Meg. She peeled back the foil, took a sprinkled sugar cookie, broke it in two, and popped half in her mouth. "Yes. I have hereby determined that we are only going to eat things off of platters from now until the end of time."

"I like the stuff people brought us," said Willie. "Not that one meat thing, though. That was gross."

Meg laughed. "It was a paté. Who needs that at a funeral? Mmmmm, delicious. Meat mousse." Meg rubbed her tummy in sarcastic delight.

"Mom!" Annie looked horrified. "That's so mean!"

"I know, I know. Everyone is trying to be so thoughtful and helpful. Seriously, though, Annie. Let this be a lesson to you. When someone dies, do not take meat pudding, meat spread, or meat mixture of any kind. Always bring sugar." Meg picked up a butter cookie and ate it whole. "See? Not meat. Sugar. I feel better already."

Meg knew she was being silly. Tired, silly, disrespectful, slap-happy, whatever it was she didn't care. She was starting to feel a little bit better, and maybe it would rub off on her kids.

Annabelle smiled. Willie ate a mini-cupcake and declared, "Not meat." Finally, Annie picked up a brownie and began to talk about her day, telling every detail about who she saw, who treated her "like a real person," and how she felt. Meg sat with her children, chatting and snacking on the treats until it was nearly time for dinner, but no one was really hungry then, anyway.

Tommy
November 5, 2013

Tommy was shocked when he passed Annabelle in the hall between the media center and the science lab. So shocked, in fact, that he did an actual double-take, like in the movies, which made Annabelle shake her head and roll her eyes. She kept walking toward her class, and he did the same, but for the rest of his class period-- Honors World History 12--he couldn't stop thinking about her and what must be going through her head. Why was she at school? Wasn't there some sort of rule? A school rule, a church rule, or just--he didn't know--a life rule or something? He wasn't sure, but whatever it was, it certainly seemed like his friend Annabelle McAfee was violating the unwritten "when to show up at school after your dad dies" rule.

Tommy couldn't tell if he was upset by her quick return, worried about her, or just still freaked out by everything that had happened. Jesus, he wasn't sure how *he* was going to make it through the day. He had never experienced death before, at least not the death of someone so close to him and his family. He thought probably that if he said this out loud, it might upset his mom and dad, because, in fact, his own grandmother—his dad's mom—had died a few years ago, and one of his grandfathers had died when he was just a baby. But Uncle Ben dying was still so much worse. His grandma had lived in Florida, so he only really got to see her on Christmas and sometimes for a couple of weeks in the summer if she went to visit and stayed with his Aunt Sarah. At the time of her death, it had been months since they'd seen her, and she was so old, it felt, somehow, okay that she died. Tommy was sure that sounded awful, but it was true. He had grown up with Uncle Ben being around all the time, like really, *all* the time. Their families went to high school games together, football, basketball, whatever. Then there were all of the holidays, game nights, and random weekday dinners with Annabelle and her family. A couple of times, Uncle Ben had even shown up at his baseball games when his own dad was out of town. Tommy would look up, and there he'd be, cheering for him just as loud as any dad would cheer for any kid. That funeral was by far the worst day of his life. He had never seen so many sad people, and he had never felt so ridiculously sad himself.

He had picked up the phone to text Annabelle that morning, before the service, to see how she was, but what do you text to your oldest friend on the day of her dad's funeral?

Are you okay? he'd typed, but it looked weird so he'd deleted it.

Do you need anything? Nope.

Thinking of you. God, no. Who was he, a goddamn Hallmark card?

Finally, he'd decided to think about what he would want to hear if he were in her place on this morning.

This totally sucks he typed. *It fucking sucks and I'll be there soon*

He hit SEND, and while he waited, he tied his tie and put some Axe gel in his hair to smooth the bed-head curls. He hoped he looked appropriate to do whatever it was he would need to do today.

Annie texted back. Tommy lifted the phone from the dresser.

ttly

Totally.

He and Annabelle had a friendship that had always comforted and confused him at the same time. In the safe spaces of their homes, on vacations, out to dinner, the two of them got along as they always had. Like a brother and sister. They talked about school, friends, about teachers, celebrities, whatever. She teased him mercilessly. He teased her back. At school, or a football game, or if they ran into each other when he was with his team and she was with her friends, she'd grow mean, or worse, sometimes quiet. He was lucky if he would get a quick "Hello." It was as if the real Annabelle came out in secret. A part of him enjoyed their secret closeness, but a part of him wished he could have her, one hundred percent, all the time. He sometimes craved their teasing, their realness.

On the night when Aunt Meg received the awful news, she had called his mom immediately, and she had gone over right away. Tommy had followed with his dad a couple of hours later, which was the right thing, he knew, but it was so weird not knowing what to do at a house which was like your second home. Annabelle was not in the family room where everyone had gathered. Aunt Meg had been crying, but it seemed to get way worse the minute that he and his dad showed up. Willie was curled up on the couch, not really crying, but his eyes were watery and his nose runny. Tommy sat down next to him and just kept patting him on the head.

"You okay, buddy?" he asked.

Willie shook his head.

"Yeah," said Tommy. "I get that."

After about a half hour of being in the family room with the adults, watching them try to make sense of the new and terrible news, Tommy whispered to Willie that he would be right back and he snuck out and made his way upstairs to Annabelle's room and knocked on the closed door.

No answer.

He knocked again.

"Hey, it's Tommy. Thomas." Everyone else in the world called him Tommy. Not her. She called him Thomas, and he let her. Long ago, she said it sounded very sophisticated, and that it reminded her of a book she had read. He called her Annabelle, in return. It was yet another special joke they shared, when they were alone, just the two of them.

He knew he should be going in to offer her comfort, but in truth, he was trying to get away from the unbearable sadness downstairs. He would find his friend, and although he knew he would find her in pain, he would find an escape. Maybe together, they could make some sense out of this horrible night.

"Come on in." Her voice was muffled, barely audible.

He cracked open the door. The room was dark, the only light now coming from the hall light that he let in, which shone onto her double bed. Annie sat rigidly on the edge, grasping a pillow on her lap. Her knuckles were white from the effort it took to squeeze the fabric. When she looked up at him, he saw her swollen face, her red-rimmed eyes.

"Oh, Annabelle."

She looked back down. He moved slowly toward the bed and sat next to her, saying nothing. She leaned into him and took a deep, shuddering breath.

He let her lean there for several long minutes, in the quiet. A few times, he patted her back, and once, he even smoothed her hair and gently rubbed her back as he did. He didn't think he had touched her since summer, not even a friendly hug, but this was so different. So, so different.

Eventually, he reached over, peeled her hands free of the pillow finger by finger, and eased her back onto the bed. He covered her with the blue-and-white striped Perry Pike High School fleece throw that was tossed at the end of her bed. She still hadn't said a word.

"You comfortable?"

She nodded, barely, reminding him of a fragile vase that could shatter and drench him with her salty tears, if pushed.

Tommy went into her attached bathroom, turned on the light, and for just one moment, he felt like an intruder, seeing all of her personal things on the counter. Victoria's Secret lotions, big, fluffy make-up brushes, glittery lip-glosses scattered everywhere. The bathroom smelled sweet and clean and faintly of vanilla, just like Annabelle. He found a box of tissues and an empty plastic tumbler. He rinsed the cup with hot water until it was clean, then filled it with cold water from the tap. In the medicine cabinet next to her mirror, he found a bottle of Advil, averting his eyes from the Midol, the Clearasil and a thousand other things he didn't want to see. He placed the tissues, the drink, and two pills on her bedside table, and turned on one low desk lamp.

"Okay?" he said, walking back over to the bed.

"Okay," she said. Her first word since he had come into the room.

"All right," he answered. He touched her lightly on her arm, not knowing what else to do, then leaned down and gave her a soft kiss on her cheek. "I'm so sorry, Annabelle." He could hear his own voice catch as he turned toward the door. He was almost into the hall when he heard her whisper.

"Please, don't leave."

It was as if she might not have even wanted him to hear it, or maybe she wasn't sure if she should say it, but either way, he wasn't going anywhere.

"Okay."

Next to her desk was a pink polka-dot chair, quilted fabric in a round frame. He dropped his nearly six-foot frame into the seat, and by the dim light of the desk lamp, he began to leaf through the teen magazines that were scattered on Annabelle's floor. "How to flirt with your guy" and "Four new ways to wear your infinity scarf" were not holding his attention, but they did distract him, just a little, from the pounding sadness of the day. Annabelle didn't move, and Tommy didn't leave, which was all she had asked.   He fell asleep in the uncomfortable chair with his head thrown back and his legs stretched out, until his mom and Aunt Meg came to wake him hours later.

Today, he felt blindsided by seeing her in the hall. Here he was, stumbling through the school day with an aching wound inside his chest, and Annabelle waltzes past, calmly, with crackers and water like it's freaking preschool snack time. She hadn't even called him to change their carpool plans; she had picked him up every morning since she got her license. His mom even slipped her a gas card every now and then, even though Aunt Meg would have told Annie not to accept. Tommy's mom had been driving him since… it happened…and had offered to start driving Annie to school when she was ready to return. She certainly looks ready, he thought. He wasn't sure where his anger was coming from. He was mature enough to know that there were many difficult emotions churning inside him right now, but not mature enough to stop himself from pulling out his cell phone, clicking on Annie's contact number and typing,

What the hell are you doing here?

He paused for only the briefest moment before pressing the SEND key.

Annie
November 5, 2013

What Annie hadn't told her mother was that she had received a text during last period. A text that took any progress she might have made during the school day, and erased it like chalkdust on the sidewalk. She had felt her phone vibrate in her pocket, but she didn't check in class, like some kids tended too. She hadn't even looked at her phone until after the period ended and she was walking to her locker to collect her things and grab her coat. What she saw didn't make sense, so she shoved the phone back in her pocket. At home, though, as she did every day, she pulled into the driveway, put her car in park, and took her phone out to read and answer any texts, emails, tweets or Facebook posts that she might have missed. But first, she revisited the unsettling text that she'd gotten during Chemistry.

What the hell are you doing here?

The text was from Thomas.

Meg
November 5, 2013

He had begged and begged, so Meg found herself curled up on the couch with Willie watching his favorite show, "America's Got Talent." They had popped up a bag of microwave popcorn, the really good, buttery, salty kind, and had the bowl between them on the blanket while they watched the performers singing, dancing, even riding trick bikes. Watching Willie eat popcorn and marvel at a cyclist's trick actually did lift her spirits, just a little.

"Thanks for the TV date," she said, kissing him on his smooth soft cheek.

"Mom!" he said, but he was smiling just a teeny bit, slurping down his can of soda.

Through the front windows of the family room, the dark sky looked particularly deep and endless. She couldn't shake the thought that she still wasn't feeling the way she was supposed to be feeling, whatever that might mean. Though she was walking around with an emptiness, with a true understanding about the word "heartache," she still wasn't noticing any real loneliness. Perhaps it was because she wasn't really lonely— Willie remained glued to her side as if they were competing in a three-legged race, and she both understood and appreciated his presence. She thought perhaps her unsettled feelings were rooted in the fact that tomorrow was the day that Ben should have returned from his trip; he would have landed about 6:30 pm. Technically, he was still supposed to be away. Maybe she wasn't prepared to miss him yet, and would feel his absence more acutely when the date of his once imminent homecoming had come and gone. Despite what they had been through, a date was a date. And so far, Ben hadn't missed a date.

She hadn't really let herself sink into the details of his death. Meg
had barely heard the police officer's description, in brief, when he had come
to the house to deliver the news that first terrible night. She had been mini-
mally prepared for the squad car in the driveway; not only had she not yet
heard from Ben--no text, no call--but the airline had called to ask if they had
the correct "Meg McAfee" at their joint address. They were sorry they could
not provide more details, they said, but there would be someone contacting
her very shortly. She was as ready as she could be, then, to hear the doorbell
ring, listen to the officer deliver the news that her husband had died. It had
always been her worst fear, Ben's death, but also explaining to her children
that their father had died in a plane crash. And here it was, right on her
doorstep, though not quite as she had imagined.

When Meg heard the story in more detail the next day, told to her
with great care in a small room at the airport, it seemed somehow worse
than anything she had imagined over the years. A chaplain was present (an
airport chaplain, she supposed), the flight's pilot, another police officer, the
flight attendant who had helped Ben, and a representative from the airline.
She was having a difficult time processing the story. Ben had been sitting in
seat 7A, an aisle seat close to the front, just like he preferred, on his flight
from Cleveland to Chicago for the International Hardware Trade Show. He
had seemed perfectly fine when he'd left the house that morning. He had
packed in about ten minutes, as always, right before leaving, a habit that
both annoyed and amazed her. She, who could spend days planning and organizing for any trip, could not wrap her mind around her husband's ability
to get ready for a week's trip in the amount of time it took her to wash her
face. Ben had said good-bye to the kids before they left for school.

"I'll see you in about a week," he'd said.

"Bye, Dad!" they'd both said, looking up from their cereal. It was
uneventful, pedestrian. He had hugged Meg, kissed her before he left for the
airport. It was definitely a ritual, even if they didn't acknowledge it.

Don't leave town without a kiss goodbye.

Don't leave the airport without a text.

Let me know when you're back on the ground.

Meg remembered that he had taken an antacid that morning, complaining of heartburn. Why hadn't she told him to stay home, call a doctor? Yet, how many other times had either of them swallowed a painkiller or popped a Tums before heading out the door? Neither of them could have guessed that it was a precursor to a nightmare.

Mid-flight, the passenger next to Ben noticed that he seemed hot, sweaty. He was uncomfortable, the woman told the crew later. She asked if he would like some water, and Ben said yes, so she had summoned the flight attendant, who also noticed that he did not look well. As she was pouring his water, Ben began having severe pain in his chest, and seemed to be struggling to breathe. The flight attendant said that she called out to him, asking if he was all right. She said that he actually answered, "I think I'm having a heart attack," but that it was difficult for him to get the words out.

A young man from the middle of the coach section came forward quickly and identified himself as a doctor. (Meg could not help but think that this sounded like a B-grade movie; the flight attendant assured her that, more often than not, there is someone from a medical field on the plane.) He took one look at Ben, quickly moved the other passengers out of Ben's row and into the aisle, laid Ben across the seats and began to perform CPR. Within several minutes, he yelled for the on-board defibrillators.

It was at this point in the story that Meg closed her eyes. She didn't want this vision in her brain. No, her worst fear had been her husband dying in a fiery plane crash, maybe going down over an ocean, into the side of a mountain. Ben dying in a plane, with strangers around him (kind and helpful strangers, to be sure) was new and horrible information to introduce into the pattern of worst-case-scenarios she had played out in the dark corners of her imagination.

The story of Ben's death settled into Meg's consciousness only as far as she would allow, which didn't accommodate the details of how Ben (Ben's body?) had traveled the rest of the way, or how he was later transported to the funeral home. Meg found herself not wanting to know the answers. So she simply did not ask for every detail, oddly comforting herself by taking business cards and phone numbers of everyone she spoke to, thinking perhaps she would call when she was ready to learn more. She preferred, for now, to view herself from the outside as the newly widowed, receiving the information at the airport, meeting the police, shaking hands, nodding when appropriate. Seeing herself in that moment, when she was forced to see the coroner, listening but not hearing, she wondered if she had been weak. Weak? A weak woman could not have identified her husband's face, seeing it in a partially unzipped black body bag in a temporary morgue in the basement of the airport. In any event, Meg decided she did not care, because in her current version of events, Ben had left for a trip and had never come home. And as long as she tucked the images of the body bag into a closed compartment in her brain, her current version was the only one that fit.

Now, Meg thought, maybe it wouldn't be until tomorrow, late evening, until the horrible reality of really missing Ben would set in like a crashing plane.

She extracted herself from the blanket on the couch, trying not to dislodge the popcorn.

"Mom," complained Willie, "it's not over!"

"I'll be back," she said. She knew he was weeks, maybe months, away from being willing to separate from her and go back to school, and that was fine with her. He was in the sixth grade. There was nothing he couldn't make up. She brushed the soft, light brown curls off his forehead as she walked behind the couch, through the family room, and into the master bedroom, where she closed the door behind her.

In the bathroom, she stood before her robe. It was hanging on its hook, innocently enough, but for a few solid minutes, Meg could only stare at the robe as if it were an actual person, daring her to make a move, challenging her to check the messages. She exhaled sharply and reached into the pocket and grabbed the phone. On the home screen, there were indicators showing activity since she had last checked.

Text from Elise
Calendar: Meeting Middle School 7:00 PM Wednesday
Missed Call Elise
Voicemail Elise
Text from Ben

Meg's stomach fell at a dizzying rate, and before she could steady herself, her legs buckled and she dropped to her knees. And there, in the private sanctuary of her bathroom, one hand clutching her phone, and the other grasping the hem of the bathrobe, Meg wept. She sobbed because she missed Ben, and she choked on tears, forcing herself to think about his last few moments. Was he scared, was he in pain? She buried her face into the pale pink fleece, gripping it tightly, and as she allowed her body to sink lower onto floor, the robe pulled off the hook and puddled next to her. Meg curled up into a tight ball. She tried to remember what she'd been unable, or unwilling, to bring forward; the last moment they were together, what had it been, really? Was she smiling at Ben when he left that morning? Did she kiss him and tell him she loved him, or was she distracted by Willie's homework or Annie's morning rush? What were the very last words they had spoken, and in the end, did it matter, or did he just know? When he was taking his last breath, did he feel her, did he say goodbye? Meg wasn't exactly sure what she believed about soulmates and afterlife and eternity (especially lately) but how could she not have felt it when Ben left the earth? How could he have died without her, without them? She cried harder and harder, her chest heaving against the cold floor, as she allowed the feelings of guilt and blame to surface. She hadn't worried enough to keep him alive.

When Meg was a little girl with an upset tummy, she'd want only to lie on the cool linoleum in the bathroom. It was like that now, only it was as if the floor and the robe had risen to meet her needs. She didn't really remember falling, or grabbing the robe, or falling apart. Meg lay in the crumpled robe until her sobs subsided. Her hand was sweaty from holding tightly to her phone. Still on her side, on the floor, she looked at the screen --the notifications were still there. She didn't know if she had wanted to receive a new message from Ben, or never get one again. Rolling onto her back, she read Elise's text first (*how are you, what do you need, call me*) She deleted the meeting from her calendar; she didn't need to go to a PPMS Fall Fun Fair planning meeting, nor would anyone expect her. She clicked "play" and listened to the voicemail from her best friend (call me, how are you, what do you need, can I pop by tomorrow and bring lunch?) All that was left was the text from Ben.

She took a breath and clicked to open the message.

Ben: Hi baby :) Are you really there? I love you.

Meg turned her face into her robe and sobbed.

Annie
November 5, 2013

The text from Thomas really, really pissed her off. Who the hell was he to ask her what the hell she was doing? It wasn't like he was hanging around trying to make sure she was okay, like he was doing a great job of being her friend at school, or her protector, or any of those things that their moms probably thought he was doing.

"You can count on Tommy," she could remember Aunt Elise saying before middle school. "He won't let any stupid guy be a jerk to you at school." Yeah, right, she thought. Now he's the stupid jerk who just sent me a nasty text.

He basically ignored her most of the time, only occasionally acknowledging that they knew each other. They hung with different crowds, were into different things. Thomas (okay, Tommy, as he went by at school) hung around with the baseball players, who in turn hung with the girls' softball team. He wore his letter jacket most of the time, even when it wasn't cold outside. He was popular and smart. They were "friends" on Facebook and Twitter and Snapchat, all the places where everyone was friends with everyone, so she knew how the girls flirted and played with him, how they included him in silly texts and how he flirted back with some, ignored others. It wasn't entirely fair to say that he ignored her, because he always answered her texts and Facebook posts, except that everything about their relationship at school felt phony. She wasn't just another girl in the crowd who was drooling over his blond wavy hair and his baseball stats, and she wouldn't pretend.

Annabelle had plenty of friends, and she was perfectly well-liked in her own crowd. She was just more quieter and reserved. She played the violin, not a sport. Her crowd had remained largely the same since elementary school, including Lizzy, and she was happier in a small group than at a big party. Annie wasn't about to send dumb messages and Snapchats to random boys, although she was suddenly beginning to understand the girls who did. Her fingers were itching to answer that ridiculous text on her phone.

She was furious that her old friend Thomas suddenly had the nerve to call her out for showing up at school today. Showing up at school had been brave. Showing up had been what she needed. Showing up was the one thing that felt ordinary. Everything else had been so wrong and so messed up, and finally, today, she felt a bit more like herself. He knew her better than that, didn't he? In the last few days, all she could think about was the night after her dad died (and if she really admitted it, the way Thomas had stayed with her, cared for her, kissed her cheek). Her feelings of sadness were wrapped up with feelings about him (again), which made his text even worse to receive.

She picked up her phone, and looked at his words.

What the hell are you doing here?

fuck you she texted, surprising and impressing herself. She turned off her phone and slammed it down, turned on her desk light, and tried to get some homework done. She glanced over at her pink polka dot chair, remembering where he sat and slept. She grabbed her fleece blanket and her books, curled up into the round chair and pretended to study.

Elise
January 2, 2002

Meg went into labor with her second child on a cold January night, three weeks early. Elise would always remember the event, not just because her best friend was having a baby, but because of the phone call that came around ten in the evening. It was snowing, and she was throwing in one last load of laundry. Thomas had been asleep for hours, and she knew that Kyle might appreciate it if, for once, she would come to bed at a decent time, instead of staying downstairs and finding a million things to do. Dishes, tidying the toys, watching the news.

She was just wiping the counters with the dishtowel when the phone rang. Meg's home number popped up on the screen.

"Hey," said Elise. "It's late for you. What's up?"

"Hey," replied Meg, her voice wobbling. "I think I'm in labor."

"You think?" cried Elise, dropping her towel and looking at the clock.

"I *think* I'm in labor and my husband is in *fucking* Chicago and my baby is asleep." Meg was yelling.

"I'm coming over. Get dressed."

Elise ran upstairs to tell Kyle, instructed him to get Thomas out of bed and bundled into a snowsuit, and they hurried through the house, grabbing coats and shoes and whatever they might need for a long night ahead. They hurried as fast as they could to the McAfees, not sure how Meg would be when they arrived. Kyle used the garage code to get in, and while he set up a bed for Thomas in Annabelle's Pack-and-Play in the family room, Elise ran through the back of the house to the master bedroom.

Meg was in the bathroom, leaning against the sink.

"Status?" Elise asked.

"Contracting," she said. "Hang on."

"How far apart?"

"Hang *on*," said Meg, doubling over, then finally relaxing out of the pain.

"So," said Elise, "that lasted about a minute. How far apart?"

"Maybe ten?"

"Okay, that's not crazy bad."

"Easy for you to say," said Meg, bracing herself on the counter. "That last one hurt like hell."

"I know, sweetie. C'mon. Let's get you there and you'll get all fixed up with some big drugs and a big doctor with his big ass hands all up inside you."

"Stop yourself," said Meg, rolling her eyes.

Elise took her arm, grabbed Meg's favorite sweatshirt and fuzzy socks off the bedroom chair, and her toothbrush, and started to lead her out of the room.

"Wait. Annie is…"

"Kyle and Thomas are here. They can stay for the night. What about Ben?"

"He got a flight out at midnight."

"Good."

"He had to buy a first class seat to get on the flight."

"It's a first class kind of a night, don't you think?"

Meg tried to smile, but it turned into a wince.

On their way through the kitchen, Elise grabbed Meg's coat, her purse, two water bottles from the fridge, then she ran back and grabbed her make-up bag and a hairbrush. Elise tossed all the supplies into a plastic grocery bag, added a few leftover Christmas candies for good measure.

Kyle looked at the two women.

"How're you doing?" he said to Meg.

"Be better soon, I guess," Meg said, shooting him a weak smile. "Hey, there's some leftover chili in the freezer and . . ."

"Oh my God, Meg, are you freaking kidding me?" said Elise.

"Kyle, feed yourself, feed the kids, we'll be home when we're home, hopefully with a baby. I love you, thanks for doing this."

"I love you, too, Kyle!" called Meg, on her way out the door.

"Good luck! Call me, okay?" Thomas was already asleep in his cozy makeshift bed, and Kyle stretched out on the sofa, grabbing the remote.

"I will. And if you hear from Ben, call my cell."

When William Benjamin McAfee was born five hours later, he was greeted first by his mom, then by his Aunt Elise, and immediately thereafter by his father, who although frazzled, had made it with a half-hour to spare.

"Ben!" Meg and Elise had cried in unison as he burst through the door, overcoat flying.

"Meg! I'm sorry!" Did I. . . Did you. . .?" He looked frantically around at the scene. A nurse was checking Meg's vitals, Elise was rubbing Meg's belly.

Meg managed a weak giggle. "Not yet."

"Not since you last texted me one minute ago," Elise said. "But soon."

Ben had sent Elise exactly thirty-one texts since he landed in Cleveland, and they'd been on the phone twice, for a few minutes each time, when Elise stepped into the hall away from Meg for a few moments.

"I *promise* I will text you if anything changes. Just drive safely. Everything is fine."

"Okay. Okay, but what if it happens all of a sudden and I miss it?"

"Ben, are you in your car and on your way?"

"Yes."

"That's all you can do. And right now, she's not even pushing, so I think we're good."

He texted her from the hospital parking lot, and then from the lobby. Elise heard him before she saw him, his dress shoes echoing in the hospital hallway as he approached the delivery suite.

"Oh, my God," Ben said, throwing off his coat. "I didn't miss it?" said Ben.

The contraction had passed, and Meg lay peacefully in the bed. She was leaning back on her pillow, holding Elise's hand. It was quiet in the room. The lights were dim, and soft music was playing in the background.

"Um, no," said Elise , glancing first at Meg's giant belly and then at the still empty bassinet, waiting by the side of the bed.

"You seem fine, though," he said, looking at Meg. "I mean, you seem really, really good."

"Epidural," said Elise, stroking Meg's hand. "And we're on a very romantic date night."

"Ah," said Ben, smiling and bending to kiss Meg.

"She's having a big one right now," said the nurse, checking the monitor and watching Meg's reaction.

"I don't feel a thing," cried Meg, gleefully, as Elise stepped back and Ben took over.

"Thank you," Ben said, to Elise. "I mean it."

"Well, I would have been here anyway. But you're welcome." Elise squeezed Ben's shoulders as left the bedside to take a break in the rocking chair.

When Willie decided to arrive, he decided quickly, and twenty-five minutes later, Meg was holding her baby boy.

Elise was the third person to hold baby William, and as she snuggled him, she whispered into his newborn fuzzy head, "Welcome into this crazy family, Munchkin."

Tommy
November 5, 2013

Really? *fuck you*? Nice. He tossed his phone onto the bed next to him and flopped back onto his pillows. Bitch, he thought. Then, in his own head, he took it back. He didn't think she was a bitch. He probably loved her. Since they had grown up together, he assumed he kind of had to love her, but it wasn't as a sister and he knew it. At school they never acted like they were very close or even liked each other that much, but everyone knew they were connected; their families always had been. Their moms volunteered as a team at class parties, their dads golfed on the weekends. They had vacationed together almost every summer, but honestly, most years, Tommy had hung out more with Willie, playing video games and Pokemon. When they got older, though, the two teenagers began to hang out a little bit more, finding things to do during the day. They did silly, vacation things, like walking to the ice cream shop for midday milkshakes, splashing in the ocean with Willie, tossing a baseball on the hard-packed sand. This past summer had been no different, until it had been entirely different. Tommy took a deep breath in, as though trying to hold onto a memory in his mind. Summer had come and gone. Uncle Ben had died. Now this.

fuck you

Last summer, on their last August day in the South Carolina beach house, he was lying on the bed in the room he shared with Willie. Annie had her own room, because she was the only girl, but he never cared. As an only child, he loved the opportunity to crash in a room with his pseudo-little brother, to wrestle and tease, to chat about whatever Willie wanted to talk about—usually Lego and Minecraft. None of it was boring to him, and as much as he knew that Willie liked hanging out with him, he wondered if Willie knew that the feeling was mutual. Today, they were lounging on their twin beds, already in their swim trunks, waiting for everyone to move it along to the beach. Tommy happened to look up from his frayed Archie comic to catch a glimpse of Annie in the hall bathroom. She was dressed in her bright blue bikini, getting ready for a day in the sun. He watched her brushing her light brown hair into a ponytail, applying her lip gloss, smoothing sunblock onto her face. He couldn't tear his eyes away, until she saw him in the mirror and he looked away, caught. Annie flipped the light off, and as she walked past his bedroom, she blew him a kiss and giggled.

At the beach, Tommy was on edge, but in the best way. It felt like Christmas Eve, when the unexpected is actually possible, and you often get what you desire. His stomach would occasionally flip, he was distracted, he was laughing loudly and tossing his hair. Was Annie flirting? He thought so. She was texting her friends using her cell phone through a plastic baggie, giggling a lot, and tossing her head back to face the sun.

When their moms unpacked lunch, Annie tossed him a sandwich. "Here, I made you a ham and cheese."

"Thanks," he said.

She sat down on the towel next to him with her own sandwich and a bag of chips to share. They sat, toes in the sand, and ate lunch facing the surf. Tommy could feel her glancing at him, surreptitiously.

"What?" he finally asked.

"What what?" she replied, innocently.

"You keep looking at me," he said, taking a bite.

"Well, you were looking at me this morning," she said, nudging his foot with her toe.

"So that's the way it is," he said, smiling.

"Apparently," she said. She got up and walked into the ocean to rinse off.

Tommy watched her from his towel. He wondered if she wanted him to follow her. He threw the last bit of his sandwich back into the cooler and headed for the water's edge with a beach ball.

"Toss?" he said.

"If you want to lose," she challenged.

They played ball in the ocean in the hot sun, splashing around, until Annabelle tired of the game and declared herself the undeniable winner, throwing her hands in the air like a true champion.

"Fine, you win," he agreed, though he felt like a champion.

It was a long and lazy afternoon. Their moms and Will had already trekked back inside. Annabelle and Tommy grabbed their towels and shook out the sand, sending grains flying.

"Hey! Cut it out!" she yelled. "I'm covered in your sand!"

"Poor baby," he yelled back, shaking his towel right at her.

She grabbed his towel, squealing, which only pulled him close to her. Was it on purpose? Tommy wanted to think that no girl in the world did anything that wasn't on purpose. So there, on the beach, with no one around and one towel between them, he leaned in and kissed her.

She did not pull away. She kissed him back. They both still held the towel, and he reached around and placed his free hand on her back, lightly touching her skin, warm and sandy. They kissed for a few minutes, nothing more, not saying anything. At one point, he thought Annie was reaching up to maybe hold on around his neck? Or touch his hair? But she didn't. "We'd better go in," she said, pulling back slightly.

"I guess so," he said.

They walked up the path to the house, where they could see the bright lights shining through the windows. His dad and Uncle Ben must be home from golf, and dinner plans must be underway. Between them, they swung the towel, almost as if they were holding hands. The last evening of vacation would soon be over, and everyone in the house would think it was a totally typical night. Almost everyone.

Meg
November 6, 2013

It was well past midnight, but Meg couldn't sleep. She was sitting in bed with her laptop on her lap, her television tuned to HGTV so she could listen mindlessly to House Hunters International. In the days since Ben's death, she'd been unable to listen to any sort of news, not national or local. In her own grief, any tragedy seemed either too big or too small to make sense of, so Meg turned it all off and watched only benign programming. Food shows, home shows, talk shows.

She hadn't checked her email in a week, and decided to avoid it, still. It was too much to think about, and although her inbox was likely filled with kind messages from acquaintances who thought they'd found an appropriate way to reach out and express sympathy, Meg was not ready to read or respond. She logged into Facebook and began to scroll mindlessly through the updates from friends and family. Every now and then she would see something about her husband, posted by a colleague of Ben's, or a friend of Annie's. She read them, found them to be kind, but found no need to reply or "like."

On a whim, she logged into Annabelle's account. She knew the password by heart, she had known it since the day her daughter first opened her Facebook account. Meg and Ben had been her first two friends on social media; those were the conditions they had set on the spot, though the technology seemed to be changing faster than they could stipulate rules. Just as she suspected, her daughter's Facebook page was flooded with messages, some from kids she recognized, some she didn't. All were thoughtful, although written in kid-speak. Annie had mentioned to Meg in passing that all of them annoyed her, and Meg understood. Perhaps someday her girl would look back and read them and find comfort in the way her friends and classmates were trying to reach out. It didn't really matter, she supposed. She was always telling her children not to put too much stock in social media, especially when the content got mean and gossipy, which it inevitably did.

"It's not real," she would say. "Conversations are real. Friendships are real. Facebook is not real. Anything you can delete with one button is not real."

She logged out of Annie's account and before turning her laptop off for the night, she noticed a new message in her own Facebook account.

Heard the news. Just thinking of you and hoping you're okay.

The message was from Jason Brinkman, her high school boyfriend. Meg was shocked. Jason had requested her as a friend on Facebook a couple years ago, and she had accepted, at first thinking very little of it. Meg had connected with most of her high school class, which had been fairly small, and she always enjoyed seeing the pictures and updates of old classmates and their kids. When Ben had heard about this particular connection, however, he'd been less than pleased. It was a memory that she opted not to re-visit now, not when she was missing Ben so much.

She'd "unfriended" Jason at Ben's request, and hadn't heard from him since. Occasionally, she saw his name or comments on pictures that mutual friends shared, and she would assume that perhaps he saw some of hers. What she received today had come in the form of a message, directly to her, via her inbox on Facebook. Her relationship with Jason was so typical high school that she could hardly even think about it without picturing herself in either a prom dress or at a football game. He had asked her to a dance her sophomore year, and they had dated until Jason graduated, a year ahead of Meg. It had been so small-town, so easy. Movies, ice cream, corsages. Of course, there was the drama that always accompanied a teenage romance; break ups, fights and tears, over--what? Meg couldn't even begin to remember. It certainly hadn't been the era of cell phones and texts. It was a time of long talks on the house phone, often dragged into the hall coat closet to find a bit of privacy. Still, if she was upset with her boyfriend, everyone in the house knew about it, and everyone knew why. His face had looked the same in his profile photo. Older of course, but kind and unassuming. He had always been a decent guy.

Meg supposed his message was thoughtful, however unexpected. Still, as with every other expression of kindness so far, she was not prepared to answer. Suddenly, she could feel her throat tighten and her eyes begin to sting, and she realized that she was not prepared for anything else tonight. Seeing Ben's name all over Annie's page, hearing from Jason, thinking about the texts--it was all too much.

Meg closed her laptop and stashed it next to her bed. She took a moment to decide against a sleeping pill and pulled the comforter up to her chin. She reached for her cell phone, and without giving it any more thought, she typed,

I'm still here. Where are you? Are you ok?

In the daylight hours, she felt better equipped to explain away the unexplainable, even if it was only in the space of her own brain. The circle of thoughts that spun endlessly in her brain were interrupted over and over by children, friends, the doorbell, a new emotion, or an unexpected fit of anger. But at night, alone, in their room, Meg just missed her husband and wanted to talk to him. Her phone glowed in the darkness on the bed next to her. "November 6, 2013," it read. "1:06 AM." Today was the day that Ben had been booked on a flight home.

Are you coming home today? she typed, as the tears bubbled behind her eyes.

She clicked SEND, and allowed herself a brief moment of believing that there was a possibility, just a small one, that Ben's spirit was communicating with her. There must be some small window, some small fissure between space and time, between alive and dead, between earth and heaven where he could be existing with the power to contact her. Is that what was happening? Right this minute, Meg hoped so. She could feel her throat clog with sadness; her temples throbbed. She tried to keep herself calm by listing in her mind all she needed to do, all the mundane things--returning Tupperware, signing insurance forms, reading cards, answering messages. As she finally closed her eyes, though, her thoughts were centered not on plastic dishes and emails but on wondering if she would receive a reply from Ben. As she rolled to her side, the tears dripped onto her pillow. She reached toward Ben's side of the bed; if he'd been there, her hand would have rested on his chest. Still clutching the phone, she settled into position, her arm draped across his empty side of the bed. Occasionally, she rubbed her thumb back and forth. In these moments, connecting with her phone, she tried not to think about Ben's phone, and where it could be.

Back and forth.

Back and forth.

With a deep, shuddering breath, she tried to sleep.

Meg was out of sorts from the moment she woke up. Annie got herself ready to go to school, but she was cranky, too.

"Breakfast?" Meg offered when her daughter came into the kitchen.

"I'm fine," Annie muttered.

"You should eat. Even Mr. Garvin said so."

"You talked to Mr. Garvin?" Annie whirled on her.

"What's the matter? I phoned him to let him know that you were headed in yesterday, and he called me in the afternoon to let me know that he'd spoken with you. It's his job to keep me informed."

"Geez, I'm fine. It's not like I'm the one who died."

"Annie!" Meg could hardly believe her daughter had spoken the sentence.

"It's true. I'm fine. Everyone should leave me alone. You, Mr. Garvin, Thomas. All of you."

"Thomas?" Meg asked.

"Whatever." Annie grabbed a water bottle and an apple and turned toward the garage door.

"Don't you dare leave like this," Meg snapped. She felt horrible yelling at her daughter in the midst of so much sadness swirling around them.

Annie stomped back to face her mother across the kitchen table.

"Mr. Garvin called to tell me that he'd seen you, talked with you, walked with you to class. He wanted me to know that I could phone him if we needed anything. It was a nice thing for him to do. The right thing." She had been impressed by the call; in fact, the counselor had contacted her on her cell phone when she hadn't picked up the landline. All the numbers were in the school file, and he felt it was important to touch base. Meg agreed.

"I'm sorry," Annie said. "It's just…a lot."

"I know," said Meg. "Please just take it down about seven notches. Have a good day. I love you."

"I love you, too." Her daughter's giant eye-roll did not go undetected, but Meg decided to let it go.

Maybe Annie was feeling the effects of the date as much as she was. She and the kids were accustomed to Ben's travel, but they were also used to him coming home after a week at most. He would burst into the house after a trip, announcing his arrival, happy to see each of them, demanding hugs, and declaring plans to go out to dinner.

It was always a mini-celebration, or at the very least, an excuse to go to their favorite burger restaurant in town. Annie would postpone her homework and Willie would be allowed to skip his bath and stay up late. Without being able to control it, Meg knew she was feeling the anticipation of Ben's homecoming. She was tidying the counters and thinking about taking a shower, making the bed and straightening the piles of books and papers in the kids' cubbies. She was mindlessly doing all the things she did whenever he was due to arrive, just so he wasn't coming into a messy house after a week in a hotel. The thought that he would not come through the door tonight made the bile rise in her throat. He wasn't coming home into a messy house, a clean house, or an empty house.

He wasn't coming home.

He wasn't coming...

He wasn't...

It was so desperately unfair, and the texts were making the desperation infinitely worse.

She checked her phone. Nothing. Well, she found herself thinking, she often didn't hear back from Ben when he was traveling.

Business trip.

Business trip.

Meg put the kettle on to make some tea, and to avoid losing her mind. She didn't even really like tea, but it sounded like the right thing to do when a person is about to go insane. Ben is not texting because Ben is dead. That one fact, that one horrible, real fact, didn't correlate with the phone in her hand and the sense of his impending homecoming.

She dialed Elise, who answered on the first ring.

"Good morning," said her friend. "How's it going over there?"

"You really have no idea." Meg knew she would have to tell Elise about the texts at some point. There was just no way around it, and no real way to handle this on her own. She absolutely could not share this with her parents, or with Ben's dad. Her own parents lived just an hour away and had returned to their home the evening of the funeral, at Meg's insistence. They had been helpful for the few days they had stayed, but if Meg shared this new development, she feared long conversations filled with "what if's" and "how's" that she would be obviously unable to answer. Her mother, a recent convert to texting, might very well try to text Ben's number herself in an attempt to "help." Meg knew she did not have the energy or patience to handle her parents, at least not yet. Ben's dad lived in the next town, and as resistant to technology as he was, she doubted that she could even explain it to him in a manner that would make any sense. She needed to check in with Ben's dad, now that she thought about it, maybe take the kids over for dinner. It was best to leave the parents out of the equation until she had some answers.

Maybe Elise would help her look at things rationally. Since there wasn't anything else she didn't share with her best friend, now did not seem the time to start hiding things.

"That sounds ominous. Well, all things considered, I guess you have every reason to sound as ominous as you want."

"That's fair," said Meg. "It's a little crazier even than it has been, if you can believe it. Do you have time to stop by?"

"Yep," said her friend, with no hesitation. "Let me get out of my jammies and I'll be over. I need to stop at the grocery for a couple of dinner things. Need anything while I'm there?"

"I don't think so," answered Meg, glancing at her overflowing countertop. "See you soon."

Meg changed from her nightshirt into some grey yoga pants and a long-sleeved white tee shirt. One of these days, she might try doing some yoga in these pants, she thought wryly. Either that, or lay off the loaves of banana bread and grief treats that were still accumulating by the dozen, no end in sight.

Meg washed her face, brushed her teeth, and put on some deodorant.

"It's a start," she thought. She headed back into the kitchen, put on the tea kettle and got out two light blue mugs. She pulled on a cozy grey wool cardigan and walked out onto the back porch while she waited for Elise to arrive. Outside, it was cool but sunny, her favorite kind of day. The small lake was rippling in the light wind, and the trees were no longer green, but vibrant shades of orange and red. Down by the dock, she could see Willie's canoe, still just tied up with rope since the summer. He would need to bring that in before it got too cold, Meg thought. It wasn't a large enough lake for any sort of motorboat, but perfect for fishing, canoes and the occasional kayaker that went by. From the very end of their wooden dock, they could see the whole perimeter of the lake, and the twenty-two homes that surrounded it. Meg loved the community that the back of her home provided— people grilling dinner on their lakeside patios, fishing off their docks, mowing their lawns. She hugged herself in her sweater against the morning air and looked around her porch. There were still pumpkins on the back steps, carved by Ben and Willie for Halloween. For the first time ever, they had completely ignored Trick-or-Treat. Their porch lights had been off, she'd had no treats to give. This was not how the McAfees did Halloween-- they dressed in costume, they decorated, they enjoyed the spooky music and creepy fun. They were never the "bowl of candy on the porch with a PLEASE TAKE ONE" kind of family, but this year, even that would have been too much to ask. She wondered if Willie had even remembered. Not that he would have wanted to go, just one day after the most devastating news, but still, he was a child. Then, late on Halloween night he quietly asked if she could get him some little Nestle's Crunch bars sometime, because those were his favorites from Trick-or-Treat. She had dissolved in tears, hugging him in his bed, promising him pounds of Crunch bars, swearing he would never miss another Trick-or-Treat ever, whatever would make him feel happy again, just one day after Ben had died. She wanted to get rid of those pumpkins and, at the same time, keep them forever. Meg supposed there would often be both big and small reminders of Ben that would make her feel pulled in two directions in the future. She sighed, imagining.

"Hey," said Elise, appearing on the porch, having come through the house.

Meg startled, lost in her thoughts.

"Sorry." Elise smiled, putting her arm around her friend. "Didn't mean to scare you!"

"Not at all," said Meg. She put her tea on the outside dining table and turned to give her friend a hug. "I'm just jumpy today."

"It's cold out here!" Elise shivered.

"I know," said Meg, "but it's beautiful and I needed some air."

"It is pretty," agreed Elise. "I put a few things away in your kitchen. Fresh fruit, milk, juice. You know, stuff you might need."

"You're the best. I needed all of those."

"I know. Now get your ass inside. I'm freezing."

Elise was sitting at the table and Meg was rummaging in the fridge for snacks when the iPhone chimed in her cardigan pocket. Meg instinctively reached to check the message, but stopped herself.

"Cheese? Fruit?" She looked over her shoulder.

"Either. Both! I'm starving," answered Elise.

Meg brought some goodies and napkins to the table, and was sitting across from Elise when the phone chimed again.

"Are you going to check that?" asked Elise.

"I don't know."

"You don't know?"

"I don't know," repeated Meg, more firmly than she meant to. "I'll get it later. I want to visit."

"Visit? We don't 'visit.' What if it's one of the schools? "

"Why would it be one of the schools?"

"Why are you being so weird?"

"Weird?"

"Yes. Why are you being so weird?"

"I don't know. Because my husband just died?" Meg sat back in her chair, hard.

Elise stared at her.

"Meg. What's going on?"

Meg just shook her head.

"What?"

"I don't know how to tell you," Meg said quietly.

She watched Elise process her thoughts, as Meg knew she would do in the same situation. In fast succession, her friend would be ticking through a list of what might be causing Meg such distress. Money issues? Something legal? An affair? No, she would cross that off. Something horrible discovered after Ben's death? The kids--drugs, sex, internet porn? Elise could be thinking the worst of any of them, though she wouldn't want to; it was just that Meg's behavior was suddenly so sketchy. Meg sighed, knowing that she wasn't doing anything except keeping a secret, and she needed to let Elise in. She looked up from her lap.

"Just tell me." Elise had softened.

Meg squared her shoulders and looked directly at Elise before she spoke, so as not to come off as any more crazy than it would already sound. She took the phone out of her pocket and placed it on the table, covering it with her hand.

"I've been getting some strange texts."

"Okay, what kind of texts?"

"I don't know."

"You don't know. Is someone harassing you? Can I see them?" asked Elise, reaching for the phone.

She reached for Meg's phone and Meg snatched it back, pulling it into her lap, now covering it with both hands.

"Don't!" she snapped.

"Jesus, Meg!"

"Just don't. You can't."

"Okay, okay, I won't." Elise sat back pointedly in her chair, hands in the air like a caught criminal. "But will you at least please check the damn phone in case it's your kids texting?"

Meg glanced down at the phone.

Text from Ben. Now?

"It's not the kids."

"Good. So what's going on?"

Meg paused. "I've been getting texts from… Ben."

Elise did not respond. Instead, she made a face that Meg couldn't really register, kind of a cross between "Oh my God" and "That seems nice and nuts at the same time," so Meg continued, quickly.

"I know what it sounds like. It sounds totally and completely ridiculous. I've gotten two, well, three, I guess. The first on the night of the funeral and one yesterday. One arrived just now. They're from his number, with his name, just like he's listed in my contacts. Just like Ben has always texted me."

"Okay..." said Elise, hesitantly.

Meg wasn't finished. Now that she was talking about it, she wanted to let it all out.

"That first night I just thought it was my imagination. I was tired, sad, delusional. I really didn't know what to think. I waited a whole day, waiting to see if it was a dream, if it would disappear, but it didn't. So, I answered him. I mean, I answered the text."

"You answered."

"I've answered the first two. Wouldn't you?"

"I ... have no idea."

Meg stopped talking and looked down at her phone.

"What's it say?"

"I haven't looked."

"So?"

Meg opened the message and read it silently before she shared it with Elise.

"It says '*I don't know. I wish I could be there, but I'm OK. How are you? I love you.*'" Her voice cracked at that point, and she started to sob. "What is going on? Who would do this to me?"

"Are you actually having conversations? I mean, are these texts answering yours?"

Meg stopped to consider. "We're having a conversation. Yes. It's definitely a conversation, just with long delays between texts."

"So can I see them?"

Meg looked genuinely frightened at the possibility; Elise seemed surprised that her question caused such a reaction.

"It's okay, Meg, you don't have to show me."

"I want you to believe me," Meg replied, convincingly.

"I will always believe you," Elise stated. "I only wanted to see with my own eyes what you're dealing with. What we're dealing with."

"Can I read them to you?" Meg asked. "I'm just so afraid that something will happen, that they'll disappear, that I'll never see them again."

"Yes, okay. If you want to." Elise sat back in her chair and let Meg recite the few texts and replies that had been exchanged so far. Elise paused and considered what she had heard.

"Meg, where is Ben's phone?"

Meg had to think for a moment. A couple of nights ago, she had noticed a large brown paper bag, crumpled at the top, shoved beneath Ben's winter coat in the back corner of their closet, her closet now. Next to that, his briefcase. The items startled her, especially coupled with the texts, but as with the many platters and trays, she just assumed that someone had brought them to the house. Meg had peeked inside, once, just to verify that it actually was a bag of Ben's stuff that had appeared on the floor of the walk-in closet, but she wasn't able to bring herself to look closely.

She had seen his wallet, his keys, and at the bottom, his raincoat, rolled up. His briefcase was, as usual, stuffed and ready to head to work. Meg was fairly certain it was heavy with papers and folders, probably his laptop. They were Ben's things, so identifiable, even without him.

"I guess it's with the things from the airport in our closet. Everything from that night is still there. Except his clothes. I mean, I have some of his clothes from...that night, but I don't have his suitcase yet."

"Oh!" Elise looked confused for a minute. "Yes, you do. It's here, but where...?"

"It's here?" asked Meg.

"Yes," said Elise. "I'm trying to remember...." She snapped her fingers. "Front hall closet! Tommy answered the door. He put the bag and briefcase in your closet, but I told him to stash the suitcase in the hall. There were people here, we didn't want to drag it around the house. Too much, you know? I totally forgot. I'm sorry!"

"It's fine. In fact, it's good. One thing I can check off my to-do list. Suitcase—done."

Elise nodded, thinking it through.

"We should look through the items, shouldn't we? Maybe you would find some answers? Maybe it would just make you feel better?"

At first Meg did not react. Then she gave the smallest of nods.

"I guess," she answered, quietly. "But..."

"But what?" Elise pushed on gently. "There is absolutely nothing you will find that will be stranger than this."

Meg agreed, allowing a tiny, wry smile.

Elise took Meg's hand and led her to the bedroom closet. The bag, marked "Property of Cleveland Hopkins Airport," was folded closed at the top, and was next to Ben's briefcase on his side of the closet, next to his shoes. Together, the friends sat on the floor of the walk-in and carefully opened the bag. Tears began to roll down Meg's cheeks as she lifted out his wrinkled raincoat, and held it in her lap, stroking it like a pet. Elise began to cry just watching, but she wiped away her own tears and urged her friend to forge ahead.

"You can do this," Elise said. "I'm right here."

Elise watched as Meg picked up the wallet first and then the keys. She held each item for a long moment, as if feeling the weight of it in her hands, briefly leafing through the wallet, fingering the keys. There was a pack of peppermint Tic-Tacs and a spearmint Chapstick. Meg shook out exactly two mints and ate them; she used the Chapstick before adding both to the small pile of examined artifacts. The bag was now empty.

"The briefcase?" asked Elise.

Meg unlatched the beautiful leather bag that had been a Christmas gift from her to him last year. Just the smell of the leather was enough to send tiny darts of sorrow through her body. She flipped through the files and folders; there wasn't much else. She pulled out and opened his laptop, but it was dead. His parking pass for the downtown garage, all of his chargers and his international adaptors. No phone. Meg breathed out, heavily. Not from frustration, but from the realization that she was surrounded by her husband's things. She could feel him, smell him, touch him.

"Are you all right?" asked Elise, reaching over to grab Meg's arm, squeeze it gently.

"I'm all right," Meg said.

"No phone," said Elise.

"No," said Meg. She wondered why she felt relieved.

"We'll figure it out, Meg," said Elise. "I promise. Should I go grab the suitcase?"

"No, no. Enough for today. I'm done," said Meg, picking herself up off the floor and brushing herself off. "Honestly, isn't it enough that he's dead? Do I have to get texts from the guy, too? And he doesn't even answer me all the time. How rude." She held her hand out to help Elise up off the floor.

Elise smirked at her friend's dark humor, and as the women walked back to the kitchen, Meg mentioned Annie's strange comment from earlier.

"Annie said an odd thing about Tommy this morning."

"About Tommy?" asked Elise. "What did she say?"

"Well, she was in a horrible mood, no surprise, and she was ranting about wanting everyone to just leave her alone. Her teachers, me, and Thomas."

"Huh. I wonder what he's doing that's bugging her?"

"Well, it could be a good thing, you know, if he's looking out for her or checking up on her, and she's just not being receptive," offered Meg.

"Could be. I can keep my eyes out at my house. Or he could have been being a dumb boy and driving her nuts."

"We both know that's not true," said Meg, smiling. "There are very few boys I would trust around my girl, and he's been at the top of the list since he was two."

"He has no idea how lucky he is," said Elise, grabbing a brownie off the tray and popping it into her mouth.

Annie
November 6, 2013

Thank God for Lizzy. When Annie arrived at school, there was her best friend, waiting at her locker with two Starbucks peppermint mochas.

"Hey, girl," said Lizzy, offering a hug and a cup.

"Hi," said Annie, hanging her coat and gathering her books for AP English. There were a few minutes to spare, so they took their time, walking slowly, sipping their warm coffees. Annie filled Lizzy in on her text exchange with Thomas.

"So you really texted him back a big FU?"

"Yep."

"And he never answered?"

"Nope."

"What will you do when you see him?"

"Don't know, don't care."

"Hm."

"Hm? Really?" Annie shot her best friend a look.

"I'm just saying maybe it's really more 'don't know, care a lot' you know?"

"No, I don't know," said Annie, walking faster.

"Slow down, slow down. I'm just wondering about ... you know... last summer?"

There it was. Lizzy was the one and only person Annie had told about the kiss that she and Thomas had shared on the beach. Not only had Annie told her, but she had shared every detail, from the morning that she caught him staring in the bathroom mirror, to the afternoon of flirting, to how Annie had almost reached and tousled his hair during their beach lunch, but she didn't. Then, afterward, she couldn't stop thinking about his hair in the sunlight. Lizzie had been captivated with the romance of it all. To think that it was really only a few months ago seemed crazy to Annie. So much had happened in an unbelievably short time, since that unbelievably perfect day. Her dad had died, Thomas had really been there with her, been there for her. School had started, and now it was like they were strangers. No, he was a stranger who sent her a mean, accusatory text, and for the first time in her life, she answered back, saying exactly how she was feeling. She had thought for a brief moment that he was really starting to like her, maybe even love her. Now she was so angry she feared she could say in person what she had already typed in a text.

"Summer doesn't matter," mumbled Annie, into her coffee cup.

"Hm," said Lizzy, again.

"Thank you for the coffee," said Annie, smiling at her friend,. "It's nice that you kind of already know everything I'm trying to say."

"You're welcome. You're a terrible liar."

"Yeah, I know."

Classes went by quickly that day. It seemed like people were treating her a little more naturally. Here, at school, she could almost forget what had happened. She could pretend that it was just another day, that she would go home to see her mom and Willie, and that maybe tonight was a night her dad was due home from a trip. If not today, she was prepared to keep pretending day after day after day.

By the end of last period, Annie was more tired than usual. Even she could admit to herself that she wasn't sleeping especially well. She stopped by the orchestra room to get her violin, then grabbed her coat from her locker on the way out of the building. From Door H, she looked out into the Junior parking lot, and she could see her VW bug parked in her regular spot, but there was someone leaning against the passenger door. The baseball jacket, the unmistakable blond hair. Certainly he did not think he was getting a ride home. Was he kidding?

As she grew closer, her anger built. When she was close enough to see his baseball number, 12, on his sleeve, she called out.

"*Move!*"

He didn't budge, nor did he turn to look at her.

By now, she was at the car, unlocking the driver's side door with her remote.

"I said, *move*," she demanded again, louder.

"Annabelle," he said, turning to her, "please." She looked at him and saw his red-rimmed eyes, his blotchy face.

"Get in," Annie sighed, sounding a little less irritated.

"I'm sorry," he said, sliding into the passenger seat.

"What's the matter?" she asked. "Why are you so upset?"

"I don't know, exactly. I think I miss your dad today. My dad was having a hard time this morning, and it all kind of freaks me out."

Annabelle nodded. She had never really stopped to consider Tommy's feelings connected to her dad. He missed his Uncle Ben. She would be devastated if anything ever happened to Uncle Kyle or Aunt Elise.

"Annie, I'm sorry I upset you," said Thomas.

"You yelled at me."

"I did not!" he said, a little too loudly. They were now face to face in the small front seat of her car. "When did I yell? Why would I yell?"

"Well, you're yelling now."

"I'm not. I'm sorry. I didn't mean to." Tommy leaned his head back against the passenger seat, exasperated.

"You sent me that mean text. That 'what the hell' text. That was yelling."

"Annabelle, I was worried about you. I really just meant, how can you be here? Are you okay? What the hell? I didn't expect to see you. *Fine.* It pissed me off that you seemed okay. I don't know why it did, but it did. I know that's not really my place."

"Okay? Am I okay? I am *not* okay, but it's none of your business."

"Really? None of my business. So that's why you told me to fuck off?"

"I did not tell you to fuck off. I said,'fuck you.'"

"Big diff."

"It *is* a big difference. 'Fuck off' would be more like, 'go away forever' and that's not what I said."

"Okay," Tommy said, starting to smile a little. "So I'm not going away."

"No," she said. "And you're not going to send me mean texts anymore, got it?"

"Got it," Tommy said.

Annie extended her hand. "Shake on it," she said. He reached for her hand but then pulled her into a fierce hug. "Annabelle, I'm sorry. I really am."

She relaxed onto his shoulder. "Thank you for being sad about my dad. I know that sounds weird. I'm sorry you're sad, but it means a lot to me."

Tommy pulled back to look at her.

"I get it," he said.

"I know you do," she said.

He leaned forward and kissed her softly on the mouth. Annie felt her stomach drop. She was on the beach.

"Now," he said, "will you drive me home?"

The drive home was like so many they had shared in the past. Thomas fooled around with her radio, plugging in his phone, playing his own music, singing loudly. Annie looked over and smiled at him, and today, for the first time in a week, she laughed.

She dropped him at his house, and before he jumped out of the Bug, he planted a quick kiss on her mouth, like this was an everyday occurrence. As if they had fought, made up, and skipped to a whole new level of closeness without even a discussion. But lately, Annie felt so far from normal that laughing in the car and kissing the one boy she had loved for so long hardly seemed something to worry about. It felt so good to feel good.

"Bye," he said, smiling. "See you in the morning?"

"Okay," she said. "I'll be here."

She pulled out of the driveway, her head spinning with questions. What in the world did this mean? If Tommy was just going to start kissing her in the car, were they a couple? Maybe they would talk at school, maybe she would wear his letter jacket. She hated when he wore his letter jacket on warm days, but maybe if she was wearing it…

She tried to stop the thoughts from turning circles in her brain, but by the time she arrived at her own house, she was even more confused. Happy, but confused. In her driveway, she pulled out her phone to text Lizzy--*oh my God Lizzy was going to die!*--but sucked in her breath when she saw the notification on her screen.

Email from Dad.

Ben
October 30, 2013

He made it through the security checkpoint without any trouble, except for a slightly longer wait than usual because of the family traveling in front of him. He watched the inexperienced dad trying to navigate the over-stuffed diaper bag and the car seat while the mom was trying to keep her hands on both babies while taking her own shoes off at the same time. Ben leaned in to hold the car seat so the father could gather his items from the conveyer belt.

"Thanks," said the dad, gratefully. "You have no idea."

"Oh, but I do," Ben said. He smiled wondering where the years had gone. He watched the young family head into the terminal. Off to Disney? Grandma's? He sighed, wishing he and his family were doing the same, thinking he and Meg were due to plan a family vacation soon.

Ben checked his watch--a little over an hour. He'd have time to grab a coffee and a paper before boarding. As he was approaching the Hudson News at Cleveland Hopkins Airport, he suddenly felt a wave of nausea come over him. He stopped and leaned against the wall to take a deep breath and then realized he needed more than a breath. He bolted into the restroom that was thankfully right next to the newsstand and vomited his breakfast into the toilet, all the while thinking that it had come out of nowhere. He splashed some water on his face, rinsed his mouth, popped a Tic-Tac, and left the washroom. He debated for about thirty seconds if he should board the Chicago flight, but he was already feeling better, and figured it must have been something he ate.

Meg
November 6, 2013

    Meg didn't know if she felt better or worse that her secret had been shared. Elise hadn't mocked her, or looked at her like she was nuts; Meg had known she wouldn't. That didn't mean Elise wasn't thinking it, or that she wouldn't later have a long conversation with Kyle about "Meg's state of mind" or "What to do about Meg."

    She was stunned to find that it was already late afternoon. The mugs from this morning, abandoned on the kitchen table, seemed to be mocking her. "See? You can't even have a regular cup of tea anymore." Meg sighed, and dumped the cold tea into the sink, and retreated to the bedroom where Ben's things were still strewn on the floor of the closet. She carefully put each item back in the bag, except for his Chapstick, which she placed into her nightstand drawer. She folded the bag closed and tucked it back under his suits in the corner

    In the front hall, Meg found Ben's suitcase, pulling it out by the retractable handle into the hallway. Willie was occupied, and Annie wasn't home yet; Meg was glad they didn't have to hear the familiar sound of their father's suitcase rolling along the hardwood floors.

    In their room, she hoisted the suitcase onto the bed and unzipped it. She wanted to open it, she really did, but she already knew what she would find. Perfectly folded clothes, socks and underwear stacked and sorted. Toiletries prepped and ready for the hotel. Ben's suitcase would look more organized and tidier than most people's closets. She zipped it back up without looking. Seeing it would be seeing Ben at his most personal. Not today. She rolled the suitcase into the closet and tucked it into a corner for another time.

    Meg glanced over at the clock on her dresser. It was 4:42 PM. His flight, the same one he had taken many times before, would have landed in Cleveland at 4:05 PM. About now, Ben would have been collecting his baggage and walking to his car in the parking garage, where he would have called her from the car at the first moment possible. His luggage had arrived safe and untouched before he was even supposed to have landed.

"Hi," he would have said, happily. "I'm on the ground, headed home!"

She would have glanced at the clock, estimating about forty minutes to his arrival in their driveway.

At 4:45 her iPhone chimed.

I'm here. Meg, I'm still here.

Elise
November 13, 2013

Did those two ridiculous teenagers really think she didn't know what was going on? Tommy was practically skipping around the kitchen in the morning, checking the window every five seconds for Annie's car.

"Didn't she text you before she left her house?" Elise asked, amused.

"Yep," he answered, shoving a giant bite of pumpkin muffin into his mouth, going to the window again, and smoothing his hair in the hall mirror.

Elise poured him a glass of milk and looked knowingly at Kyle.

"What?" said Kyle, not picking up on anything.

"Tommy," said Elise. "Slow down. Drink some milk. She'll be here in a second. Are you in a particular hurry this morning? Do you have an early meeting at school? Homework to finish?"

"Nope," he said. "Just an everyday kinda day."

Tommy looked out the window again.

"Hmm."

"What are you two talking about?" asked Kyle, looking between his wife and son.

"Um, I'm pretty sure we're talking about school," said Tommy, slurping his milk.

"I'm pretty sure we're talking about Annie," said Elise, pointedly.

Tommy's neck started to turn red. "Why would we be talking about Annie?" He went to the window yet again. "Hey! She's here. I gotta go!"

"Bye, honey. Make it a great day," Elise yelled after her son. "Love you!"

"You too," he called, slamming the door.

"Annie?" asked Kyle, catching on.

"Annie," stated Elise.

Meg
November 13, 2013

"Hey," said Elise as soon as Meg picked up the phone. "How's it going over there this morning?"

"Good, I think. Did the kids get off okay from your house?"

"Um, I should say so! A little more giggly and happy than usual."

"What are you talking about?" asked Meg, standing at the counter, picking at the last bits of a cookie platter., then shoving it away. "Stale."

"I do believe my son is smitten with your daughter."

"No!"

"Yes!"

"Finally!" Meg said, exaggerating. "That took long enough!"

Elise dissolved in laughter. "We'll just have to watch how this plays out," she said. "And let me know what you start to see on your end."

"You know I will!"

"So what else is new?" Elise asked.

Meg actually laughed at the question.

Obviously, their conversations certainly couldn't skirt the topic of what felt less like an elephant in the room, and more like an elephant in Meg's pocket. Meg was quite aware that Elise's innocent "What's new?" meant a lot more than "What's new?" used to mean.

At the question, Meg pulled the phone out of her sweatshirt pocket and checked, just for good measure. Meg was never without her cell phone anymore; therefore, she was never without clothing with pockets. It had taken her forever to dig out this old Miami University sweatshirt from the back of her closet, but it was a chilly morning, and she knew it had a front kangaroo pouch. Meg wasn't certain if she was afraid to miss Ben's next text or if she was afraid that someone would find the phone and see his number. She wasn't ready to explain to anyone else. What if the phone was somehow erased or lost? In the end, she decided that it didn't matter and the phone remained with Meg. If it wasn't physically on her, it was on her bed at night, on the bathroom counter, and in the car. At one point, she realized that she had been physically closer to her cell phone than she had been to Ben for any stretch of undivided time. Two weeks. That was a record.

"No," Meg said, "not since a week ago." Thinking back to the text that had arrived at the exact moment she had been reflecting on his non-arrival still sent a shiver through her body.

"Did you ever text him back?"

"I didn't," she said. "I was trying not to. You know, to wait it out, and see what happened. I guess I wanted to see if it would stop. If he would stop, I mean, if I would stop. I don't know what I mean."

"So, *have* you stopped?"

"I don't know." Meg was clearing the breakfast dishes as she talked. Fred the panda was on the counter, and she petted him on the head, as if he were real. Sometimes she felt as though he was, the way he showed up these days, on the sofa, flopped at the end of her bed, here, in the kitchen. Once, she caught herself carrying him around on her shoulder; she had meant to take him back up to Willie's room, but somehow, she'd gotten distracted, and before she realized, she was going through the morning newspaper and mail piled on the counter while absently patting a stuffed panda on her shoulder. She really was losing her mind.

Willie had gone back to school this week, and it seemed to be going smoothly. Both of his team teachers had called her midmorning on Monday, and they each said he was quiet, spending his study halls with his iPod, headphones in, but they weren't worried. There was no pressure in the sixth grade to complete any missed work; he was only to do whatever he needed to feel caught up and ready to move forward. They offered him any extra help he needed. He was a good kid, they said, and they were both so sorry, for him and for her. She was grateful for their calls, but mostly so grateful to hear that Willie was making it through the school day. By the time he came through the front door on that first afternoon, she nearly toppled him in relief.

"Mom, geez," he said, but he didn't stop hugging her.

"You're okay?" she asked.

"Mmm hmmm," he mumbled. "It was okay. Kinda weird."

"I'll bet. It's all kinda weird. It will get better."

"I guess. Can I have a snack?"

"Sure. Hang up your coat. I have a little surprise for you."

His eyes lit up. "Really?"

Meg went into the kitchen, and Willie stampeded through with his coat and backpack, now in a huge hurry to put his things away. In a flash, he was back at the table.

She presented him with a glass of cold milk and then, from behind her back, a bag of mini Nestles Crunch Bars.

"Mom! I love these!"

"I know, kiddo." She couldn't not smile at his joy.

From his seated position, he threw his arms around her waist. She was amazed at how little it took to remedy a tiny sadness, and only wished she knew how to fix the bigger ones. Meg tore open the bag and sat at the table and took a moment to celebrate the ordinary.

Now, midweek, it was more routine for him, and that made it more routine for Meg. The subject matter with Elise, though, was anything but.

"I do want to answer him, but I'm afraid. I think I'm setting myself up for something. A disappointment? The truth? I don't know." Meg sighed, loading the last of the breakfast dishes into the dishwasher.

"At very worst, you'll get closer to figuring out who's on the other end of this nonsense."

"Right," said Meg softly. At very worst.

After they chatted a bit more about the possibility of Tommy and Annie falling in love and living happily ever after, Meg hung up and decided to finally face a few unpleasant tasks and decisions that she had been putting off. The sooner she tackled this sad to-do list, the sooner she could start checking boxes. First, she gathered her laptop, her phone, a fresh legal pad and a pen, and set herself up at the kitchen table. She checked every voice-mail on her landline. Twenty-six messages. When she entered her cell phone password, she was informed by a pleasantly bland computerized voice that her voicemail inbox was full.

"No surprise," she thought to herself. Almost every message was a call from a friend or coworker of Ben's, or a friend of hers, all saying the same things in different words. Meg jotted down names and numbers just in case she needed to return any of the calls. A message from their insurance agent, needing her to sign some forms, he said, in order to eventually collect on Ben's life insurance policy. Meg's first fleeting thought was to text Ben and ask his opinion on the matter. Can you collect an insurance policy on a husband who's maybe not quite dead? Perhaps she should wait a bit to answer that message.

There had been a funeral.

A casket.

A body.

She had been there and had seen people crying real tears. For God's sake, she had planned most of the service herself, with the help of the funeral director.

Meg picked up her phone, and as if the message from Bob Kratz, Stafford Insurance, had been all the impetus she needed, she sent a text, and for the first time, she didn't dwell over it or think it through. She texted her husband as she had texted him thousands of times before. Quickly and without thinking, just because it had to be done.

What's going on? I need to know. I miss you.

SEND

Like so many messages before.

Do we have dinner plans Saturday?

Did you grab the dry cleaning or should I?

The kids want Chinese tonight. Me too. Will you be home?

She put the cell phone down, finished sorting through voicemails, and moved on to the basket full of sympathy cards, beautiful handwritten notes, and floral enclosure cards. Elise had been careful to keep everything sorted for her during those first few days. Sympathy cards had arrived in droves, and tiny cards had come with flowers and platters. Some, like the card—letter—from Sophie, she'd had to fold and put away to read again and again. He loved you from the first moment he saw you, Meg. I was so happy to have been a part of your story, and if you hadn't snagged him, I would have. I love you, I miss you. Sophie's card made her weep and laugh, providing a welcome release.

Neighbors had been helpful in such unexpected ways--bringing in their garbage cans and raking their leaves. Each of these kindnesses had been meticulously cataloged on a page by her best friend.

"The family of Ben McAfee appreciates your expression of sympathy during this time of..." She was sending the preprinted cards, provided by the funeral home, to most everyone. Then she came to a card from Kate. Kate from The Crooked Nook. She opened the card knowing that the words inside would be exactly perfect.

Meg, darling. I am so sorry to hear about your excruciating loss. Ben was such a wonderful man. Sometimes friends will say they understand, and you may feel that they don't, even though they are trying. I truly do. Call me if you need to talk, or if I can do anything at all. Pop in and see me anytime. Thinking of you, with love always. —Kate.

Meg's eyes filled with tears. She saw Kate fairly often, since Kate still owned the bookstore, but Kate worked less and less, and her daughter was primarily on site these days. Ben and Meg would never have bought books, calendars, or stationary anywhere but Kate's store, and Meg still treasured the time she had spent there. She had worked part-time through Annie's toddler years, but once Willie was born, she'd decided to stay home full-time. Then, she would often stop in with both kids to say hello, buy a picture book, visit with Kate and Piper while her children harassed Bookmark.

On a whim, she picked up the phone and called the store.

She felt a pang of--homesickness? longing?--when she heard the familiar voice of Piper, Kate's daughter, answer the line. "The Crooked Nook, may I help you?"

"Piper, hi. It's Meg."

"Meg! Oh, Meg, I'm so glad to hear your voice! How are you? Oh, crap. I'll bet you're so sick of hearing that. I'm so sorry. Oh, God, there I go again. I can't help it, seriously, how are you? How are those beautiful children? God, Meg, I've been thinking of you. I have a card right here for you that I keep meaning to mail. Shit, I'm a terrible friend. My mom has been just crazy worried about you. Jesus, Meg. It's just so awful. Oh my god, like you didn't know that already. I'm so sorry, I am just the absolute worst at this. Shit."

Meg laughed, a deep belly laugh, and it felt like her soul was coming back to life, just a little bit.

"Piper, you are perfect. I hope there are no customers at the desk listening to you."

"I'm in the back sorting out the new shipment for Christmas. Oh, goody, a new Nicholas Sparks." Sarcasm hung on every word.

Piper had always been a book snob. She and Meg were almost exactly the same age, and they had gotten along famously ever since meeting in their early twenties during Meg's first years at the store. Back then, Meg was a newlywed, dressing fairly conservatively (or as Piper used to say, "straight out of the Preppy Handbook, I see, Muffy.") Piper tried hard to achieve a punk look, but it never really suited her, and eventually, her spiky blond hair and studded leather jackets settled into short trendy haircuts and beautiful edgy clothes. She was a striking, petite girl, with pale skin and blue eyes. Kate had always just let Piper do her thing; in fact, she encouraged it. After Piper graduated from Perry Pike High School, she'd pursued a degree in art history. While some parents might have pushed for a more marketable degree, Kate solidly supported a liberal arts education, especially if Piper would choose to own the Nook one day. Since her graduation, Piper had also tried her hand briefly at acting (deemed "adventures in waitressing" by her mother) and a brief stint at a culinary school, but she always ended up back home. As Kate said, she always returned "more Piper than ever", and with more knowledge to share with their customers. Meg always hoped to be a mom like Kate. She was open and loving to Piper, open and accepting of her dreams, and she had been warm and welcoming to Meg, as well.

It was hard for Meg to admit that, in Kate, she had sometimes seen glimpses of the type of mother she wished she'd had. More warm than judgmental, more traveled than closed-minded. When these thoughts crept into the periphery of Meg's brain, she would brush them away, knowing that in the moment, Kate was simply a mother-figure in her life, and her own mother wasn't nearby often enough to even compete with those nagging notions.   Piper and Kate did not have the perfect mother-daughter dynamic by any means. There were days when Meg was first working at the Nook when she would tiptoe past the back room, lest she interrupt a "conversation" about Piper's short skirt or about Kate's "unreasonable" response to Piper's comings-and-goings at the house. Or maybe, Meg realized later, they actually had achieved the perfect dynamic. What Meg coveted then, and sometimes still, was their closeness. Kate was always willing to listen, whether it be about an outfit, a curfew, a degree, or a matter of the soul. Kate had a gift, and Meg was lucky enough to often be on the receiving end of Kate's generosity.

"Darling girl," she would say. "How can I help?" Meg's eyes filled, even now, remembering. She had been overwhelmed one day. With just a few more pages to finish in the conclusion to her thesis, Meg had been up late typing. Annie had missed her morning nap; she was teething and no amount of soothing or frozen bagels were helping. Meg had dropped her fussy, clingy daughter at pre-school and for the first time, she was behind the counter of the Nook wishing she were anywhere else.

"I don't know, Kate," Meg sighed. "It was just a long night and a longer morning, you know?" Meg looked away, feeling foolish at the tears pooling in her eyes.

"Oh, I do know," Kate said. "Listen, there's no one here. Take a few minutes. Go take a walk. Get a coffee and some fresh air."

"I've only been here for five minutes," Meg laughed. "I hardly need a break yet."

"Well, I need a coffee. You need to peek in the preschool window to see how Annie is doing, and by the time you get back, the world will be rosier."

Meg had nodded, collecting herself. "Okay. Okay, then."

She walked the two blocks up Center Street to Perry Pike Presbyterian on the corner, where the preschool was housed, and with a quick glance into the picture window by the back entrance, she could see the three-year old class on their carpet squares. It was sharing time. Annabelle was clapping her hands together and smiling delightedly. The sun and the air were natural refreshers as she walked to the local coffee house and ordered two black coffees. Within fifteen minutes, she was back at the store, pink in her cheeks and drinks in her hands.

Kate looked up from the front desk. "Better, pet?"

"So much better. Thank you."

"It's why some women are older than other women. We know things." Kate had tapped her forehead, and nodded, smiling.

"Hey, save me a copy of the new Sparks book," Meg now giggled into the phone to Piper. "I could really use a sappy novel about now."

"Wo-ow. You must really be bad off," said Piper. "But does that means you're coming in to see us soon?"

"I was hoping you'd ask," said Meg.

Annie
November 13, 2013

It had been a week since she had first kissed Thomas in the car and received the email from her dad. That day, it had felt like her life was about to take a big turn in some direction or another, but in fact, things were staying pretty calm. Perhaps this was her own fault, because she had yet to tell her mom or Lizzy about either of these two seemingly life-altering events. She both imagined and feared that once she spoke of them out loud, life would actually change a great deal. Her mom and Lizzy would freak out on both counts.

Annabelle was in study hall, staring at her math homework, but she couldn't concentrate. She didn't know if she should be able to focus yet after … her dad … so she kind of gave herself a break. She wasn't sure if she could blame her distraction on her grief, on the email from her dad, or on making out with Thomas, which she was doing every day after school. Oh my God, who knew that making out could be so awesome? Annie had kissed boys before, and she'd even made out with one or two, and while it had been nice, even fun, it hadn't been like this. When comparing notes with her friends at sleepovers, all the girls said the same things: no one liked wet kissers, sloppy kissers, or boys who groped (too much.) There were a few boys in the junior class who had reputations as great kissers, and Thomas was one. In the past, Annie had brushed off that piece of information, rolled her eyes, claiming that she didn't want to know. Now, though, she was on the short list (she hoped it was short) of girls who had kissed one of the best. His reputation was well-earned. When he kissed her in the mornings before school (quickly) and in the afternoons after school (longer) she didn't want him to leave.

Was Thomas her boyfriend? The new coupling of "Thomas" and "boyfriend" was hard to grasp, yet at the same time, the idea resonated with an inner comfort and easy familiarity. She was definitely enjoying the secret they were keeping. It felt especially illicit, she thought, since they had been friends for so long, and any news of them being "more than friends" would certainly surprise their classmates and their families. At the thought of "families," Annie felt a pang in her stomach, a flash of uncertainty. Her family didn't feel whole, that was sure. Did a not-whole family still go on vacation together? Did a not-whole family have happy holidays? What if she and Thomas were to get married one day? It would be such an amazing wedding, filled with squeals of "Can you believe it!" and "It was always meant to be!" But without her dad. She could feel the pounding sadness start in her heart, and she tried to shake it off, before the tears could sneak into her eyes. Wedding? God. Her emotions really were all over the place.

She pulled her headphones and her iPhone out of her backpack to turn on some One Direction, anything to stop this crazy train. As she scrolled through her playlists and her songs, she started thinking back to the email she had received a week ago. Obviously, it had shocked her, seeing her dad's name among the other senders in her inbox. She wasn't frightened; she was more surprised at her own reaction. Seeing his name on the screen had instantly filled her with happiness and heartache simultaneously. He had been a chronic emailer, and she'd already been missing their correspondence. Funny forwarded jokes, questions about her schedule ("When is your next orchestra concert? I want to put that in my calendar") or just a silly YouTube video. She had opened the email sitting in her car in the driveway.

Ben McAfee, marked unread. Dated 11/06/13, 2:57 pm.

Hi, honey. It's Daddy. I'm still here. I miss you.

It was from his email address, even though Annie would have assumed that an email account gets automatically cancelled or voided when a person dies. It seemed real. Maybe, she thought, it could be some internet error that had caused his email to be sent late and arrive late. Seeing the words had both startled and comforted her, and while she wasn't quite sure what to do with the email on her phone, she certainly knew she couldn't tell anyone. Her dad was dead, and she had received a message from him in her inbox. How could she even say that out loud? Here she'd been thinking that her big news was all about Tommy. If she thought that was going to cause some major ripples, how could she drop a bomb like this email?

Later, she thought. She would figure it out later.

She turned up her music, opened her math book to the right page, and got to work on a solvable problem.

Meg
November 20, 2013

12:15 pm
Ben: I miss you so much. I'm not sure where I am. Do you know?
Meg: You died. We thought you died. Can you tell me where you are?
Ben: I don't know. But I'm here. Don't worry.
Meg: Can we keep talking like this?
Ben: Yes
Meg: I love you.
Ben: I love you 2
Meg: Are you ever coming back?
Meg: Do you think you are close to me? Are you in heaven? Ben,
where do you think you are?
12:20 pm
Meg: Ben?
12:27 pm
Meg: Ben? Are you there? I'm still here.

At one point, she almost texted *are you a person?*

Meaning, are you a body, a soul, or a spirit, but somehow asking something so specific felt like it could cross the line of whatever conversational tone had just been established, or maybe end it completely. She didn't know the rules. It was the first actual back-and-forth exchange that they had had, and although there was still no real information, Meg felt lightness inside that she had not experienced since the first terrible moment on October 30th. She clung to the phone like a lifeline, and reread the words hourly, at least. She wished he could answer her question. If Ben knew where he was (if in fact, he was somewhere) and if he could tell her, it would calm so much of the unsettledness surrounding him. If in fact, *he* was *Ben* at all. *Regardless*, she was grasping whatever connection she was being given, and she was determined to keep it as real, albeit private, for as long as she was allowed. Believing in something so nebulous was against her character, but this felt so good in the moment, and she was willing to look past her normal sensibilities and act on her instincts of faith. She had considered, very briefly, going to speak to the pastor of the church where the kids had been baptized, but it had been so long since she and Ben had been in regular attendance, and she couldn't quite imagine how to start this particular conversation. When thoughts of heaven and spirits pulled close, she just let them come, and her childhood faith took over. Willie had asked her recently if his daddy was in heaven.

"Of course," she had answered. "Of course he is."

"Do you get your stuff in heaven?"

"What stuff?"

"I don't know, your favorites?"

"Oh, I hope so," she had answered. Willie hadn't seemed to want to talk anymore, but Meg realized that she'd wondered something similar. Where was Ben's phone? Certainly, she didn't think a very physical iPhone could travel to the spiritual realm, but she found herself unwilling to dig deep into the thought process.

When she walked into the bookstore a few days later, Meg was still waiting to hear from Ben again, yet she felt more at ease than she had in weeks. That morning, she had pulled her favorite tights and sweater dress out of the closet, realizing immediately that both seemed a bit looser than usual. That seemed odd, in that she was existing solely on cookies and muffins, but perhaps this was the silver lining of her grief. It felt good to wash and dry her hair, put on her make up, find a chunky bracelet, add a bit more makeup (God, she was pale) and then toss on a long necklace for good measure. As much as her mother had tried, Meg had never really believed in the adage that "less was more," especially where accessories were concerned, and in the last three weeks, she had truly ignored some of her favorite things. She stepped into her favorite tall black boots, zipped them up, and took a look in the full-length mirror. It was slightly disconcerting to see herself dressed and put-together. She hadn't left the house much, and had been comfortably uncomfortable to muddle through the first weeks of grief in leggings and pajama bottoms. Meg didn't blame herself for choosing forgiving, kind clothes with elastic waists and soft linings , no more than she blamed herself for feeling guilty and strange about getting dressed up in this moment. Ben's texts seemed to be the encouragement she needed in order to walk into the world. Not that she could ever tell anyone (not even Elise?) but it was still far too easy to envision Ben alive.

Sometimes, when she allowed her mind to wander, she could imagine a world in which she was the only one who knew this truth: that Ben was very much alive and he was depending on Meg to be the heroine and save him from whatever fate had apparently befallen him. Other times, she acknowledged that if the truth lived inside some dark recess of her mind, or inside the mind of a horrible unknown person playing a trick, she would have to come to terms with it eventually. Either way, she was unable to deny that the communication was helping. The messages on the phone were not "the texts" they were "Ben's texts," and the newest, more conversational exchange had elevated the possibility of her virtual relationship.

She spritzed on a little Flowerbomb perfume, a gift from Ben for her forty-fifth birthday in July. She remembered opening the box, and smiling.

"My favorite!"

"Mine, too," he had said, with a sly grin.

She sometimes found it hard to believe how long they'd been together. The fact that they had known each other longer than they had not provided an odd comfort to her now, somehow keeping the imaginary teeter-totter of her life balanced a bit toward the positive. She placed the perfume back on her dresser, wondering how she would feel when the bottle was finally empty. Meg was already beginning to resent everyday items and tasks that were drenched with deeper meaning; what she resented most of all was that she was the only one who seemingly felt the painful twinge of these tiny memories, sharp pangs that surprised her everywhere. Empty perfume bottles, or even the potential for empty bottles, Ben's dirty t-shirt that she was unwilling to wash, a book open to a certain page, a memory of the last time they sat together at the kitchen table, a favorite food, an open shampoo bottle in the shower, the windbreaker tossed casually in the backseat of her car, and endless other small bud indelible reminders of her husband's daily life entwined with hers.

Meg knew one thing for sure. As she stood on the sidewalk outside of The Crooked Nook, Ben would be happy with her at this moment. She pushed open the old wooden door, and the bells on the handle jingled, happily heralding her entrance. Both Kate and Piper turned to look.

"There she is," said Kate, softly. She walked over to Meg and embraced her in a deep, real hug. Piper stood behind the register and tried not to cry, while Meg dissolved into gut-wrenching sobs.

"I know, darling girl. I know. Shhh, shhh. It's okay."

"But, K-kate. I was happy this morning. I mean, I was even h-happy right outside. I'm okay. See? I'm even dressed. In *real* clothes. Oh, shit. I'm crying all my make up off."

"Oh, Meg, that sucks," said Piper, leaving her post and reaching out to wipe the corner of Meg's eye with her own fingertip.

"This is how it happens," Kate said, giving Meg one hard squeeze, then pulling back to hold her firmly by the shoulders. "You'll be fine one minute, a wreck the next. It's not easy, and it's not always fast. Sometimes it was hard for me when I saw friendly faces, other times being around people would help. Who could say?" Kate threw up her hands, questioning.

Meg nodded. "That's it exactly."

"You're not on anybody's timeline," Kate said.

Meg sighed, and instinctively rubbed the phone in her coat pocket with her thumb, back and forth. Every now and then, when Meg caught herself in the act, she wondered if it was a similar feeling to praying the rosary, the almost meditative action, the sense of calm she could invoke.

"Thanks," said Meg, pulling her hand from her pocket to wipe her cheeks with a tissue handed over from Piper. "Okay." Meg took a deep breath in and exhaled slowly. "Okay." She held her hands up as if a cease-

and-desist were in order. "Girls, let's talk about why I'm here. Because it's not to cry on your shoulders, although that may happen from time to time."

"That's fine," nodded Kate.

"Can you still use me?"

Kate had been asking Meg to come back to the Nook for years. Part-time, full-time, whatever would work for her schedule. Meg had no idea what made her think that now was the time, but being alone in the house while the kids were at school was not currently appealing. In fact, it was rather appalling. She saw Piper and Kate exchange a quick glance, questioning.

"I'm fine," Meg said, quickly. "I mean, obviously, I'm not fine, but I would love to be here again. And I will be fine."

Kate looked at her, long and hard, and then nodded.

"If this is what you want, what you *need*, then not only would we love to have you, we can use you

"Weekdays? Does that work?" said Meg.

"She's already asking for weekends off," Piper said, nudging Meg with her shoulder.

Meg smiled. "I may keep trying to set you up with good-looking, preppy boys. Or, men. I'm still an excellent matchmaker." Meg looked pointedly at Piper.

"Oh, yes *please*," cried Kate, and Piper rolled her eyes.

, "You scarred me for life with your plaid blazers and sensible shoes."

"Those were Topsiders. And anyway, not anymore," said Meg. She shook a stylish riding boot in Piper's general direction.

Piper gave a half smile. "Still needs a little work."

"Well, good thing I'm here then," Meg said.

Meg reached back into her pocket and pressed the phone tightly against her thigh, wishing she could tell Ben.

"Okay, then," said Meg, smiling. "I'll start tomorrow."

"It's good to have you back from your fifteen year vacation," teased Kate.

"You can't even imagine," said Meg.

"Bring the kids by," said Kate. "I need to see my babies."

"The baby is almost ten," said Meg, wincing, "and I'm fairly sure the teenage girl is making out all the time with Elise's son. Is there a book for that?"

"Not Annie!" Kate exclaimed in mock horror. . Kate and Piper knew Elise through Meg, and because Elise shopped at the Nook like everyone else in town.

"I have no proof, except that a mother knows what a mother knows." Meg was still waiting for Annie to fess up, but so far, nothing.

"Bring them soon, Meg. I want to see them, plus I have a great new series that I think Willie will love."

"Perfect," said Meg. And she began to craft her new ordinary day.

Elise
November 20, 2013

"Did she show you the texts?" asked Kyle. They were sitting at the kitchen island before dinner. He had loosened his tie after work, and quickly poured a glass of wine for himself and one for Elise, once she'd started talking. He'd innocently inquired about his wife's day, and certainly had not expected to hear the story that Elise presented, one that she'd apparently already known for at least a week. Now, though, Elise was worried. She shared with Kyle all she could remember about the details of Ben's texts. Elise hoped that she wasn't trampling on Meg's confidence, but she knew without a doubt that her concern trumped their code of secrecy. If the situation were reversed, Meg would be having the same discussion with Ben.

"Not exactly," Elise admitted. "I tried to get a look, but she guards the phone like it's a newborn baby. No, it's different—I held her babies all the time, but I can't get one finger on this phone. She was reading the texts to me, and I guess I just trusted that she read me everything."

"Do you believe her?"

Elise gulped her Pinot Noir. "Do I believe ... what? That there are texts on the phone? Sure. Do I believe that there are texts on the phone from Ben? Okay, maybe, yes. Still, I think she and I might disagree on how they arrived, or when, or I guess, who sent them. At least the recent ones. Oh, my God, do you see what a mess this is?"

Kyle shook his head sadly. "So ... Meg thinks Ben is sending her messages from ... where? Heaven?" He paused. "Earth?"

Elise shook her head slowly, sadly, not really knowing the answer.

"She claims she understands that it could all be a trick, or some sort of mix-up, but if you could see her face, Kyle, that's not what she wants. It might not really even be what she thinks. It's like, I have this feeling that she's trying to say all the right things, but the entire time, she's just waiting for the next text from her dead husband. She's got her hands on that phone every second, and she's answering the messages, Kyle! She's communicating with Ben ... or whomever ... whatever.... It has to stop." Elyse gave a heavy sigh, shaking her head. "It really has to stop."

Kyle sighed. "God, it's so sad. I'm sure we can't really understand the grief, you know? We lost Ben, but she lost her husband. Her husband." Kyle emphasized both words.

"She also seems happy to hear from him, you know? I almost think she's doing better because of it."

"Maybe you're right. I mean, joke or whatever, is it helping somehow? Even just the distraction?" Kyle looked at Elise, questioning his own statement, and took a sip of his wine.

"But what if it's not Ben? I mean, of course it's not Ben!" Elise shook her head, hard, at her own statement. "It's false hope. It's nothing, right? Meg's going to end up hurt one way or the other. It's going to feel like losing Ben twice." At the thought, Elise's eyes filled with tears.

"How can I help?"

It was the sentence that she both loved and hated. There was no way for Kyle to fix this. If ever there was uncharted water, they were definitely swimming in it.

Elise had been tossing around an idea in the back of her brain--she knew most definitely how it would be received by Meg, but she was unsure how it would be received by Kyle. "What do you think about me making an appointment with Sarah?"

Kyle didn't answer.

"For Meg, I mean. About all of this."

Kyle's youngest sister was a well-respected psychiatrist in Cleveland with a thriving practice. Dr. Sarah Parker had rightfully earned her stellar reputation as one of the younger physicians circulating among the more established doctors in the mental health community. She had been featured recently in *Cleveland Magazine* among "The Fresh New Faces in Medicine." Elise wasn't sure of the scope of her sister-in-law's practice, but

Sarah had known Meg for years, so if she couldn't offer the necessary services, she could absolutely recommend the right therapist.

"God, I don't know, baby. She knows Sarah, she knows what Sarah does. Don't you think she'll reach out if she needs help?"

"Meg is texting her dead husband, for Christ's sake! Someone has to make this stop!"

"Okay. Take a breath, " Kyle said. "Or you'll end up killing me, and I won't even try to text you because you're being a bitch."

Elise had to smile. She took a breath and a gulp of wine.

"Fine."

"Why don't you offer the number, or Sarah's card?" said Kyle. "Don't step on her toes, baby. Just tell her that we are all here if she needs us, including Sarah." Elise nodded, and Kyle continued. "Meg's been through a lot, and she definitely needs to feel like you are one thousand percent on her side. I'm on her side, too, you know. And yours."

Elise nodded, biting her lip. "I know."

"Do you think this is some sort of breakdown? Is she imagining it?"

"She's definitely not imagining it," replied Elise. "That's one thing I'm sure of."

Meg
Early June 2011

She had always loved summer vacation. While some mothers count-ed down the days until the big yellow bus rolled around in the fall, Meg dreaded the beginning of the school year each August, and she couldn't wait until the last day of school. No more schedules, no early mornings, no homework. Swimming pools, popsicles, sleeping late and bright afternoons. The summer was stretching out its arms, waiting for them to relax into the warm, endless days ahead. It was finally here, a long-awaited old friend greeting her on the doorstep.

She made Annie and Will the traditional last-day pancake breakfast (chocolate chips and strawberries) before they headed off to their last day of school. They were both dressed in blue and white for their respective field days. Annie would do the hurdles, an unexpected talent discovered last year, and Willie was ready to run the three-legged race for his class. Ben was headed to the office, and Meg was already eagerly anticipating the kids' ar-rival home in the afternoon. She had promised to have the pool bags packed and ready to go (Annie had requested her new striped bikini; Willie had begged her to remember his diving torpedoes.)

Meg opened her laptop to check her email before jumping in the shower. Not much excitement in her inbox. A group email from Annie's high school orchestra director offering summer lessons, two messages from Old Navy, an end-of-the-year email from the school district, and several Face-book notifications.

Jason Brinkman has requested you as a friend on Facebook.

Jason Brinkman. His name conjured up feelings from a time she hadn't revisited in many years, and Meg smiled, remembering how young she had been. Just seeing his name on her screen threw her instantly back to the angst of high school romance, 80s love ballads and late night, driveway breakups. She was, in her memories, always wearing a lavender shaker-knit Forenza sweater, the one she was fairly certain first offered Jason the opportunity to feel her up at the movies. A soundtrack of Chicago and Aha! played on a loop as the scenes from her youth scrolled past, as if they were only just barely tucked away from her everyday life. Yes, without a doubt, she remembered her time with Jason, but she had been a child. Now she was a grown-up, a wife, a mother. For heaven's sake, she and Ben both had friends of the opposite sex on Facebook and in real life; it would be good to reconnect with Jason and see how he was getting on. She clicked "Confirm request" and pointedly closed the laptop.

She dialed Elise while she was rinsing the breakfast dishes.

"Good morning," Meg said cheerfully. "Happy summer vacation!"

"It kills me how happy this makes you," said Elise.

"I love it! Pool today?"

"Of course. We'll meet you there."

"Good." Meg paused.

"What?" asked Elise.

"Nothing!" said Meg.

"You want to say something, I can tell."

"Well, a weird thing happened this morning," admitted Meg.

"Weirder than this being the last day of school and that we only have six more hours until we are invaded by small aliens who want to take over our homes and lives and our laundry rooms for the next ten weeks?"

Meg giggled. "I think you're the one who needs a summer vacation most of all. No, the weird thing is that my high school boyfriend contacted me on Facebook. We're 'friends.'"

"Reeeeaaally?" crooned Elise. "Now that is interesting. What happens next?"

"I'm not sure. Nothing, probably. If he chats with me, I'll say 'Hi,' I guess. I can't imagine having some big conversation. That would be wrong, right?"

"Right," agreed Elise. "Wrong. What would Ben think?"

"I don't think Ben would mind. He's friends with lots of people from high school. So am I."

"This is a little different though, isn't it?" asked Elise.

"I guess so. Like I said, I'm not looking for a real friendship."

"It's not what you're looking for that worries me, Meg. So naive."

"Ohmygod, stop. Now, what should we pack for our first poolside afternoon?"

"Vodka?" suggested Elise, sighing into the phone.

"Whatever it takes," said Meg in a singsong voice. "Whatever it takes."

As the end of the school day drew near, Meg gathered the pool bags, towels, and cooler. She was so happy to be dressed in flip-flops and a sundress. Ben had texted earlier that he would meet them at the pool for dinner, so all that remained was to meet the bus.

Everything was ready to go and waiting on the counter. She glanced over at her laptop. It wouldn't hurt to check Facebook to see if anything was going on in the world of social media while she waited, would it? Meg opened the screen and saw that she had several Facebook notifications, and one private message.

She opened the message, and Jason's face popped up next to the words.

"Crap," thought Meg, feeling both weirdly happy and angry at herself at once. She'd opened the door.

Meg—so great to hear from you. I hope you and your family are doing well and enjoying the start of summer. You look great. Let me know what's going on with you when you get a chance. I have two girls

—can't believe how fast time has flown. Have a great day, and again, let's catch up soon.
Jason

His visage was right there on the screen, but she still pictured his high school face. The message made her happy; she was glad to hear he was doing well, and his words certainly seemed innocent enough. So, that was that. She closed the laptop and checked the clock. The bus should be coming any second. She grabbed the bags from the counter and went to the garage to load the car and wait for her children outside. The sun glinted on the lake, sending slivers of light in waves across the water. It was a picture-perfect day to start summer vacation. She heard the bus before she saw the blinking lights stop at the corner. Willie, then Annie, walked carefully down the bus steps, then sprinted toward the house, free at last.

"No more school!" shouted Will, hurtling himself onto the lawn, tossing the backpack into the grass and kicking off his shoes. Annie's reaction was less physical, but her relief was palpable.

"It's summertime, my babies! Take five minutes, get your suits on, and we're going to the pool!" She saw an elderly man walking a dog smile as he watched them whoop with delight.

"Looks like the start of summer," he called.

"It is!" called Willie.

"I remember those days," he said, walking by, tipping his cap. "Those were the best."

Meg smiled at him. "They really are, aren't they? Have a lovely afternoon!"

The man smiled at their mayhem.

"Who's ready for summer vacation?" she called. "Let's get this party started!"

Tommy
Thanksgiving, 2013

Tommy rolled over in bed, instinctively reached for his phone to check the time, worried for just a moment that he had overslept. But the smell of turkey was already filling the house, and he stretched out on his back, remembering what day it was, enjoying not having to rush out of bed.

Tommy: You up?
Annie: Yep
Tommy: Happy Thanksgiving
Annie: Thx you too
Tommy: What time are you guys coming here
Annie: Not sure. Afternoon I think
Tommy: I think my mom is making turkey for breakfast.
Annie: lol
Tommy: See you soon, turkey.
Annie: xo

Tommy threw on a pair of jeans and a flannel shirt, and headed downstairs. As he had suspected, his mom was already in the kitchen, surrounded by pots, pans and bowls.

"Good morning!" she opened her arms, but her hands were covered with sticky bread. "I'd give you a hug, but I'm making the stuffing."

"That's really okay," he said, dipping a finger into a bowl of pudding.

"Is it good?"

Tommy nodded.

"It's for the pie. Do you want to help me make it?" said his mom, nudging him with her hip.

"It's just so much better when you do it," he said, scooting out of the way.

"Oh, so that's how it is," she said, smiling.

"Where's Dad?"

"He went to get a bag of ice and a can of cranberry sauce, if he can find anywhere open this morning. Meg is bringing drinks and mashed potatoes."

"Sounds good. Do you know if my khakis are clean?"

"Oh, um… they should be. Hanging either in your closet or on the rack in the laundry room."

"Thanks."

"Do you need a shirt ironed?"

"Probably not. I think I'm going to wear that light blue one that has buttons down it."

"The button-down."

"That's what I said."

"That will look nice."

"I'm not really trying to look nice, Mom. It's not a big deal."

"I didn't say it was a big deal, Tommy. Why are you so touchy?"

"I'm not."

"You are. Now stop it. It may not be the easiest day for Meg and the kids. I want you to be especially nice to Willie and"—

His mom stopped short.

"And?"

"And, nothing. Just be nice to everyone, you know, thoughtful. This is the first real holiday since Uncle Ben—died— and we just need to be extra sensitive. You will be, I know it."

"Okay, I'll be extra sensitive."

"How's Annie doing?"

"Fine. I don't know, good."

"Okay, just checking. Is she talking to you about stuff? Like, when you drive to school together?"

His mom was acting like she did when she already knew something, but she was trying to get him to tell her anyway; one of her oldest tricks.

"I mean, a little. She's doing a little better, I guess.

"Good."

"Good." His mom turned to check the bird in the oven, and Tommy took the opportunity to retreat from the kitchen and the questioning.

A few hours later, he was dressed in his khakis and blue shirt and seated at the table next to Annie, who had arrived with Aunt Meg and Willie in a swirl of hugs and kisses and even more bowls and casseroles. God, she smelled delicious.

"This is one full table," said his mom, looking around. She looked like she might cry.

"I'm starving," said Willie, who looked uncomfortable in his dressy clothes.

"Willie," said Aunt Meg.

"Me too, Buddy," said Tommy.

"Okay, okay," said Tommy's dad. Let's say a quick grace and then we'll eat. Can we hold hands?"

Tommy saw his dad and mom holding hands, and he saw Aunt Meg reach for Willie's hand, and he was so suddenly struck by missing Uncle Ben at the table that he sucked in his breath. He felt Annie squeeze his hand, hard.

"I know, I know," she whispered. He should have been comforting her.

He squeezed back, and then he squeezed the hand he held on his other side, Aunt Meg's. She looked at him, and nodded. Her eyes were full, but she was holding it together.

"Dear Lord, we are grateful for this meal, for our friends and family, for our many blessings. Please watch over each of us, and watch over"—his dad's voice broke—"watch over Ben. Amen."

"Amen," Willie whispered.

Tommy's mom sniffled, and Annie just took a deep breath.

"Thanks, Kyle," said Aunt Meg.

Tommy's dad wiped his eyes with his napkin. "Pass the stuffing, please. It's time to eat Ben's favorite meal."

Tommy released Annie's hand, picked up the stuffing to pass, and the barrier of the first holiday had been broken.

Meg
December 2, 2013

Nowhere in Perry Pike did the Christmas season shine brighter than the Crooked Nook window display. This year, Piper and Meg had trimmed the window with twinkling white lights, framing a perfectly jolly snowman who was reading a vintage copy of <u>Twas The Night Before Christmas</u>. At the base of the snowman were piles of books—new holiday releases, old favorites, classics, children's books, and seasonal cookbooks. The window's side walls were decked with holly, and there was even a small table in the corner, with a plate of cookies and a beautiful snow globe. More often than not, Page, the new bookstore kitty, made a bed for herself amid the fluffs of snow in the front of the window—a live attraction for window shoppers.

"Who could resist this?" asked Piper, hands on her hips, admiring their work.

"No one," agreed Meg, putting the final ribbon touches on the shop's wreath. Up and down Main Street, garlands were draped and lights were shining. It was Meg's favorite time of year. She patted her phone, tucked inside her bookstore apron pocket.

The texts were more regular now. She had begun to spend less time thinking about their origin and had learned to depend on them. It felt like she was texting Ben out-of-town. Just this morning, they had exchanged:

> *Ben: Is it December already? I know you love this time of year.*
> *Meg: It's December 2. I do love it!*
> *Ben: I miss being there.*
> *Meg: I miss you so much.*
> *Ben: This is good, though.*
> *Meg: Yes, I guess it's good enough.*
> *Meg: Ben, how is this happening? Where are you?*
> *Meg: Ben, I need to know something, anything*

Then, nothing. She peeked at her phone now, just in case. No notifications. It's okay, she told herself, even as she was praying for his next text
to arrive. At her worst moments (or her clearest moments?) she would try to
remember that her husband was dead, and to be grateful for any tiny morsel
of communication she received. At her best moments (or were these her
clearest?) Meg would also try to remember that this communication was not
from her husband.

Ben.

Is.

Dead.

Whatever this turned out to be—pure insanity or a horrifyingly nasty
prank—the virtual conversation was still only temporary. Unfortunately, she
could only make herself remember this (believe it?) for the briefest periods
of time: the time it took to walk from her bedroom to the kitchen, the time it
took to drive from home to the high school, the time it took to come in from
outside the bookstore into the warm interior. The time it took before she
could check her phone again, waiting for the next message from Ben. Her
clarity was increasingly fleeting.

At the bookstore, Meg felt at home, sometimes more comfortable
amid the novels and the new young adult fiction than she did in her house
without Ben. She and the kids were slowly beginning to adjust to some mo-
tions of their new life, if not to the actual idea of Ben being gone. She imagined that the kids were using the same tools that she was; pretending that he
was away in a hotel was easy. Annie and Willie had both, on separate occa-
sions, expressed to her that sometimes they forgot that their dad wasn't coming back, and they worried that their feelings were somehow terribly wrong
or disloyal. For one brief moment, Meg considered telling them that she felt
the same way every second of every minute of every hour, but she was
afraid she would give away her secret. She assured them that their feelings
were not only appropriate but allowed.

Here at the store, she could busy herself recommending bestsellers, placing orders for customers, and visiting with friends from town who popped in to buy Kite Runner for the Freshman reading list requirement.

Toward the end of the day, Piper headed to the storage room to check on the shipment of handmade Christmas cards for display on the rounder in the front of the store. Kate was out for the day, meeting some old friends for a monthly lunch and round of shopping, and Meg was looking forward to going home and making a warm chili dinner for herself and her children. Snow had started to fall, Meg noticed, as she petted Page.

"Pretty kitty," Meg purred, rubbing the cat who preferred to stay on the counter and sit right in front of the register. "Look at the snow outside, kitty." Meg was paying no attention to the door, and didn't hear the bells ring. Suddenly, a customer was standing right in front of her.

"Excuse me," he said.

"Oh! I'm so sorry," Meg said, startled, looking up. "Hi! Can I help you?"

"Hi," he said, looking at her, expectantly.

"Hi," she repeated."

He stared.

Meg paused for a moment, then recognition dawned. "Jason," she said.

He nodded.

"Jason. What are you doing here? I mean, here in town?" He was standing very close to the counter, hands in his pockets. Something wasn't registering comfortably deep within Meg's gut, and she stayed behind the counter. Although she had recognized him when prompted, he was disheveled. Jason's tan windbreaker was wrinkled, and his dress shirt underneath was untucked from his jeans. His longish, dark hair was unkempt, and he seemed on edge.

"Oh, seeing my dad at the nursing home, helping him out with his house. Just thought I'd say hello. You know, just hello. So, hi. I never heard from you after I sent you that message on Facebook, but still…"

"Oh, yeah. Sorry about that. It's been a little bit of a tough time lately," Meg said.

"I know," said Jason. "I did hear about your husband. I was sorry, like I said when I wrote to you. I think I had tried to get in touch a couple of years before that, too."

"Had you? I don't remember." Meg frowned and looked down at the cat on the counter. She looked to see if a customer needed help.

"Yeah," he said. He hadn't moved from the counter. He continued to stare at her, and she wasn't quite sure what her instincts were telling her. It wasn't necessarily bad, but her guard was up.

"How did you know I worked here?"

"Facebook," he answered.

"I didn't put this on Facebook," Meg said, starting to feel more panicked than uncomfortable.

"Your daughter did," said Jason, very nonchalantly. "It's so easy to find stuff out online, you know?"

"You're Facebook friends with my daughter?" said Meg.

"No, but I was trying to find you. You should check her privacy settings if you don't want people knowing stuff about your family."

He wasn't wrong, but she didn't like his tone, and she didn't like how she was feeling in his presence.

"Hey, can you excuse me one second?" she said. "I just need to grab something out of the back room."

"Sure," he said, making no move to go anywhere.

Meg walked quickly to the storeroom where she found Piper cross-legged on the floor amid stacks of beautiful cards, laser-cut and glittered.

"I need you," said Meg, quickly and firmly.

Piper rose to her feet, hearing Meg's tone. "What's wrong?"

"A guy showed up here. My high school boyfriend. I'm sure it's nothing--actually, I'm not sure--but I'm just getting a creepy vibe. Can you come out with me?"

"You got it."

"Okay. Give it thirty seconds and then show up next to me."

Meg returned to the front, where Jason was still at the counter, petting Page. Meg stepped back behind the register and pulled the cat into her arms.

"Everything okay?"

"Fine." Meg nodded. "My co-worker was in the back, and her break is over."

"Yep," called Piper, appearing at Meg's side. "My break is over!"

"Piper, this is Jason. An old friend of mine from high school," said Meg.

Piper extended her hand, but Jason did not even look in her direction.

"An old friend?" he said, in an amused tone. "I think it was a little more than that, don't you, Meggie?"

At the use of her nickname, Piper stole a quick look at Meg.

"Well," said Meg, "I guess that's true. We were high school sweethearts. It was such a long time ago. We certainly had good times." Meg smiled as nicely as she could.

"Yes," Jason said, very slowly. "We had good times."

Piper was still standing with her hand extended, but she withdrew it slowly.

"Okay, then," Piper said. "This has been so great, catching up and all, but Meg, I think we better start closing up, don't you? Why don't you go get the broom from the back, and I'll start locking up."

"Enjoy the visit with your dad, Jason," Meg said, turning to leave.

"Well, I won't really get to see…"

But Meg was already halfway to the back storeroom.

"Good seeing you," she called over her shoulder.

"You too," he called back. "My girls are with their mom this weekend, so…"

Piper rolled her eyes. "Great story, dude." She motioned to the door.

"Just stopping in to see an old friend," he said.

He turned slowly and walked out of the shop. Piper locked the door quickly behind him and whirled to face Meg, who was now standing in the doorway between the two rooms of the store.

"What the hell was that?" said Piper, her back against the door, as if to protect the entrance.

For a long moment, Meg couldn't answer.

"I really don't even know. Let's just hope it's nothing."

Piper narrowed her eyes. "Let's hope."

She knew exactly why she hadn't answered the first message from Jason. It had caused an enormous fight between Meg and Ben on the first night of summer vacation just a few years ago.

Annie and Willie had been swimming with Tommy all afternoon, enjoying the hot sun and the feeling that only the last day of school can bring. They had eaten ice cream cones from the Snack Shack and still had a patio dinner to look forward to. Meg was lying contentedly on her favorite lounger, tucked under a giant sun hat, reading her first beach book of the year. Elise was right next to her, occupying the same chair that she would claim all season, skimming through the newest *People* magazine.

"I think Angelina is so beautiful," she sighed.

"Ick," said Meg, not looking up.

"Ick? You've got to be kidding."

"Nope. I will never understand how Brad left Jennifer for her. Jennifer Aniston is gorgeous. A perfect beach beauty."

"Please. Angelina is a classic beauty. Jennifer is like a teenybopper. There's no comparison," laughed Elise.

"It's Angelina. Hands down," said a male voice.

"Ben!" Meg smiled, looking out from under her hat. "How was work?"

"Brutal," he said, loosening his tie and bending to kiss his wife. "I'm ready to change into my swim trunks and have a beer. Will you order me one, and grab one for Kyle, too? He's on his way. I called him on the way over."

"Great," said Elise.

Soon after Kyle arrived, they were seated around a poolside table crowded with salty fried food, cold drinks, wet children and damp towels.

"Did Meg tell you about her stalker?" asked Elise, shoving a French fry in as she asked.

"No," said Ben, eyebrows raised.

"Oh my God. He is not a stalker." Meg rolled her eyes.

"'He' who?" said Ben.

"Jason sent me a message on Facebook. It was just to say hello, and now we're friends. Not like real friends, just Facebook friends."

"Jason-old-boyfriend-Jason?" Ben took a gulp of his beer, and set it down, pointedly.

"Yes," said Meg. "Jason-from-high-school-Jason. It's nothing. Why is everyone making such a big deal about it?"

"I'm *not* making a big deal about it. I didn't even know about it," Ben said.

"Please," Meg sighed. "We're all connected with old friends on social media."

"Whatever," Ben said.

"If you don't want me to be his 'friend,' I won't," Meg said, looking directly at her husband.

Elise shot a glance at Kyle, acknowledging the awkward moment. She busied herself by asking the kids if anyone needed a soda or more chicken nuggets. Kyle quickly headed to the bar for another round.

"Okay," Ben challenged. "I don't want you to be his 'friend.'"

"Really?" said Meg sarcastically.

"That's what you said," said Ben, "and that's how I feel."

"What about how I feel?"

"Why would I care about how you feel about your old boyfriend?"

"That's not what I meant," said Meg, feeling her eyes start to fill with angry tears. "You're really starting to piss me off, Ben. I'll 'unfriend' him when we get home, if that's soon enough for you. Can we drop it, please?"

"Fine."

"Fine."

"Can we swim again, Dad?" begged Willie, appearing at Ben's side, ketchup smeared on his mouth.

"You can," nodded Ben.

The evening continued painfully— Elise and Kyle attempted to make conversation about anything else—the weather, vacation plans, even a paint color they were selecting for their garage walls. The couples limped through the meal until the check finally arrived.

"I'll get it," said Ben, grabbing for the bill.

"Thanks, Ben," said Kyle. "I'll get it next time."

"Sure," said Ben abruptly, "no problem." He was not himself.

Elise locked eyes with Meg, who looked back at her as if to say, "I don't know. What do I do?" Elise subtly motioned toward the locker room.

Inside, she grabbed both of Meg's hands. "I am so sorry. I would never have brought this up. I was only teasing, Meg, I swear."

"It's not your fault," Meg said.

"I feel like it is. What can I do?"

"Honestly, no worries. We'll figure it out. I mean, really, there's nothing to figure out, right?" Meg kissed Elise on the cheek, and they finished changing.

Eventually, the kids were dried , pool bags packed, and flip-flops found. The first day of summer was officially in the books.

Meg and Ben drove home separately, since they had arrived in separate cars, and by the time Meg had reached the house and unloaded the kids and their inordinate amount of stuff, Ben was already parked and inside and waiting by the kitchen counter. Annie and Willie both went to their rooms to change into sweats or pajamas.

"Thanks for that," Ben said, nastily.

"What in the world is going on?" Meg said, truly dumfounded.

"Thank you for embarrassing me in front of our friends."

"You have *got* to be kidding me. You caused a scene at the dinner table over something that meant nothing. I'm the one who was embarrassed, and Elise feels terrible," argued Meg.

"Right. Elise knew. Who else knew that Mr. High School Boyfriend was now your married-woman Facebook friend?"

"Seriously, Ben, you are way out of line," Meg said, turning away.

"So delete it."

"What?"

"Delete the message and the contact. Don't be his 'friend.'" Ben was looking at her with a serious stare. "Any guy who gets in touch with an old girlfriend, an old girlfriend who is married, is a total loser. Even if you were his 'friend,' you'd be 'friends' with a loser. Delete it."

"Fine, Ben. Do you want me to do it now?" Meg stared back.

"Now."

"Don't you trust me?" Meg said softly. "Don't you trust my judgment? Just so you know, I'm going to delete him from my contact list, just to put this behind us, but the fact that you're standing here, demanding it, makes me think you don't trust me." They had never had a conversation like this before.

"I trust you. I just want it gone. I want him gone." Ben was still stone faced.

Meg walked to the laptop on the counter. She opened her Facebook page, scrolled until she found Jason Brinkman, and clicked "delete friend."

"Happy?" Meg asked.

"Yes," he said, "Thank you." He moved toward her, softening, obviously seeking some sort of reconciliation.

Meg stared at him, the despondency she felt masked by the hard glare she flashed. She turned and walked away. For the first time in their marriage, she slept on the couch.

Tommy
December 2, 2013

He'd been on his knees, digging in the back of the hall coat closet, searching for a pair of warmer gloves (he lost at least one glove every season) and a decent hat that didn't have a pom-pom or a knitted tassel. Ski Club would start at the high school soon, but even now, the early morning drives to school were bitter cold--it was time to layer-up. Tommy yanked out his dad's hideous scarf, moved two tennis rackets, and was about to give up, when the back of his hand scraped against a sharp edge beneath the hanging winter coats. He pushed the clothing aside and found a metal storage box. Nothing fancy, no lock, no label. Tommy slid the box out of the closet; maybe his mom was storing extra winter stuff in here. He sat back onto his heels, and opened the lid. No gloves. Just a few things he might have expected to find in a closet—some out-of-date electronics, extra batteries, a few old pictures and even some 35mm film canisters. There was a knot of old phone chargers, and he spent a few moments trying to sort it out—he was always losing his cords—but they were all useless. In the very bottom of the box, was a stack of correspondence, tons of postcards, and a pile of letters. He picked up the postcard on top of the pile, carefully, and looked around to see if anyone was watching (even though he hadn't done anything wrong—he'd stumbled across a storage box). The card depicted the St. Louis arch against a bright blue sky. He turned the card over and read, "Wish you were here, angel—I love you! Love, Daddy." It was addressed to his mom, dated when she would have been seven, maybe eight. The next card was from the Cincinnati Zoo. "I didn't get to see these white tigers this time, but we should come back here sometime! Miss you! Love, Daddy." Hundreds of cards, all with cityscapes or funny pictures, all sent to his mother over the span of her childhood.

The letters told a different story. They were all unopened, all sent from his mother to his grandmother at an address he'd never heard of. The first (and only) letter he opened, the one with the most recent postmark, contained a brief note, and his own school picture.

Hi Mom.
 Just wanted you to know that Thomas started his junior year today. Here is our address and phone number.
 Love, Elise.

His mom had included a folded piece of paper with all of their contact information. It was separate from the letter, as if she thought maybe it had a better chance of surviving. The picture and the letter felt oddly weighted in Tommy's hands.

The letter was dated September 2013. "RETURN TO SENDER" was stamped in bold red ink across the envelope's address, and on every envelope in the box. There were at least a fifteen more unopened letters, and though he didn't dare open more, he held one, then another, up to the hallway light above. Some held pictures, some newspaper clippings. The postmarks dated back to the early nineties, all sent to his grandmother, returned to his mother, unopened, unread.

Tommy knew that his grandfather had died before he was born, but he had been told only that his grandmother was not in his mother's life. For years, he'd been too young to need any further explanation; however, now seeing the years of one-sided correspondence, his heart broke for his own mom. He picked up the one envelope he had opened and studied the address, tracing his mother's handwriting with his fingers, the recipient's name so oddly unfamiliar. The thought of his mother tucking the unread letter into the box was so unsettling to him, so sad, that he shoved the letter back into the pile so he didn't have to see it anymore, didn't have to hold it in his hand. He rearranged the items in the box as best as he could remember, and slid the box back under the coats, forgetting entirely about his gloves and hat.

Annie
December 2, 2013
10:15 pm

Every now and then, Annie looked at the email, thrilled each time to see her dad's name on the screen. Perhaps it was the secret she was keeping, perhaps it was that he was choosing to communicate only with her. Even if it wasn't her dad (please be her dad) she really liked thinking she had received a message from him after he … well, after. As with all things electronic, she knew there was always the chance that the message could be gone forever in the blink of a power outage or a computer failure. Tonight, as she was revising her English paper, she decided to print out the email and keep it, just in case. After the last page of her essay on *Gatsby* fed through her wireless printer, she opened the email and clicked "print." And there it was in her hands, a hard copy of questionable origin.

Hi, honey. It's Daddy. I'm still here. I miss you.

Now that she had it, what would she do with it? She folded it in half, then in half again, and then clipped it closed with three pink paperclips. She tucked it into the front pocket of her backpack, along with her wallet, her keys, her Midol, her pens and pencils, and her Victoria's Secret nude shimmer lip gloss. To anyone who happened to see, it could be a schedule, a homework paper, or a love note. They would never guess, and all that really mattered was that Annie knew. One sentence that she could carry close to her at all times. Date stamped, printed, saved.

Her phone chimed with an incoming message.

Hey

One word from Thomas. Her heart skipped a silly beat at the thought of what they were about to do.

Hey she texted.

Can you? he texted back.

Annie took a breath before answering and stopped to listen to the sounds of the house around her. It was after ten, so Willie had been asleep for at least two hours. Her mom had been up to check on her and to say goodnight a full hour earlier. She had seemed particularly edgy, and had even asked to take a look at Annie's Facebook page, scrolling through the feed, while Annie sat back in her desk chair and rolled her eyes. Not that Annie had anything to hide; it was just unlike her mom to be so blatantly nosy--she usually did her spying in private. But once her mom had made her upstairs rounds, she had turned off most of the downstairs lights on her way back to her bedroom on the first floor. Even if she wasn't yet asleep, she wouldn't hear if Annie slipped out the back door.

She paused to consider another thing as well. Could she?

I think I can she texted.

Five minutes Thomas replied.

Annie pulled a white Aeropostale hoodie over her leggings and long-sleeved tee and found some heavy socks. She edged open her bedroom door a crack, listened again, and heard only the sounds of a house that was resting for the evening. She turned off the light in her room and closed the door behind her.

Annie tiptoed down the stairs and crept through the kitchen to the mudroom, where she grabbed her winter coat and slipped into her fuzzy Ugg boots. Carefully, she unlocked the back door and shut it softly behind her. She would be gone such a short time, she told herself. There were mittens in her pocket, which she put on as she walked quickly to their meeting spot, at the corner of Church and Division. Thomas was already there, just like they had planned, standing directly under a streetlight, shivering even in his navy parka. A very light snow was falling.

"Hi," he said, smiling, reaching out to take her hand.

"Hi," Annie answered.

"C'mon," Thomas whispered.

He led her down the sidewalk, their boots leaving tracks in the very new snow. Just down from the corner was an empty house, an old Victorian. It had been for sale forever, it seemed, but now the sign was down and it had fallen into disrepair. Thomas said he had heard that some kids had gotten in a couple of weeks ago through an unlocked basement window.

"Are you scared?" he asked her.

"A little," she admitted.

"Don't be. I'm here. No one will ever know."

"I probably shouldn't stay too long," said Annie, looking around the dark yard and the suddenly imposing house.

"Me either," Thomas said, squeezing her hand. "We should check it out, though. I mean, if you want to. Do you want to?" He seemed so nervous that Annie had to laugh.

"I'm here, aren't I?" Annie gestured with her palms upward, shrugging. The fact that she was defying the rules was adding to her excitement and heightening her nerves. "Let's go before I freeze to death!"

Thomas grinned and they snuck around to the back. The autumn leaves were partly frozen and crunched under the snow and the weight of their boots. The small, rectangular basement window was above a window well, and popped open with just a push. Thomas helped Annie slide through; inside, under the window, was a chair, which allowed her to lower herself into the basement. Annie wondered how that had happened. Maybe the kids partying here had come up with an entry and exit system? Thomas followed her, turning on his bright phone flashlight. A few beer cans, some trash, a faint smell of smoke. An old pool table, a pingpong table, and several storage boxes stacked against the wall. In one corner was an old sofa and a dinged-up coffee table that had not traveled with the owners to their new destination. On the couch, there were a few decent toss pillows and a couple of blankets. Annie also noticed a candle and some matches on the table, and she looked suspiciously at Thomas.

"I came over earlier, just to make sure the place wasn't too gross."

"Too gross for what?" Annie asked.

"Too gross to … come here and hang out."

"Got it," she confirmed, smiling.

Annie took off her coat and moved over to the couch. It was cold in the basement; she was glad Thomas had thought to grab a couple of blankets. She grabbed one to snuggle under while he stood, watching.

"So are we gonna hang out?" she asked.

"Yes," he said, not moving. Annie felt like she was seeing his nerves in the shape of his person.

"Yeah, I mean, of course, yes, " he said again, putting his phone on the table, shrugging off his own coat, and joining her on the sofa. She lifted up the blanket so he could get underneath, and she cuddled next to him.

"Nice," she said.

"Mmmm," he answered, stroking her hair.

"Do you want to light the candle?" Annie asked.

"Sure," Thomas said. He disentangled himself and reached over to strike a match and light the wick. There was just enough light with the candle and his phone to see each other and their small space in the corner.

He leaned back, she leaned forward, they were kissing. It was different from their usual kisses in the car, more urgent. Annie had had several opportunities to be alone with Tommy since they'd became an official couple but something was new. Perhaps it was the aura that surrounded this particular night. They were sneaking out, meeting up, with the intention of … doing what, exactly? Neither of them had said, but today at school, when he had proposed the idea of meeting up after bedtime, she had certainly agreed, and quickly. And here they were. She knew Tommy wouldn't push her too far; she was fairly sure of her own self-control. She was so extraordinarily happy just to be alone with him, that sneaking out was already worth every potential punishment that she might suffer.

She felt his mouth open, just a little, and his tongue played along her teeth. She sighed, letting her tongue flicker lightly in his mouth, and it was perfect and soft and she wanted more. Thomas pulled Annie closer and slowly began unzipping the sweatshirt she still wore. She didn't protest. The hoodie now hung open, and their tongues continued to lightly tease each She wore a pale pink shirt under her sweatshirt, and she knew Thomas could see the outline of her bra though the tee. He moved his hand to her cheek, where he began to caress her, softly. Her skin was so, so soft. She sighed again, and continued to kiss him, her hand on the back of his neck, tickling. She noticed that every time she sighed, he squirmed, and it made her feel like some sort of superhero.

Thomas moved his hand slowly down her neck, and then to the neckline of her shirt. She tensed, just the slightest bit, as he slipped one finger under the elastic strap of her bra, but she didn't pull away. Instead, she felt herself pull a bit closer to him, one hand still on his neck, and her other resting on his thigh.

She was barely breathing, and she couldn't hear Tommy breathing at all. They had never been together this long without saying anything, but she couldn't speak, or move, or even open her eyes. She felt him slowly inch his left hand down from her collarbone until he was cupping her breast, keeping still. Annie c her breath, and then she dipped her head and kissed his neck. He gently moved his right hand to her other breast and began caressing her. Tommy pulled his lips away from Annie's, and she was glad to see his face. She looked into his eyes while he was touching her.

"Is this okay?" he asked her.

"Yes," she whispered.

"You're beautiful," he said.

"I'm not," she said quietly, looking down.

"You're the most beautiful girl I've ever seen," Thomas whispered.

"Do you want to see me?" she said. She couldn't believe her own words. Annie, always more shy than brave, was being aggressive and bold, and she knew it. What she was feeling felt different, but exciting. It was good, and she wanted more.

"Annie, don't do anything you don't want to do," Thomas said softly, meaning it.

"I want to."

Annie leaned back from Thomas's hands, peeled off her sweatshirt, and dropped it behind her on the couch. She pulled her pink shirt over her head. She knew he was seeing her in her bra for the first time, and as she let the shirt drop to the floor, her hair mussed, she smiled, and reached behind her back to release the clasp. Annie felt she was giving him a gift, and she reveled in the power she was feeling.

"Wait," Thomas said.

Annie cringed. She had gone too far. She looked away, embarrassed.

"I just want to look at you for a minute."

He stared at her, sitting on that old sofa in the dark basement. Annie sat quietly in front of him, leaning in to kiss him every now and then. Finally, after she kissed him once too many times, teased him with her tongue on his lower lip one too many times, he pulled her in, and stroked her lower back, stopping at the clasp of her bra, and undoing it. Her bra fell forward, onto her shoulders. Thomas eased it off, and looked at her.

"Take your shirt off, too," Annie whispered.

He did, and she traced his chest with her fingers, dropping a light kiss onto his shoulder.

"Of course, you've already seen me like this," he said.

"What?"

"At the beach." Tommy flexed, actually being silly in this otherwise very serious moment. Annie let out a big giggle, relieved that they could still be themselves.

"You're right. How could I forget?" But, suddenly self-conscious, she covered herself with her arms. "It's different for me." She smiled, shy again.

"Don't. Please don't." Thomas peeled her arms away from her chest, while pulling her down onto the couch. He covered them both with one faded, chambray comforter, and let his head fall onto the arm of the old sofa as Annie's head rested on his chest. Annie was tossed in a space between bliss and sleepiness as they continued to kiss and pet under the covers.

"I should probably go," she finally said, quietly.

"I don't want to leave you," said Thomas, kissing her, his hand still touching her breast.

"Me neither, but it's later than I thought. It's almost midnight.

Something about midnight made her want to be home and in her own bed.

"Okay, Cinderella. Let's get you home." Thomas daringly bent to place a soft kiss on Annie's breast. She looked startled at first, and then she smiled. She had a lot to learn, and she wanted to learn it with Thomas.

Once they were dressed and walking home, they were quiet, but content.
The snow had stopped falling, and the trees and streets were lightly draped in a lacy coverlet of white.

"It's beautiful," Annie whispered.

"You're beautiful, Annabelle," said Thomas, squeezing her hand.
Annie grinned.

He walked her past the meeting place and all the way to her house. No lights were on; no one had discovered she was gone.

At her back door, Thomas leaned down to kiss her goodnight. She kissed him back, and it felt different, stronger.

"See you tomorrow," she said, finally pulling away.

"Tomorrow," he said.

Annie turned and reached for the doorknob, beginning to turn it quietly.

"Annie," Thomas whispered behind her.

"What?" she turned and looked over her shoulder.

"I love you."

She dropped her hand from the knob, and turned to face him, and smiled.

"I love you, too."

He moved toward her and pulled her close for a hug. She burrowed into his coat for one last time before the evening ended.

"Thomas," she said very, very quietly.

"Hm?" he replied, into her neck.

"I got an email from my dad."

Meg
December 3, 2013

"Hi, buddy," Meg said, as Willie shuffled into the kitchen. He threw himself into a kitchen chair, crossed his arms on the table and laid his head down.

"Hmmmfph," he mumbled. "Tired."

"I can see that," she said. "You went to bed early, though. Why so sleepy?"

Meg was a little worried about Willie. He'd been adjusting fairly well, although she had gotten a call from his teacher last week.

"I completely understand," Mrs. Simon had said, "that this is a tough time for Willie, and for all of you. I'm just noticing that he seems a bit distracted. He's daydreaming a bit, wearing his headphones in study hall. Just a little less engaged than before. It's nothing to be alarmed about, especially given the circumstances, but I wanted to check in with you, of course."

"I'm glad you did," Meg said. "And I'll keep an eye out at home."

"I think that's all we need to do," his teacher said. "He's such a good kid, and I don't want him feeling any more pressure than he needs to right now. Let him know he can come to me if he needs any extra help."

Meg had appreciated the call and the kindness.

Now, she regarded her sleepyhead at the breakfast table.

"Tired, honey?"

"Annie woke me up last night," he said, paying more attention to his Coco Puffs than to what he was saying.

"What? What do you mean?"

"I don't know. In the night sometime I guess. I heard her talking on her phone when she was coming up the back steps. Can I have some strawberries, please?"

Meg's stomach rolled. After the uncomfortable encounter at the bookstore, she'd been on edge. Now she walked quickly to the back hall, almost tripping over Annie's wet boots, carelessly kicked into the corner.

"Annie!" she yelled loudly. No answer. "Annabelle!"

The door at the top of the stairs flew open.

"What? What is it? Geez." Annie was in a towel, water dripping from her hair onto the floor.

"Hey." Meg could feel herself relax at the sight of her daughter. "I just wanted to see if you were, um, up and getting ready."

"Yes," Annie said, "like every morning."

"Don't be rude. See you in a few minutes."

"Yep." Annie closed her door, and in a few seconds, Meg heard the buzz of the hair dryer.

Willie was still at the table when she returned.

"Hot chocolate?" she offered.

"Yes, please," he mumbled.

"So, you heard her on the stairs last night? Late last night?"

Willie shrugged. "Not sure."

"No big deal. Maybe she came down for a snack." Meg turned away from the table, trying to act like it was not an important conversation. Something felt off, but she was innately aware that "off" was her current state of mind.

"I guess. But I don't think so. I heard her on her phone and stuff."

"I'm sure she'll tell us," Meg said, forcing a smile.

What the hell had gone on last night?

Where did she go?

Why did she go?

Meg cut up some strawberries for Willie, and helped him through his morning checklist--backback, lunch, snack, and coat. He had plenty of time to eat and watch some morning television, while she went up to investigate.

"I'll be right back," she told him. "Eat."

He nodded, already engrossed in SpongeBob.

Meg quietly took the back staircase and stopped outside her daughter's room, where she could hear Annie softly giggling. She knocked once, opened the door, and Annabelle turned, startled. She was still wrapped in a bath towel.

"Mom! I'm not ready!"

"I can see that. Perhaps you should get off the phone, with…?"

Annabelle glared at her. Into her cell phone, she said, "I have to go. See you later." She slipped the phone into her backpack pocket.

"Who was it?" asked Meg.

"Why?"

"Because I'm asking."

"It was Tommy, okay?"

"Tommy?" Meg was confused. She had assumed that Meg was on the phone wasting time with Lizzy or one of her girlfriends. "Our Tommy?"

Annie rolled her eyes. "Yes, *our* Tommy."

"Annie, why is it a big deal if you're talking on the phone to Tommy … unless … unless it *is* a big deal. Annie, what's going on?"

"Mom it's nothing. I don't want to talk about it."

"I didn't ask you if you wanted to talk about it. We also need to talk about last night."

Annie's face paled. "What about last night?"

"Why don't you tell me?" said Meg, sitting down on the edge of the bed.

With all that they had been through, it wasn't Meg's intent to trap her daughter in a lie; it was her intent to find out where she had gone, and why.

"Did you leave this house?"

Annabelle looked back at Meg, obviously trying to gauge how much was already known. Could Meg have already spoken with Elise, would Thomas have spilled?

"Yes, but…"

"I can't imagine there's a 'but' that could make much of a difference," said Meg, quickly realizing that if she wanted Annie to supply the truth, she'd better stop sounding like her own mother. She took a deep breath and backtracked.

"Why would you leave the house without telling me?"

Annie appeared to be thinking fast. Meg had never worried about Annie lying--not about the big stuff, anyway. It just wasn't the nature of their relationship. She was the girl who said too much, whose conscience wouldn't allow her to carry any kind of guilt. Itty-bitty regular lies, but only rarely. Meg knew that when Annie grudgingly grabbed her winter coat off the hook in the mornings, she likely left it in the back seat of her car, even though she swore she wore it into school. She knew that Annie didn't always eat her fruit at lunch, or that she stayed up far later texting and chatting than she was supposed to (especially lately).

"Mom, I only went out to my car late last night to get something. I ended up staying out there for a while, longer than I planned. I have some stuff to figure out. I'm still not sure what to do."

"What did you have to get? What could be so important that you had to go outside without telling me? Was the house locked up? Were you alone?"

"I was alone. The back door was unlocked, but only for a little."

"Back door? If you were going to your car, why didn't you go through the garage?" Meg asked, actually impressing herself with her own inquisition skills.

"Mom, I didn't want to wake you," Annie insisted. "The back door was closer and my car was in the driveway. Really. I just needed to grab something, and I stayed out longer than I meant to. I'm sorry."

Meg wasn't sure she believed any of it, but Annie needed to get ready for school, and she needed to get Willie on the bus.

"So what was it?"

Annie walked slowly over to her backpack in the corner. Meg watched as she carefully sifted through a few items in the front pocket. From behind the phone, she produced the folded paper with the clips on it, and handed it to her mother.

"Here."

Meg took the paper, slid off the pink clips, and unfolded it. She stared at the email, reading it, then reading it again, before she looked up at Annie, wide-eyed.

"What is this?" she asked softly.

"I think it's an email from Daddy."

Meg looked back down at the paper.

"When did you get it?"

"Last month."

"Annie," whispered her mom, sitting down slowly on the bed, "why didn't you tell me?"

"Because it can't really be happening, right?" Annie was speaking at a frantic pace. "I didn't tell you because it's not really happening. Last night, I just wanted to see it again. That's it, I swear. I swear, Mom."

Meg couldn't be sure if it was a lie of epic proportion or just a tiny stretch of the truth but she knew the paper she'd been handed was significant, regardless.

Meg smoothed the crumpled note on her lap, almost meditatively. She could sense Annie watching her, perhaps anticipating a flip-out, some sort of massive mom-breakdown. But Meg simply kept reading, re-reading.

Annie stayed silent. Meg was highly aware of her daughter's worry. The probable lie was almost visible around her--surely there was more last night's story--but now this email was the priority.

Meg suddenly looked up. "Can I see your laptop?" she asked her daughter.

"Mom!" Annie began pacing around her room. "Mom! Why don't you believe me? I said that I. . ."

"I do," Meg said. "Calm down, please."

Although Meg actually wasn't completely convinced, she didn't have the wherewithal to investigate Annie's story at the moment.. "I do, Annie. This isn't about that."

"What, then?"

"Laptop?"

Annie took her laptop from her desk and handed it over to Meg, who was still sitting on the bed.

Meg clicked on the Facebook tab, forever present at the top of Annabelle's Internet browser, and Annie's homepage opened.

"Mom?" asked Annie, impatiently.

"Just checking something."

Meg scrolled through Annie's friend list looking for Jason Brinkman, or any Brinkman for that matter, and found nothing. A cursory glance at her home page didn't give Meg any reason to worry.

"Annie, just let me know if anything strange ever pops up here, okay? Like always, I mean. I want to know what's going on in the big wide world of Facebook. Lots of creepers out there." She smiled at Annie.

"I'm not friends with any creepers, Mom," said Annie, rolling her eyes.

"Roll your eyes all you want, Anniegirl. I'm just doing my job."

"So what about the email?" Annie sat down next to Meg and took the note from where it lay open on the comforter.

"Well, that's kind of my point," said Meg. "I would hate to think that someone out there is lying to you." In her robe pocket, Meg's fingers wrapped around her own iPhone, protectively.

"My friends would so not do that, Mom," Annie said, almost angrily.

"I don't think so either, Annie. But there are mean people in the world. People who take advantage of sad situations."

"It came from Daddy's email account, Mom. I don't understand."

"I don't either." Meg sighed.

"It makes me kind of happy to see it. Is that weird?" Annie's eyes teared up.

Meg put her arm around her daughter. "Oh no, it's not weird. It's not weird at all."

Texts from Meg:

9:02 am did you email Annie?
9:04 am She's worried. She is a child.
9:06 am answer me, Ben. Please

Elise
December 3, 2013

The Purple Onion was one of their favorite lunch spots, and Elise was happy to see Meg walk through the door, looking like her old self, her cheeks pink from the cold, rubbing her mittened hands together as she approached their table.

"Brrrr!" said Elise. "You brought the cold in with you!"

"Sorry," said Meg, sliding into the booth opposite her friend. "It's so warm in here. I'll never want to leave."

"I ordered you a diet Coke," said Elise, motioning to the drinks already on the table.

"Perfect," said Meg, opening the menu, and then closing it. They both always ordered the same thing.

"So," said Elise. "The love story continues. At least at my house."

Meg laughed. "Well, it would appear so. There's been lots of giggling and texting, but she hasn't actually told me yet."

"Who would have ever thought?" Elise shook her head in disbelief.

"What do you mean? *We* thought! Haven't we been waiting for this since their first hiking date? Isn't this the wedding we've always dreamed about?"

"Oh my God, a wedding!" Elise shrieked, just as the waitress came by for their order, then clapped both hands over her mouth, giggling.

Meg handed her the menus and said, "Two turkey clubs, please, wheat, no ham, extra avocado. One order of fries, one order of onion rings." She looked at Elise.

"Yes?"

"On the money."

"Thanks, ladies," said the waitress, smiling, taking the menus and retreating to the kitchen.

"Well," said Meg, "so far it seems innocent enough on Annie's end. What about at your house?"

"He's like a puppy. Running around, paws on the window, panting, can't wait for her to get there, can't live without her. Ridiculous. Well, not ridiculous at all, obviously. She's fabulous. We've all known that forever." Elise smiled. She loved Annie like her own daughter, and Meg understood.

"Can you imagine if this were actually to go somewhere? I mean, I know they'll probably head off to different colleges—"Meg speculated.

"Which is probably for the best--" Elise interrupted.

"I agree," continued Meg. "So a wedding may be a bit in the future, but there is prom!"

"Oh my God, *prom!*"

"Perhaps we're being slightly crazy," giggled Meg.

"Only slightly!" Elise slurped her soda.

They chatted about dresses, corsages, and limos until their food arrived. The sandwiches were stuffed full of delicious veggies and fresh turkey, and the onion rings were hot, and piled high on a plate. Elise squirted a pile of ketchup for the fries and looked at Meg.

"What else?"

"What else what?" Meg asked, popping an onion ring into her mouth, whole.

"You said on the phone that you had a story about the bookstore."

Meg nodded, chewing.

"Oh, I do." She swallowed and then began to retell the story of Jason, starting from his unexpected arrival at The Nook, including every detail, while Elise ate and listened, her jaw dropping in all the appropriate places. When Meg finally reached the point in the retelling where Piper locked the door behind him, Elise had stopped eating all together.

"I cannot believe what you are telling me," said Elise. "What are you going to do?"

"What can I do? It's over, it happened, he's gone. And he said he's leaving town."

"No," said Elise. "Not enough. He knows where you work, he probably knows where you live. You at least need to contact the police."

"And say what? A guy came into the bookstore where I worked and was annoyed that I didn't answer him on Facebook? It's not like he threatened me. He just made me uncomfortable."

"Kate and Piper know never to let him in again, right?" asked Elise.

"I think Piper might put a hit out on him before that could ever happen," said Meg. She picked up another onion ring.

"Are you worried about him coming to your house? I'm not trying to scare you, Meg. I'm just thinking about you and the kids."

"I have the security alarm set every night. I really do think he's gone, and I don't want the kids to have another thing to worry about, you know?"

Elise considered. "I do know. Just keep your eyes open. It's weird, isn't it, that Ben got so crazy mad about Jason when he first contacted you?"

Meg nodded slowly, considering. "Ben was never a fan of hearing about old boyfriends, and it seems like ages ago, you know?"

"It's still strange that Jason would show up here out of the blue," Elise said. "It just feels like kind of an odd coincidence."

"It's not, though. Is it? He said he's here seeing his dad." Meg paused, considering. "And it's not like Jason would have known Ben was angry. And even so, what would it mean?"

"I'm not really sure," answered Elise. "I just want you to watch out for that guy."

Meg nodded.

They finished their lunch, briefly revisited the topic of Annie-and-Tommy, both agreeing to watch for signs of escalating teenage romance— or worse, teenage angst—at their respective homes and to report to each other immediately. For once, in the weeks since Ben had died, Meg did not check her phone for texts, and Elise didn't ask about the messages. It wasn't until Meg was driving home that she realized that she had completely forgotten to tell Elise about the email that Annie had received. God, she thought. How crazy was her new life that she could forget such a significant detail?

Sarah Parker
December 4, 2013

Dr. Sarah Parker swiveled her chair toward her panoramic window. Maybe some wouldn't be wild about a city view of Cleveland, she preferred it over all other options. During the day, she could watch the city moving below her like a constant movie, people hurrying, cars maneuvering in and out of downtown. When it grew dark, she loved to watch the lights, especially in December. Today, it was like being inside a snow globe. Big, white flakes fell past the glass and onto the street below. Shoppers were toting bags and balancing boxes. Policemen were already directing traffic in the intersections—Sarah wondered if there was a basketball game or a concert in the city this evening--and she could see cars backing up on the streets. Holiday wreaths dotted the restaurant doors and sparkling lights shined on the trees in store windows. Sarah could hardly wait to leave the office; she had her Christmas list in her briefcase and she was in the mood to shop. She checked her watch. 4:07 PM. Just a while longer, and a short break before her next appointment. She had started to rise from her desk to head to the staff lounge when there was a soft knock on her door. Her sister-in-law, Elise, peeked around the corner, bearing a bakery bag and two styrofoam cups.

"Time for a quick coffee?" Elise asked. "The receptionist said you didn't have a patient."

"Oh, my gosh! Perfect!" said Sarah, taking the drink and giving Elise a kiss on the cheek. "It's so good to see you! How did you know exactly what I needed? Sit." She motioned to one of the two deep, comfortable chairs opposite her desk, and she took the other. "What are you doing all the way downtown?"

Elise sat, taking in Sarah's pretty office surroundings, and the stunning view behind her.

"God," said Elise, smiling and procrastinating, "you look great with the big city behind you!"

Sarah laughed. "Why, thank you!" She tossed her auburn curls over her shoulder, dramatically. "So, what's up?"

"Well," said Elise, "I need to ask you about something."

"Ask away," said Sarah, digging into the bag for a muffin.

"It's Meg," said Elise. "I'm worried about her."

"God, Elise, I'm sure. It's so terrible." Sarah had been at the service; she had known Meg and Ben for years. Together, they had celebrated many of Tommy's birthdays, cheered at baseball games, and visited at family gatherings. "How is she?" She took a sip of her coffee. "Ah, so good," she said.

"I mean, pretty well, you know, all things considered." It appeared to Sarah that Elise had more on her mind, and Sarah wasn't at all surprised.

"Of course," said Sarah. "It's been, what? Just a little over a month?"

"Right. Yes, that's right." Elise looked perplexed about what to say next.

"What is it?" Sarah asked, sure now that Elise was here for more than a hot drink and a quick question.

Elise paused before responding. "It's just that…well, I'm not sure I'm supposed to say anything."

"But you came here to ask me about something, right?"

"Right, but it's going to sound so…so…"

"Elise, I've had all kinds of conversations in this office. Confidential conversations."

Elise nodded, and fidgeted with her coffee, busying her hands by adjusting the lid.

"I know."

"But?"

"Sarah, I know there's this rule about doctors not seeing patients in their own family, so I wasn't sure about coming here, but I do have a problem."

"I can absolutely refer you to the best that I know if you need someone to speak with, Elise."

"It's not me, it's still about Meg."

"Okay, does she want to come in? And if she feels to close to me, we can get her a referral, no problem."

"I haven't asked her yet."

"Elise, what's worrying you?"

Elise met Sarah's eyes, and didn't waver as she spoke.

"Meg has been getting text messages from Ben," she said quickly, then exhaling sharply.

"I'm not sure I know what you mean," said Sarah, her voice measured, nonjudgmental. Her practiced tone was meant to put Elise at ease, and was a large part of why she was earning her reputation.

"I'm not sure I know what I mean," Elise said. "Messages are showing up on her iPhone from Ben's number, with Ben's name, and she's answering. Ben is dead, Sarah."

"That's true," Sarah said. "So, this must be very difficult for her."

Sarah tried to appear unruffled; it was part of the job. She hoped she was coming across less flustered than she felt. Was Elise *really* sitting across from her talking about texts from Ben?

"Yes," said Elise, "it is. Well, it is and it's not. But this is crazy."

Sarah laughed. "'Crazy' isn't a word we throw around here lightly."

Elise clapped her hand over her mouth. "Sorry! I just mean, you and I both know it's not Ben. How do we get her to know it, too?"

Sarah sat back in her chair and took a sip of her hot drink. "What do you mean 'it is and it's not' difficult for Meg?"

Elise paused. "It's like, she didn't want to tell me about the messages because she was worried I wouldn't believe her. Which I totally understand. But then once I knew, and she would tell me when they arrived, I could see that she was looking forward to them. Waiting for them, you know? And then sometimes they have conversations. Meg and Ben. Or Meg and … whoever. God, I don't know. She gets upset when he doesn't answer right away, almost like a teenage girl. So how do we make it stop for her? Or at least make her understand it's not real?"

"Why do we have to?"

"Oh, my God, you sound like Kyle."

"Elise, I'm just saying that, first, we can't do anything unless Meg wants to do something on her own. Have you asked her if she wants the texts to stop? Have you discussed the idea of an appointment with her? You can't drag her in here and make her talk to me. Second, it sounds like it might actually be helping, not hurting, her. Is it slowing down her acceptance of his death? Maybe. Is she hurting anyone? No. Is she suicidal? It doesn't sound like it. Is it probably a cruel joke? Yes, probably."

"'Probably'?" said Elise. "What do you mean 'probably'? And it *is* hurting someone? It's hurting Meg!"

"She thinks it's Ben," said Sarah. "Who are you to tell her it's not?"

"It's not what?"

"Who are you to tell her it's not Ben?" asked Sarah. "How do you know?"

Elise stared at her. "How do I know?" she asked incredulously. "Because Ben is dead, Sarah." Her tone was becoming increasingly angry.

"Elise, I'm only saying that Meg is grieving, and however she is perceiving this and processing this … "

"I'm her best friend. I want it to stop.

"Why?"

"I just told you! It's hurting her."

"How?"

"I … I don't know. How can it *not* be hurting her to think that her dead husband is texting her from, I don't even know where?" Elise's voice was raised, she sounded frantic. "From beyond?"

"Why is it bothering you so much?" asked Sarah.

"I'm her best friend."

"And?"

"And when did this become about me?" Elise retorted, now with a fierce edge to her voice. "It's bothering me because I love Meg. It's bothering me because I'm afraid this could go on for a lifetime and keep her in some suspended universe. Now it's bothering me because I thought you could help and obviously I was wrong."

"If she's being harassed on her phone, she could call the police."

"She won't. In her world, she's texting Ben. If she calls the police, it might stop. She doesn't want this to stop."

"You want this to stop."

"Yes, I want this to stop. Why is that so wrong?"

"Elise, I love you, and you know how I feel about Meg. I would do anything to help you."

"Help *her.*"

"Yes. Help her. Trust me on one thing. Attacking her and dragging her to a psychiatrist right now will make her more confused and sad than she already feels. You know that. Just love her and let her talk to you, at least for now, before you bring in a professional."

"I wasn't going to attack her," said Elise.

"That's how she would have viewed it."

Elise nodded, acquiescing.

"I have a patient coming in soon," said Sarah, glancing at her watch. "I wish I had more time. But I do have one question. Think about this for a while, and then call me later if you want, okay?"

Elise nodded. "Okay, what is it?"

Her sister-in-law, the psychiatrist, looked her right in the eye.

"I mean this, Elise. I love you, and this doesn't change anything. But if you're so worried about how these texts are hurting your best friend," asked Sarah quietly and unfalteringly, "then why are you texting her from Ben's phone?"

Elise
December 4, 2013
4:43 pm

    She sat in her car in the underground parking garage of the Cleveland Clinic Medical Center, and sobbed deep, choking sobs until she thought she might actually die. After what seemed like hours and hours, she reached into her purse for a tissue. She pulled her phone out, turning it on first to shine some light into the interior of her handbag, and then to check for messages from home.

Text from Meg: Hey— How's your day? Rough one here, but I guess that's normal. Tis the season. Call me. xo

Text to Meg: Hi-- so sorry you're having a tough day. How can I help? xo

Elise lay her head back on the car's headrest and cried like she had lost her best friend.

Meg
December 4, 2013
5:14 pm

Text from Ben : Don't worry, baby. We'll figure it all out. I love you.

Annie
December 4, 2013

She was waiting for him by her locker after the student council meeting. Annie saw Thomas at the end of the hall, coming toward her, and she
smiled. It was as if she had a new sort of radar; she could sense when he was
nearby and feel when he was about to leave her side--a sense of impending
loneliness--even if they were only going to be apart until the ride to school
the next morning.

"Hi," he said, by her side, at last.

"Hey," she said, shyly. "Do you want to grab dinner?"

"I have a baseball team meeting now," he said, looking disgruntled.
"I think I'm going to be in the gym for a while."

"It's December," she said, incredulously. "And you just came from
the gym."

"I know, but we have to pick apart those freshmen," he teased.

"So, you're not here to ride home with me?" she said.

"I can't. But I wanted to see you."

Annie blushed.

"Okay," she said. "Call me later?"

"I will. Hey, um, do you want to talk about that thing you said?
About the email?"

Annie still felt terrible about lying to her mom about sneaking out,
but showing her mom the email had felt like breaking the water's surface
after too much time spent on the pool floor. It had been an opportunity
seized. She might be ready to have the conversation with Thomas.

Annie shook her head. "Not here."

"But sometime?"

"Sometime."

He leaned in and gave her a quick kiss--in front of people!--and took off for practice. Annie felt herself blush. Lizzy was just heading toward her, grinning at what she'd seen, when Thomas came running back down the hall. He had almost reached her locker when he yelled out to her. "Annie!"

"What?" she called.

"Here! In case you're cold."

He tossed her his letter jacket and ran.

Meg
December 5, 2013

The text yesterday afternoon had started a new conversation, but the tone had changed.

> *Ben: Don't worry, baby. We'll figure it all out. I love you.*
> *Meg: I love you 2. Figure what out?*
> *Ben: This whole thing.*
> *Meg: Where are you?*
> *Ben: Where am I?*
> *Meg: Are you asking me? I don't know.*
> *Ben: Don't worry. It will be all right.*

Where are you? Such a simple question with no answer. She'd been asking it in her head and out loud since late in the afternoon of October 30th, when she didn't hear from Ben shortly after his flight had landed. Now she was asking it of her dead husband, or of a stranger. She asked the question to herself as she lay in bed trying to sleep, when she drove, when she tried to work, in the shower.

Asking.
Asking.
Always asking.
Where are you?
Where are you?
Where are you?
Business trip.
Business tri…

Business…. The pretending was getting more and more difficult, and the never-ending questions were beginning to wear on her. She knew, didn't she? Ben was dead, his spirit wasn't texting her, he was not alive, as much as she wished it to be true. She wanted to exit this crazy train she had accidentally boarded. The email to Annie had cast a new light; someone was playing a hateful joke on her, and now on her daughter. Someone had breached the circle of protection she tried desperately to keep around her children. With Annie involved, this shameless infringement on what should have been a private period of mourning seemed suddenly beyond contempt, and Meg was tired.

She checked the clock on her phone. It was after 9:00 am. The kids were already at school, and she was due at the bookstore around ten. She clicked to open her text messages.

Nothing from Ben. (It was not Ben.)

Not Ben.

Not Ben.

Not Ben.

Not since yesterday.

Was she brave enough to send the text she knew she needed to send?

We need to stop, she typed. Then she deleted it, and started over.

You need to stop.

She looked at the words. The idea of telling Ben (not Ben) to stop sending her messages filled her with unexplicable sadness. It could be the last time she ever heard from her husband.

Not Ben.

Not Ben.

Not Ben.

She said it over and over in her head. The last time she had truly heard from *her* Ben, she reminded herself, had been on October 30, before

he boarded his return flight home. *Her* Ben had texted that he loved her. In
the few seconds before she hit the button, she permitted herself one more
minuscule heartbreak; she mourned the loss of his name ever again being on
her screen.

And she pressed SEND.

She dressed for work quickly, in a comfy, gray cable knit sweater
and black leggings. She slipped on a pair of clogs, and did a quick fluff of
her hair and a quickie make-up refresh before she ran out the door. Thank
God this wasn't a corporate job, she often thought; she loved looking and
feeling like herself at the bookstore.

"You look like hell!" Piper exclaimed, as Meg burst through the
door, not wanting to be late.

"Well, so much for me trying to pull it together," Meg said, a bit rue-
ful.

"No, you always *look* good, you just look like *hell*, you know?"

"I really don't."

Piper sighed. "I'm just saying you look a little tired. Or upset. Are
you okay? Coffee? Oh, and I just got a great eye gel sample. Wanna try?"

"Yes, I'm okay. And yes, to everything," Meg replied, always
amused by Piper's lack of subtlety.

Much to Meg's surprise, she actually felt better than she had in quite
a few weeks. She wasn't waiting for texts, she wasn't on edge. Once she got
a mug of hot coffee and had applied Piper's Clinique under-eye cream, she
felt almost refreshed.

Around eleven, the door flew open, the bells jangled, and Meg
looked up to watch as Kate greeted an elderly man, a regular customer of
theirs. The energy that surrounded Kate was contagious; she always provided just the right touches to ensure that every customer had a memorable experience in her shop.

"Mr. Avery!" said Kate, as he entered. "I was so happy to see you
ordered the *Hunger Games* series for your grandson. Let me show you an-

other new series that's just arrived. I think he'd love it!" Off they went, chatting amiably.

Just this morning, Kate had worked her magic to get a textbook overnighted to the Goodman's daughter in her dorm, and she had fixed a glitch with a Christmas shipment that had been suddenly delayed until January. "I'm so sorry," Kate had said, "but that simply cannot work." She was never nasty. Firm, but friendly, she maintained easy working relationships with all of her loyal vendors.

Kate was now on a stepladder behind the register, organizing the shelf where all orders were held for pick up. Currently, there were more than seventy-five copies of <u>Romeo and Juliet</u> waiting for several sections of eighth-grade English. There were stacks of books marked with Post-it notes, so that Kate, Meg, or Piper could identify a pick-up for a customer. Mr. Avery (<u>Hunger Games</u>), Mrs. Stewart (two cookbooks and the new Danielle Steele.) There were more copies of <u>Fifty Shades of Gray </u>behind the counter than Kate would care to count, but a sale was a sale. Meg perused the orders so she could be prepared if anyone popped in. That's when she noticed a stack of Young Adult fiction labeled "Brinkman."

Meg picked up the stack and shuffled through the books.

"Kate, do you know when this order was placed?"

"Let's see...the other day, I think. Yes, maybe on Tuesday. A gentleman called in and wanted to order some Christmas gifts for his teenage daughters. He asked me if I would put together some age-appropriate novels. You should go through them, though, Meg, and see if I picked good ones, ones Annie would enjoy."

"Oh, I'm sure they're all great." Meg was quickly trying to piece together dates in her mind. Tuesday was the day that Jason had shown up in the store. He had said he was leaving town after one night, hadn't he?

"He wasn't local. I didn't know him. He said he was in town, staying with family over the holidays." Kate was chatting, still straightening the piles of books.

Meg grew silent, holding the stack of books and staring at the name and the date on the Post-it.

"Kate, that's Jason."

Ben
July 2006

He couldn't wait to get Meg out of here and back to their hotel room. When his own high-school reunion invitation had arrived, he'd tossed it in the garbage; now, he couldn't believe he'd been dragged to Meg's twentieth. Now he was trapped at a corner table, drinking a watery vodka in a dated ballroom, while Meg squealed and gossiped with her friends on the dance floor.

"Please?" she had begged him when the tacky invitation had arrived a couple of months ago. "I really want to go."

"Meg, really?" He'd taken the invitation from her, reading it aloud in the kitchen, with exaggerated formality, and a British accent, if he remembered correctly. He couldn't exactly say why, but it had amused him in the moment. "The Class of 1986 invites you to attend your twentieth high school reunion. Dinner and dancing at the Ramada Inn Northeast. Class photo at 9:30 PM. Cost $125 per couple.

"Seems a little pricey for the Ramada, don't you think, Meg?" He was having fun taunting her, because although he had no desire to go, he had every intention of taking her.

"Ben," she implored, "you know you'll be the cutest, most successful man in the room. None of the girls will be able to take their eyes off you. Me included." She gave him a suggestive glance. "I'll make it worth your while at the fancy Ramada."

"Promises, promises," he said, swatting her on the behind with the invitation.

"I promise," she said, kissing him smack on the mouth. "I'm making the reservation."

So here they were: Meg enjoying her walk down high-school memory lane, and Ben, leaning against a high-top bar table, sipping a cocktail, watching her in her splendor. He had always known she was exceptional, but seeing her here, among others she had grown up with, learned with, been raised among, it was easy to see that Meg's star beamed brighter. Her laugh sparkled above the crowd like champagne bubbles, fizzing and popping, and she tossed her head back as she enjoyed the moment. She looked young, she had on a short (but not too short) pink cocktail dress and a great pair of heels. In an ocean of black dresses, Meg was the shiny lure.   Some of these people were already starting to look like grandparents, Ben thought. Hell, some of them might be. He hoped he was as attractive to his wife as she was to him. He was just about to go grab Meg off the dance floor, whisper something sexy in her ear to lure her away, when another man joined him at the otherwise empty table. Must be another abandoned spouse, Ben thought.

"Hey," the stranger said, setting his beer on the table, "these things can be rough, huh?"

"Sure can," Ben said.

"You're Meg's husband, right?"

"I am," said Ben, slightly confused. "Ben McAfee." He extended his hand. "And you are?"

"Jason Brinkman." The two men shook hands. "I saw you two come in together. Boy, she hasn't changed a bit."

"Nice of you to say so," said Ben, trying to keep the conversation brief. Something about the guy rankled.

"You guys been married a long time?"

"Yep," Ben said, suddenly offended and entirely unwilling to engage.

Jason nodded. "My wife couldn't come tonight."

"Too bad," Ben said, chugging the last of his vodka and tonic.

"I've thought about her a lot over the years. Meg. You know how it goes."

"Not really," said Ben, putting his own drink down rather hard and pushing his chair back.

"Dude," said Jason. "I didn't mean anything. I'm just saying you're a lucky man. I never should have let that one get away."

"Dude," Ben said pointedly, throwing Jason's word back in his face. "That one got away a long time ago." Ben stood up and walked angrily away from the table, on a mission to find his wife and to take her away from this room full of people he didn't know or care about. He wanted to buy two more bad drinks from the overpriced bar and take them upstairs to the hotel room. He wanted to leave all of their clothes in a heap on the floor and he wanted to make love to Meg, hard and fast, on top of the bed, and then again under the blankets, because that's what she would want. Ben intended all of it to be a giant "Fuck you" to the man he had met at the table, and he knew that Meg wouldn't mind, even if she knew. He found her on the dance floor, whispered in her ear and made her blush, before firmly taking her by the hand. He watched as she waved goodbye over her shoulder to her friends before clinging to his hand and planting a kiss on his cheek. He watched their feet as they approached the elevator. He watched the elevator door open and their reflection in the mirrored interior as they entered. As it closed, Ben McAfee watched Jason Brinkman surveying the whole scene.

Meg
December 5, 2013

> *Ben: Stop? Why?*
> *Meg: Just stop. Please.*
> *Ben: But what about Willie. You should talk to Willie.*
> *Meg: What about Willie?*
> *Ben: You know about Annie. Check Willie's iPod.*

Check Willie's iPod? Meg could feel her stomach contract. She shouted to Kate that it was an emergency, and she bolted from the store.

As she drove faster than she should toward home, her thoughts swirled. What had she missed? What was happening with Willie? Meg checked the dashboard clock. 3:10. She still had time to make it home before the bus arrived.

She pulled into the driveway, threw the car into Park, and ran inside. Meg took the stairs two at a time up to Willie's bedroom. Legos, playing cards, toy dinosaurs, and all other things that screamed "nine-year-old boy" were scattered on the bed and the floor. Where was his iPod? Maybe he had taken it to school. No, she had told him not to, after his teacher had said he needed a bit more focus. So, where? She searched his desk, going quickly through stacks of origami paper and school drawings; she opened a few drawers and shuffled through socks and belts. Nothing. Then it dawned on her. She threw back the messy blankets on the bed, sending some small plastic dinosaurs flying. There it was, tucked into the pillows with Fred and assorted animals, headphones plugged in.

Sitting down on the bed, Meg powered on the device and saw that Willie had fallen asleep to Queen, his favorite "new" band. She glanced out the front window to ensure that the bus had not yet arrived. She clicked the icon for iMessage, the application on Willie's device that allowed him to send texts to just a few people, including her, Ben, Annie, and a few other friends and family.

It was the next best thing, Willie said, until he was allowed to have a real cell phone.

"Ah, the old cell phone discussion," Ben would tease, knowing full well that he and Meg had already planned it for his big Christmas gift this year.

"Everyone has one, Dad!" he would whine.

"So will you, when you're 21," Ben would say.

"*Dad*!"

Meg felt her stomach recoil when she saw his name on Willie's phone.

Dad.

There it was, a text conversation that in any other reality would have been completely unmemorable, but here, in their new world, was unthinkable. The exchange between Ben and Willie had seemingly been going on for months--Meg scrolled quickly through to get an idea of the content. The first text had arrived on November 5th, the day Meg had been stunned to received her first message. Had Willie been as shocked and scared as she had been? Why hadn't he come to her, or worse, why hadn't Meg thought to check his phone? Because, she told herself, what mother thinks to ask her child if he's been communicating with his dead father? She should have thought, she chided herself.

Her texts from Ben, and Annie's email. Of course Willie was in the mix of this nightmare. In her own grief, consumed by the texts and desperately attached to her own phone and her own story, what had she missed? Oh God, what had she missed? What other lines had this perpetrator dared to cross?

November 5
Dad: Hey buddy, I miss you. Everything is going to be fine.
Willie: Dad? Where are you?

Her heart broke as she read the first exchange, which was so similar to the messages on her own phone. As the texts went on, the messages grew more conversational.

November 13
Dad: How was school?
Willie: Okay. I had art. I hate art.
Dad: I know you do. Are your grades good?
Willie: Yep.
Dad: I'm proud of you :)

Every now and then, a few days would go by with no communication, a pattern Meg found familiar. Then Meg would read a short exchange, or a longer conversation. At some point she began to cry while she was skimming the messages, knowing she would go back through and dissect them word for word. How could she possibly explain this to Willie, when she had no idea what was happening, and worse, no idea what she wanted the answer to be?

December 1
Willie: Dad, are you there?
Dad: I'm here.
Willie: I miss you. Can you come home?

Nothing since. Meg set the iPod down on Willie's nightstand, took a deep breath, and started to stand. As if her body was telling her what her mind wouldn't accept, her knees buckled beneath her, and a sob started so deep inside her that Meg had no choice but to let it come up. There, on her knees in Willie's room, she gave up trying to figure it all out, and wept. She was still there when both Annie and Willie arrived home from school. Although she'd had every intention of being in the kitchen to greet them, to find a way to approach this topic calmly, here it was, suddenly upon her, as her children piled into the bedroom.

"Mom! We've been calling you. Mom? What's wrong?" Annie dropped her backpack and fell to the floor next to her. She took Meg's hand, stroking it as if Meg was a child in need of comfort.

"Mommy? Are you okay?" Willie stood back a bit, appearing to assess the situation in his bedroom. He hurriedly grabbed his iPod from the bedside table and put it in his pocket before tucking in next to Meg on the carpet.

Meg rocked back into a cross-legged position and wiped her eyes with her fingers.

"Oh, my babies. Oh my gosh. I'm all right. I'm so sorry." She reached out to each of them, pulling them even closer to her.

"Mom, what is it?" Meg could heard the worry in her daughter's voice.

"Well," said Meg, the word a giant exhale. "I think we have a bit of a mystery on our hands." She glanced at her daughter first. So many questions were evident on Annie's young face. Willie stared at the carpet. When Annie did speak, it was if she was asking the question that Meg was thinking.

"Mom?" she asked, are you sure?"

"It's all right, Annie," she said, sending her daughter a reassuring look and placing her hand firmly on Annie's knee. It was time, Meg decided, that she bring the three of them together to discuss what they had each been dealing with separately. She had tried to keep her secret, and in doing so, she had been blind to the fact that her secret was also theirs.

Meg looked at them both, one at a time. "I want you both to know something. Since Daddy died, I think maybe something a little strange has

been going on." She noticed Willie reach instinctively into his pocket, a reaction she found heartbreakingly familiar.

"Am I right?" she looked at them, waiting.

"Yeah, our dad's dead," said Annie, "and it sucks."

"Yep. It really does. What else?" Meg paused, waiting. Both of her
children remained quiet. Meg wondered if they were afraid to say out loud
what she had been thinking for months--I've been getting messages from
Dad--or if maybe, at least in Willie's case, he wasn't even sure any more if
his communication with Ben was strange. They'd all adapted in different
ways to their new life. Willie was adapting by texting with his father, and
she was about to explode his world, yet again.

"Okay," she said firmly. "I'll start." She hoped she sounded braver
than she felt. "Mommy has been receiving some text messages in the last
few weeks, and they seem like they're coming from Daddy's phone."

She saw Willie's head jerk up. He opened his mouth as if to say
something, but then closed it, and looked down, still just listening. Annie,
however, was glaring at her, which was unexpected.

"You've been getting messages?" Her daughter's voice was icy.
"How could you not tell me? How could you sit there and read my email
from Dad and not tell me that it was happening to you?"

"Annie, I wasn't ready to--"

"You got an email from Daddy?" Will said softly, looking at his sister.

"Yes," Annie said. "I got an email a few weeks ago. What the hell is
going on, Mom?"

Nothing else from Willie, but now he had pulled his iPod from his
pocket and was scrolling through screens. So Meg took a breath and continued, knowing he was still listening.

"I got the first message from Dad the night of the funeral, and it
freaked me out. Sometimes I get a few messages at once, and sometimes I
don't hear anything for days at a time. Sometimes I answer."

"You do?" said Willie, looking up at his mother.

"Yes," admitted Meg, nodding, "I do." Annie was now silent, listening.

"What do you say?" asked Willie.

"I guess it depends. Sometimes I ask him questions, sometimes I say I miss him. A few times I've asked him to tell me where he is, because that's what I really don't understand."

Willie nodded, nearly imperceptibly.

"But it's not him," said Annie loudly, "so why are you answering? Why are we even talking about this? This is so fucking stupid!"

"Annie!" Meg grabbed her daughter's hand and squeezed it, hard. "Stop. I know this is difficult, but stop. Please. Let's just talk about it."

Annie ripped her hand away and turned her back on her mother, but she stayed in the room, on the floor.

"Willie," said Meg. "I don't understand where the texts are coming from, or who is sending them, but sometimes it just feels so good to think I'm texting with Daddy."

"Are you sure it's not Daddy?" his brown eyes filled with tears.

"Oh, baby. I'm sure. At least, I'm sure in my head. It never feels really sure in my heart."

Willie's tears rolled out of his eyes and down his cheeks.

"Mom, stop!" yelled Annie. "You are making this a million times worse."

"Shut up, Annie!" screamed Willie. "Daddy was texting me and now it's probably not even Dad, so just *shut up*!" Annie looked stunned at his outburst, or shocked at the admission. Meg couldn't be sure.

"Dad was texting you?" Annie almost whispered the words.

Willie was sobbing now, and Meg gently took the iPod from his hands.

"Can I?"

Willie nodded, head down, his fists digging into his eyes.

"I'm sorry, Willie. I didn't know," said Annie. She scooted next to him, and began to gently rub his back, up and down, up and down. Annie rubbed his back softly, while Meg took her time to look more closely at the texts that she had barely glanced at minutes before.

"So who is doing this to us?" asked Annie, quietly now.

"I really wish I knew," answered Meg, still reading.

"I wish it was Daddy," said Willie.

"I know, baby. Me too."

"Why did I only get one email?" said Annie. "You both got more messages. Didn't Dad want to keep talking to me?" As soon as the question was out of her mouth, she was shaking her head at the ridiculousness of her words.

"It's not Daddy, baby," said Meg. "Remember?" Annie nodded, taking it in. Even after her anger just minutes before, it was too easy to feel connected to the name on the page, the name on the screen. Ben. Dad. Daddy. As much as they all tried to understand, their broken hearts simply couldn't comprehend the truth.

Piper
December 6, 2013

She saw him come in the front door of the shop and immediately she was on edge. Meg was gone for the day, for which Piper was immensely grateful. Jason was wearing jeans and a denim shirt, both visibly stained with paint or mud. His parka was unzipped and he looked sweaty, even on this cold afternoon. His hair was just a bit too long, his eyes tired.

She couldn't bring herself to offer a sincere greeting; her mother would have been appalled. Then again, her mother hadn't been in the store the day Jason had raised the creep meter. If Kate had seen that, she might have banned him herself.

"Can I help you?" Piper said, coldly.

"I have some books to pick up," Jason said, nodding to the orders behind the counter.

"Last name?" Piper asked.

"Brinkman. Jason."

"Ah, how could I forget," she said, turning to find his novels.

"Is there a problem?" asked Jason.

"Nope."

Jason reached for his wallet and pulled out a credit card.

"Is Meg here today?" he asked, looking around.

"If she was, I wouldn't tell you," Piper retorted, looking him dead in the eye, sliding the stack of books toward him.

Jason leaned across the counter. "Just tell her one thing for me. Tell her that her daughter's been seen around town, if you know what I mean.

From one concerned parent to another, I thought she'd like to know. She should get that girl of hers under control before she gets a bad reputation."

"I don't know what you mean, and I don't like what you're implying," said Piper directly.

He signed his receipt while Piper glared at him.

"I'm only saying…"

"Get out," she hissed. "Don't come back."

He turned slowly, his work boots making heavy footsteps across the store.

"Merry Christmas to you, too," he called back, before the door closed behind him, jingling merrily.

Piper thought briefly about calling Meg but decided not to upset her needlessly. Meg would be at the bookstore soon enough.

Annie
December 6, 2013

She didn't want him to stop. They were snuggled together in the front seat of her car, parked at the end of Thomas's street. The snow was falling in the streetlights, then landing on Annie's windshield, snowflakes splattering into beautiful messes on the glass. They hadn't ventured back to the empty house on the corner, not since Annie had nearly been caught. She hadn't liked lying to her mother, but this--making out with her boyfriend in a warm car--this, she liked.

Annie was wearing Thomas's letter jacket, but underneath, she was nearly naked from the waist up. Sweater open, buttons unbuttoned, hooks open. Tented by the warm, heavy jacket, she felt safe and protected as his hands moved freely over her shoulders and breasts. She kissed Thomas as she knew he liked and reached over to run her fingers down his chest. Annie had been waiting for this--this time alone with him, this moment right now when he was kissing her neck--since they had arrived at the theater for the early evening movie. When she wasn't thinking about her dad, she was definitely thinking about this. All the time.

She played her fingers through the placket on his shirt, teasing and tickling.

"God, Annabelle," he whispered.

Daring herself, she dropped her hand to his waistband, then a little lower, until her hand was resting lightly on the crotch of his jeans.

He kissed her urgently, moving against her hand. Annie wasn't exactly sure what to do, so she just touched him in the same way he touched her, softly and gently. It seemed to be working; Thomas moaned and pulled away.

"We have to stop. Now."

"Stop? Why?" Annabelle was surprised. "Am I doing something wrong?"

Thomas groaned from deep in his throat.

"Oh, my God, no. You're perfect. It's just that," he seemed to be choosing his words carefully, "if we don't stop now, I won't be able to, um...stop. You know?"

"Oh. Oh!" she exclaimed, understanding "I'm so sorry," she said. "Is there something I should do?"

"No. Not yet. And definitely don't be sorry." Thomas pulled her to him and kissed her. "I love everything we're doing. I can't believe I'm saying 'not yet' but it's because it's you, Annabelle. In a million, trillion years, I would never want to be in this car, in the dark, saying 'not yet' to anyone but you."

She sighed and leaned back against the headrest.

"I get that," she said, smiling at him across the front seat.

"Okay?" he said.

"Okay. Not yet."

They buttoned themselves back up, and Annabelle smoothed her hair in the car mirror.

"Hey," said Thomas quietly, "what about that email from your dad?"

"Not much to tell. I got an email from my dad. And it doesn't make any sense."

"Do you want to talk about it?"

"Not really. It makes me feel weird. But you can see it." She reached into the back of the car and grabbed her backpack.

"You don't have to, Annabelle. I was just wondering."

"No, it's fine. It's easier just to show you."

He watched as she unzipped the outer pouch of the bag and reached in, grabbing the folded paper easily, as if she knew its place by heart. She removed the three pink paper clips, and unfolded the worn, white printed paper.

"Here you go." She handed it to him.

He looked it over.

"See?" she said. "His name, his email address, the date, everything."

"I do see."

"But I kind of like it, you know?"

"I get that," he said, handing the note back and watching her remake the folds.

"Maybe you should have answered it," Thomas continued. "Just to see what would have happened."

"How do you know I didn't answer him?"

"Him?" Thomas looked at her.

"My dad. How do you know I didn't answer the email from him?"

"I guess because you didn't say that you did." Thomas had a strange look on his face.

"I didn't say anything about it at all," Annabelle said.

"Okay, sorry," Thomas replied. "I didn't mean anything by it. I'm just saying that if you answered, maybe you'd get a better idea of who had sent it to you."

"Maybe," said Annabelle, still irritated. "Maybe not."

"Okay, okay. I was really just trying to help." Thomas sighed in resignation.

"Well, stop trying. You don't know a thing about it, Thomas. Just leave it alone. I'll figure it out and it will stop."

"Stop? You mean it's still going on?" Thomas looked at her incredulously. "You've gotten more emails?"

"Not emails, exactly. And not me." Annabelle hesitated.

"What?" Thomas pressed. "Annie, you can tell me. I can help you."

Annie shook her head, back and forth, as if she were shaking away the question.

"Annie! Tell me what's going on. Please!" He reached over to grasp her by one shoulder. "Annie!"

"Okay, *fine*." She whipped around to face him. "It's my mom and my brother. They've been getting messages. And they've both gotten way more than me, like real conversations. It's freaking everybody out, but you cannot tell anyone. I mean it. No one." Annie grabbed his hand and looked him straight in the face. "*No one.*"

"What kind of messages?"

"Texts. Messages from my dad's number. From his phone, I guess."

"Texts. From your dad. Like your email." Tommy was looking right at her, but not in a way that made Annie feel any crazier than she already felt.

"Yes. But you can't say a word. Not even to your parents."

"But … "

"Tommy ohmygod I never should have told you." Annie put both her mittens up to her face.

"Annie. C'mon. I won't. I swear." But Tommy sounded unsettled and looked more upset than Annie would have expected.

They sat in the dark for a few long moments before Annie spoke again.

"It'll be okay, Thomas, right? I mean, I'll figure it out. We have to. I have to."

"You know I'll help you."

"It's weird, you know? I'm kind of sad that I haven't heard from him again."

Tommy looked at her. "Maybe don't think of it like that. None of this is real, Annabelle. Just try to remember all the good stuff your dad always told you instead. Like how beautiful you are, and how you were his favorite girl."

"Oh my god, please don't."

Her eyes were filling with tears. The memories were too much, and somewhere, in that very, very protected part of her being, the one that she reached into when she was alone, she wanted to believe that her father was emailing her from…somewhere. The belief lay tucked deep down inside the part of her heart that had once believed so wholly in flying reindeer, in pinky swears, in unicorns. Annie wasn't ready to let go of her Dad.

"Annie, someday the good memories will help. And yes, we will figure this out. Okay?"

Tommy looked at her and waited.

Annabelle nodded, staring straight ahead, unconvinced. She started
the car and drove from their dark parking spot back up the lighted street to
Thomas's house, where he kissed her goodnight, told her not to worry, and
headed in through the garage.

Tommy
December 6, 2013

Annie had barely pulled away, but now, in the confines of the dark garage space, alone between his parent's cars and surrounded by gardening supplies and baseball equipment, he allowed himself the worry and—was it fear?—to creep over him like rash. The thumping in his chest echoed the chaos in his thoughts. Tommy was not sure how long he stood there; his brain was garbage. Text messages too? Holy shit. Why had he believed his mother?

Tommy
November 30, 2013

He still couldn't understand what he had found, even though he was holding it in his own hand. Why did his mom have Uncle Ben's phone? He'd only come into their bedroom after school to grab his mom's phone charger—which he always borrowed—and when it wasn't on her nightstand, he pulled open the drawer and recognized Uncle Ben's phone right away. He had the coolest case—it was this cool bright blue, like shiny metal. He picked it up and pressed the home button, just to be sure. So weird, seeing all of Uncle Ben's apps pop up. The home screen photo was a family picture, which made him smile, but in a sad way. He wasn't sure why he pressed the email icon, but when he did, it was the sent folder that filled the screen. An email to Annie was at the top. Sent November 6, 2013.

"Wait," he thought. "What?"

He checked and re-checked the date, the timestamp, turning the phone over and over in his hand. And then he clicked to open the email.

Hi, honey. It's Daddy. I'm still here. I miss you.

So, maybe his mom was using Uncle Ben's phone. Maybe she was holding the phone for Aunt Meg. Maybe the email was something that his mom had forwarded to Annie for some reason.

No.

No.

None of it made sense.

He put the phone back exactly where he'd found it. Up in his room, he thought about calling his dad, and then his mom, and then instead he picked up his own phone and dialed his Aunt Sarah at her office.

"Tell me again," she'd said. "Slow down. Take a deep breath."

"I found Uncle Ben's phone in my mom's drawer."

"Okay. So that's not a giant problem, right."

"Right. But there's an email on the phone to Annie."

"Go on."

"And the email is from her dad and it was sent just a couple of days ago."

"Okay, well, this could be a lot of things. Maybe your mom was forwarding something she found on the phone?"

"No. I thought of that. It's like he's writing to her *now*." Tommy was pacing, trying to explain.

"Tommy, honey, I need you to calm down a little. Was there something in the note that especially worried you? Do you think Annie is in danger?"

Tommy had taken such a deep breath—he remembered closing his eyes and allowing himself time to feel the entire exhale before answering the question.

"No. I don't think my mom would hurt her. Not ever."

His aunt had seemed particularly shocked at his answer.

"But you do think that your mom sent this email to Annie."

"I do," he said. "But I don't know why."

Eventually, Aunt Sarah had told Tommy exactly what he didn't want to hear. "You're going to have to ask your mom, Tommy. Tell her about what you've found. Ask her what the email is about. Maybe there will be an answer that we just haven't been able to come to without having all of the information. And call me if you want to tell me about it, or if you just need to talk."

"You won't tell anyone that I called, right?" Tommy trusted his aunt. He knew she would help him without treating him like a kid. Plus, there was that doctor-patient thing, right. He wasn't really a patient, he guessed, but still.

"I will not," she said. "But listen, above all, your mother loves you. And I know how much she loves Meg and those kids. I promise this is going to be okay."

He was waiting in a kitchen chair when his mom returned from the grocery store, Ben's phone lying conspicuously next to his own on the table.

"Hi, kiddo!" She came in from the garage, two plastic grocery bags swinging from each hand, her purse thrown over her shoulder, sunglasses on her head. "How was school?"

"Can you sit down, Mom?" he said, calmly, which was weird. He did not feel calm

"Honey?" she set the bags on the counter. "Are you okay? Can you help me get the rest of the groceries and then we can … "

"I think the groceries will have to wait."

Elise looked at her son and then looked at the phones on the table. Elise sat down.

Willie
December 6, 2013
10:27 PM

> *Willie: Dad, are you there?*
> *Willie: Dad?*
> *Willie: Daddy, are you there? Is this you, Daddy?*
> *Dad: I'm here, Buddy. I'm here.*

Willie exhaled the breath he had been holding. He placed the phone face down on his nightstand, turned off his light, grabbed Fred the Panda, and closed his eyes.

Elise
December 6, 2013

Elise was still up when she heard the garage door opening. She had been cozied up on the couch most of the evening, not really waiting for Tommy to get home from his date, just relishing a relaxing evening of television reruns and a pile of magazines. She was padding through the kitchen in her fuzzy socks to turn off the last lights before bed when he came storming through the door.

"*How could you?*" he screamed. "*How could you?*"

Elise, startled by his entrance and outburst, dropped the water glass she'd been carrying and it splintered into hundreds of shards beneath her feet. There was no time to try to fix the mess; Tommy was enraged, and Elise was scrambling to get to him across the room. The broken glass and his anger were keeping her at bay in her own kitchen, away from her own child.

"How could you keep torturing them like this? Aunt Meg and Willie too? Are you freaking crazy? What is *wrong* with you? I mean, seriously, what is *wrong* with you? You said you *stopped*!" Tommy was shrieking now. Out of control, pulling at his hair, like he used too, as a child, when he didn't like a food, or an idea, or he was terribly uncomfortable. Elise tried to go around the counter, the other way, toward Tommy and away from the glass, but he held up both hands, palms out, two stop signs.

"Do not touch me. *Do. Not. Touch. Me.*"

It was the worst thing she had ever heard from her child, but she stopped.

Tommy pounded his fists on the granite counter.

"Why? What could you possibly be thinking? One email was bad, I mean really really really bad. But … "

He pounded the counter top over and over, and Elise could do nothing but watch as her son grabbing at his own hair in frustration, nearly pulling it out in front of her. "What the fuck, Mom? How could you do this to them?"

"Tommy, *stop!*" she screamed. "I can explain!" She was sobbing. In her desperation to get to her son, she'd walked over the broken glass; almost instantly, her feet were bleeding.

"*I don't want to hear it!*" he shouted, still keeping her at arm's length, even though she had managed to cross to the same side of the room as her son, her baby.

"Tommy!"

"*There is nothing you can say!*" He was sobbing and yelling, now. His rage was like that of a man, but his voice, choked with tears, she recognized. It shocked her to think that she had frightened her son so badly, but also to imagine that she had induced this sort of reaction.

He was shaking all over as he continued to yell and she continued to cry. "I asked you, Mom. I *asked* you right to your face what was going on and you told me. You said you made a mistake. You were just thinking of Annie and you thought it might be good for her to hear from her dad. That's *weird,* Mom, and it was a huge mistake. But you said you would never do it again. You *lied!* Were you doing this all along? The whole time?" He finally stopped yelling and stared at her. Tears were running down his cheeks.

"Tommy," she whimpered, sobbing in desperation, trying to touch his arm, but he shoved her away.

At that moment, Kyle came running into the kitchen, stopping short at the scene. He must have seen her then, reaching for their son. There was blood on the kitchen floor, Tommy was hysterical, physically shaking, pointing at his mother.

"My God!" Kyle screamed. "What is going on here?"

"It's *Mom!*" Tommy was screaming. "She said she had *stopped!* But she's sending the messages to Aunt Elise and Annie. And oh my God to Willie. *Willie!* He's like a *baby!*"

It was at that moment that she heard it, a shrieking, desperate sob. Tommy stopped yelling, and Elise saw Kyle turn to stare. Annabelle was standing in the door of the mudroom, wide-eyed, both hands covering her mouth as if trying hold in the unbearable pain. She had dropped Tommy's gloves on the floor in front of her, left behind in her car, like a sad sacrifice.

She fled.

Sarah Parker
December 7, 2013

There wasn't much that Sarah loved more than a Saturday with not one event on her calendar. She stretched out in bed, enjoying the luxury of the still-dark room, the warm duvet, the soft pillow. The sun was peeking through the floor-length drapes, so it must be getting later in the morning. Sarah rolled over and peeked at her clock. 8:37 AM. Perfect, she thought. She had slept almost ten hours, and she could even close her eyes again for a while.

Sarah drifted back off, her peace uninterrupted until her doorbell rang at 9:15 AM. At first, she wasn't sure if she'd even really heard anything; maybe she'd been dreaming. Sarah lay still in her bed, until it rang again, accompanied by frantic knocking.

She grabbed her robe from the foot of her bed and ran down the hall, nearly tripping on the stairs trying to get to the door. Through the glass panels framing the entrance, she could see her nephew, looking wild. His face was streaked with tears.

"Aunt Sarah, Aunt Sarah! I need you!"

She opened the door, and he fell into her arms, sobbing.

Meg
December 7, 2013

The house was too quiet.

"Breakfast!" Meg called for the second time. She had already flipped the pancakes and they were warming in stacks in the oven. The bacon was sizzling, and she had poured the juice; she was only waiting on her children. Just as she set the syrup on the table, Willie shuffled into the kitchen in his flannel pajama pants and a Lego Minecraft thermal shirt.

"You look cozy," she said.

"You do, too," Willie said, sweetly.

She smiled and ruffled his hair. He was going to make someone the perfect husband one day, she thought.

"Pancakes?" Meg asked, pulling the hot platter from the oven.

"Yes, please."

"Any sign of life from your sister's room?"

"Nope," said Willie, slathering his pancakes with butter and syrup. Meg suddenly realized that Fred hadn't joined them for breakfast. Maybe Willie was trying to find some way back to his sense of "before," but strangely, Meg missed seeing the fuzzy soft panda face at the breakfast table.

"I'm going to go check on that crazy sleepyhead. Be right back."

Willie nodded, mouth full, his mouth already covered in a sticky mix of citrus and syrup. Meg wiped her hands on the dishtowel and headed up the back stairs.

"Annie? Honey? Are you up?" Nothing. Meg and Ben had always been firm believers in letting the kids sleep late on the weekends, a habit that would have driven her own mother crazy. "It's eleven o'clock in the morning, Meg. You kids would have been up doing chores by eight," she would have said. Ben believed that if the kids were sleeping, they needed sleep; they had their whole lives ahead of them to be a slave to the alarm clock. She would just check on her girl to let her know that breakfast was ready. Meg also wanted to hear about her date with Tommy. She still really couldn't believe this was happening between Annie and the boy they had all loved for most of his life. Annie must have come in a little later than curfew last night—Meg hadn't heard her come in—but it wasn't a habit. Meg could guess where they had been. She would have called Elise if she'd been terribly worried.

Annie's bedroom door was ajar.

"Annie?" Meg said, peeking around the doorway, into the room. The bed was made, her room looked as if she had just left for her date. School clothes were tossed on the floor and her favorite make-up and hair products were strewn across her desk. The room smelled like Annie-- a mix of Victoria's Secret body sprays and her lotions--but she wasn't there.

Meg walked further into the room. No Annie. She didn't see her purse, or her phone. The phone charger, as always, was plugged in by the bed.

"Annie!" Meg called, not calm any more, not yet screaming.

No answer. Meg yelled down to Willie. "Willie, is Annie downstairs?" Maybe she had somehow gone down the front staircase in the brief moment she had come up the back.

"No," he answered, completely unaware that something might be wrong.

"*Annie!*" she yelled, now in a full panic. Meg ran from room to room upstairs, finding nothing. Back downstairs, she checked every room, looking for--what? Her daughter, whom she might have accidentally overlooked somewhere in the house? Hurt and lying unconscious somewhere right in their own home? A sign? A clue? Jesus God what was going on? She had a sudden flashback, more of a remembered feeling, to a moment when she was a teenager and they couldn't find their family cat, Matilda. They looked all day, everywhere. Her mom had called outside, left food and water, while Meg had searched the house top to bottom, finding nothing.   Finally, in the early evening, her dad had called the local police department to report a lost kitty. Meg remembered the worried, helpless feeling. Matilda had been a house cat. How would she fare alone in the dark, cold night? Later that evening, when Meg went to the linen closet for a clean towel before her shower, she was greeted by her kitty (who gave her a big sleepy yawn) curled up on a pile of clean towels. The one place Meg hadn't looked.

Where was the one place Meg hadn't looked? Ben, where do I look? I need you, Ben. The thought was so heavy on her chest that she felt she might collapse.

Instinctively, she reached for her cell phone in the pocket of her fleece robe. There was one unread text from Annie. From Annie?

3:45 AM
Annie: *It's Elise*

(Oh, God, thank you, Ben. She rubbed the phone, as if it were a magic lamp, and Ben her personal genie, guiding her to her daughter.)

But what the hell did that text mean? She texted back.

10:57 AM
Mom: *where are u?!*

She dialed Annie's number. Voicemail.

What did the text mean, and where was Annie at 3:45, and—God!—where was she now?

11:01
Mom: *Where are you? Pls text me RN*
11:02
Mom: *Are you OK? You are not in trouble. I love you*

Was Elise texting from her daughter's phone, letting Meg know "It's Elise"? Meg's imagination jumped to the worst possibility, which, given all the recent events with Ben and with her phone, was not unexpected. Elise had taken Annie to a hospital and tried to reach Meg from Annie's phone. No, Elise would have called her over and over on every line and from every phone if it was an emergency, and she would have given her more than "it's Elise" on the message. What if Elise and Annie were lying in a ditch somewhere? What if everyone at the Parker house had expired from carbon monoxide poisoning, including her daughter? Elise was trying to text her at three in the morning while she took her last breath. Meg knew she was really reaching, really getting inventive, and she needed to find her daughter and stop the peripheral craziness in her brain.

Meg texted Elise with their emergency signal.

Meg: *911*

And she waited one minute.

Nothing.

She waited one minute more.

Nothing from Annie or Elise.

At 11:06 she dialed Elise's home number and Kyle picked up.

"Meg?" he said. His voice was almost strangled.

"Kyle." Meg didn't mean to cry, but something about hearing his voice made her start. "Is she there? Is Annie there?" She could barely believe she was saying the words.

"No," he said, in a worried whisper. "I was hoping she'd have come home to you. I thought Tommy might be there, too. He's been gone since early this morning."

"Come home to me? What does that mean?" Meg shrieked. "Why are you whispering?"

"It's Elise. She had...a bad night."

"What happened? Wait. I mean, is she okay? God, I'm sorry, but you'll have to tell me later. Where are the kids?"

Kyle paused. "Tommy won't answer his phone. Meg, I'm guessing they're together, but I'm not sure. A lot happened over here last night—God, you don't know. You don't know. I'm coming over. Have you heard from anyone?"

"One text from Annie, at about four o'clock this morning. Kyle, she's not here. I have to do something NOW."

"Can you wait until I get there. Give me five minutes."

"Kyle, what is going on?" Her panic was rising like tidewater.

"I promise I'll fill you in," Kyle said. "Just tell me, what did Annie's text say?"

"It said, 'It's Elise.' Was Elise texting me from Annie's phone? I can't figure it out." Meg was still trying to decipher it all as she described the message to her best friend's husband.

"I wish it were that simple, but it's not. I'm coming now. Keep trying Annie, see if you can get anything. I'll do the same with Tommy. I promise we'll find them. Meg, I'm so sorry."

"Sorry for what? Kyle, Annie is gone! I don't think she's been here all night. And Tommy— Kyle, we can't just sit here. I have to call someone, do something. Kyle, I don't know what you're talking about, but I'm calling the police."

"Meg, I did hear from Tommy. If you can give me five minutes to get to you I'll tell you what I know, but I want to do it in person. I swear it will be better that way. Can you keep it together for just a few more minutes? Meg, I am so sorry this is happening. I need one sec to get Elise settled and I'll be right there."

She swallowed hard. "Okay. Come fast. Give Elise my love."

Meg heard Kyle make a noise, almost like a sob, before she put the phone down slowly. Get Elise settled? What was going on?

Meg sent three texts to Annie.

Mom: *Are you okay?*

Mom: *Call me*

Mom: *I love you. Whatever happened last night, it's okay. I will come wherever you are*

She tried to call her daughter's cell phone several times in a row, but each call dropped straight to voicemail.

Meg texted Elise.

Meg: *Are you okay?*

She got an instant reply.

Elise: *Don't hate me*

Don't hate me?

Meg: *I could never hate you. I love you*

Then, nothing.

She quickly pulled on jeans, a bra, and a red thermal shirt and slipped into a pair of old slippers. Willie had finished his breakfast, including most of the bacon.

"What's wrong, Mommy?"

She debated trying to cover this up, whatever this was, but there had been so much in their world lately, too much for one little boy to have to try to sort out on his own, or with his panda.

"You know what? I'm not sure. Annie and Tommy seem to have gone off somewhere, but Uncle Kyle says not to worry. He's on his way over, and we're going to figure it out. Annie texted me this morning, so that's good news." She could hear her own words, sounding fast and anxious. Her breath felt ragged. She tried to slow it down for her son. "Anything you see or hear, just let me know, okay? Like a spy."

Willie was quiet, taking it in.

"Will she come back?" He looked at her with real worry, needing a real answer. Meg could feel the hurt like a paper cut slice through her heart.

"Yes," she said, smoothing his curls, "for sure. Why don't you go get dressed, in case we have to go get Miss Annabelle somewhere."

"Okay." Willie slid off his stool and retreated upstairs, leaving Meg to pace in circles, waiting.

She checked her phone. Still nothing from Annie or Elise. Meg busied herself by scraping the leftover pancakes into the garbage and wiping the table, until there was a knock at the door. Kyle. It was so good to see his face, the face of someone who loved Annie, who loved Tommy, who would step in and help her in the same way that Ben would have handled this situation. She opened the door and Kyle held out his arms.

"I'm so glad you're here," she said. "Where did they go?"

"Meg," he said. "Meg, oh my God."

"What? Kyle, what? Did something happen?"

"No, no. I haven't heard from the kids. But we need to talk about last night."

"I don't understand," said Meg, turning and walking into the kitchen. "I'm sorry you guys had a bad night. But we need to handle this now. This first. Kyle, it's our kids. "

"I think last night has a lot to do with today," Kyle said slowly, closing the front door and following her.

"What do you mean?"

"I…I don't know where to start. I'm so sorry, Meg.. I'm just so sorry." Kyle looked pale and afraid. He dropped into one of her kitchen chairs. "I didn't know. I swear, I didn't know."

"What are you possibly sorry for? What didn't you know?"

"The texts. I can't even imagine ... losing Ben ... and then …. how could someone do this?"

Meg suddenly realized what Kyle was talking about.

"How do you know about the texts?" Meg grew cold inside, and her voice was quiet and shaky.

There was no time for Kyle to try to cover, nor any reason anymore. "Elise was worried about you, at first."

"At first? What does that mean?"

"Of course she's always been worried about you. That's not what I meant." Kyle shook his head back and forth; he wouldn't look her in the eye.

"What then?" Meg sat down in the chair across from him.

"She told me about the texts because she wanted to help you, somehow. But…"

"But?"

Kyle looked at Meg pleadingly.

"What, Kyle? What is it?"

"It's her," he whispered. "Elise is the one who's been texting you. She's been texting you this whole time. Elise is Ben. That's what Annie meant this morning when she texted you. *It's Elise*. It's Elise."

Meg looked at him, and shook her head incredulously. Then she laughed.

"Kyle!" Meg felt almost hysterical in her reaction, yet she couldn't control her own laughter bubbling up through the waves of panic in her stomach. "That doesn't make any sense. That doesn't make any sense at all."

"I know, but you have to listen to—"

"No!" Meg emitted a strange, choked sound, something between a yell and a sob, which, even to her own ears, sounded almost insane. "No. No no no no no. What are you talking about, Kyle? That's the wrong answer. Elise is not Ben. Elise is Elise. Elise texts me as Elise. My God, she texts me all the time. You know that, Kyle! Don't be crazy. Someone is texting me from Ben's phone. Elise texts me from Elise's phone. You are so wrong. Someone has this very wrong and now you have this really, really wrong. Elise loves me. She's my best friend." Meg heard herself make that terrible noise again, the choking, crying gargle.

"Meg, I know. But just this morning I cleaned and re-bandaged your best friend's injured feet. Do you know why?" He could see Meg staring at him, and he continued.

"She sliced them open on broken glass. A glass that shattered all over the kitchen when he accused her, or I guess, exposed her." Meg covered her mouth with her hands, and Kyle kept talking.

"She was trying to get to him, to explain, but he was just screaming and screaming. That's when I ran in, to see what was wrong. Oh, God, Meg. There was blood, and she was crying and Tommy was screaming. And then Annie..." He looked up at her.

"Annie."

"She came into the room, she came back to give him gloves, she saw the worst, she knows."

"Oh, my God."

"She ran, and Tommy followed her."

"Kyle," she said loudly, almost a scream, standing. She slammed her hands on the table.

"We have to find them. I'm not sure where all this Elise stuff is coming from, but ...."

He removed her hands from the table and held them tightly in his own.

"I know, Meg," he said softly. "I know it still makes no sense, but Tommy is the one who figured it out, it's why he was so, so angry."

"Tommy?"

"He told me very late last night that he found Ben's phone in Elise's nightstand. And an email to Annie. From Ben."

"What? How?" Meg shook her head violently, shaking off the information, not wanting to connect any dots about an email to Annie.

"He was looking for a charging cord and ..."

"Ben's phone?"

"I'm so sorry. He said he took the phone to Elise and showed her. She tried to deny it at first; she acted confused, but then finally, she admitted that she'd sent the email to Annie. Said something about thinking it would have been nice for Annie to hear from her dad after he was gone. I don't really know more than this, but apparently she fell apart in front of Tommy and promised she would give you Ben's phone and stop. But after Annie told him that you and Willie had been getting messages... Annie and Willie?" Kyle's voice trailed off, as if the thought of her kids was too much.

"You need to tell me everything," Meg said. "Please. Now."

Kyle took a deep, ragged breath. "Well, I guess that's when he realized it had been so much more than that one email. That Elise had created an identity out of...out of Ben. Or Ben's phone? And that she hadn't stopped communicating. God, Meg. You should have heard him last night. I've never seen him like that ... like ... completely insane. I thought he would hurt her, or himself. That's the scene Annie walked in on, and then ran away from. I'm so, so sorry."

Meg's head felt as if it was spiraling back to the night that Ben had died, to sobbing in Elise's arms on the bathroom floor, to . to the texts she had finally shared, the belongings they had sorted, the advice and comfort she had received from her best friend. And before that, to vacations, holidays, secrets, phone calls.

Best friend.

Best friend.

Best...

And it had all been lies. Lies?

"We need to find the kids," she said, suddenly, as if snapping herself out of a bad daydream, which wasn't entirely untrue.

Kyle said, "Tommy's been gone since this morning, but he texted and said he was going to get Annie. I assumed he was coming here, but now we both know that didn't happen."

"Text him now, please, Kyle," Meg said.

Kyle pulled out his phone and she pulled out hers to text her daughter, yet again.

Mom: *Annie, where are you? I love you*

Mom: *Annie, I'm with Uncle Kyle. I know everything*

Mom: *Annie, it's okay. Where are you? I love you and it's all okay.*

"Meg," Kyle started, "Elise would want you to know … "

"Kyle, I don't care about Elise. I need to find Annie and you need to find your son. In about two minutes, I'm calling the police."

A knock at the door startled them both. Meg ran to the front hall, hoping to find Annie, Tommy, or both. When she opened the door, she was completely shocked to see Kyle's sister, Sarah. Sarah spoke quickly.

"Meg, I'm so sorry. I'm pretty sure you're having an awful morning. I have Tommy in my car, and he says he knows where we can find Annie."

"You have Tommy?" Kyle reached to grab his sister's hand with both of his own, just as Meg threw her arms around Sarah.

"Thank you," Meg said. "Thank you."

"Let's go," said Kyle, slamming the door behind them as they all ran to the car.

Annie
December 7, 2013

She was alone. She was also cold, and the sofa was rougher than she remembered. Annie had a sweatshirt and a coat, but it was freezing in the basement of the house. It was weird, she thought, that she was wearing the same white sweatshirt she'd worn the last time, the only other time, she'd been in this basement. She hadn't expected to stay long; she had just needed a place to go, and for the first time in her life, she felt like she had nowhere. She certainly hadn't been ready to go home and tell her mom about the scene she had witnessed. Annie still couldn't believe it herself. She wouldn't stay at Aunt Elise's house, even though they had all begged her; she could hear Thomas calling after her when she ran to her car. She didn't want to be anywhere near him, ever again, and it had been too late to go to Lizzy's. She wanted her dad. If her dad was here, he would tell her what to do. If her dad was still here, none of this would ever have happened.

I want my dad.

I want my dad.

I want my daddy.

The words were spinning in her brain, and the tears threatened to spill. No more creepy texts, no emails, no screaming fights in Thomas's kitchen, no funeral, no broken glass, no cookie platters, no no no no. Where did her life go? Where could she go? Annie wasn't warm enough to stay any longer, so she probably had to go somewhere.

She was untangling herself from the blanket when she heard a noise on the floor above her. Footsteps? Maybe Thomas had figured out her hiding space. Well, Annie thought, it wasn't as if she'd planned to stay forever. She hadn't even planned on staying the whole night, exactly, but in the end, she had been curled on the old couch, just thinking and crying and worrying. Adding insult to injury, she'd dropped her phone on the hard basement floor as she climbed through the window, cracking the screen. For a while, it was still fairly functional, at least as a clock and a bit of light, but after a few hours, the phone had died, so she'd lost track of time and just stayed. Eventually, she'd dozed a little.

Had she run away? She didn't think so, not really. The mountain of sadness towering over her was about to tumble, and she felt like there was nowhere to hide. She'd planned to be back before morning, before her mom even knew she was gone, but seeing the light outside the window, she knew she'd blown it.

More footsteps. She stood up and prepared for whoever had finally come to find her, and was likely really, really mad. Annie didn't care, because buried within her sadness was a bitter anger. She was ready to tell Tommy and Aunt Elise to go to hell, and her mom would do the same, once Annie was forced to tell the horrible truth. Aunt Elise was a liar. More than a liar, she was cruel and hateful. Annie nearly crumbled, thinking of what her mother was about to face. Another huge loss.

Tommy had known all along. Annie had heard him say it, crystal clear. "It's Mom. She said she had stopped. She's sending the messages." There had been more, probably, but it had all ended for Annie in that moment. She had dropped his gloves in the mudroom and run, knowing she would never see him again.

She stood, shivering, wrapped in the blanket. It was not quite so dark inside now; the sun was shining, sending a narrow slice of light through the small windows, reflecting a bit off the broken glass from her phone.

She heard the door at the top of the steps open and someone began to descend, heavy steps.

"Mom?" she called softly. "Tommy?"

She didn't realize that she was only prepared for the known, but when a man stepped off the last step and into the dusky light of the basement, the unknown presented itself, with Annie at her most vulnerable.

Annie took two steps back. "Who are you?" Her voice shook.

"I think I should be asking the questions, don't you?" His voice was gruff, but he wasn't threatening.

She didn't want to say her name.

"Is this your house?" she said, her voice barely audible. Annie backed up further, sitting on the couch and shrinking into a corner. She picked up her phone, instinctively, even though it could provide no assistance.

"I'm sorry," Annie said. "I didn't know anyone lived here. I didn't mean to trespass. I didn't have anywhere to go."

The man just stood there, watching her, saying nothing. His hair was straggly under his baseball cap, which he wore backward. He wore a winter coat, but no gloves; his hands were shoved into his coat pockets.

"I really am sorry. I'll go now. I'm sorry." Annie was babbling. She stood up quickly. Suddenly, after wanting nothing but to be alone, she wanted only to be out of that damp basement and back in the comforting warmth of her family room, watching television with Willie, eating breakfast with her mom. She took a few steps forward, away from the couch, but then she realized that in order to get out of the basement, she'd have to move past the stranger, or go back out through the window. Neither option seemed feasible, since she didn't know who she was dealing with. She stood still, not sure what she should do. She was considering bolting for the steps, and then he began to inch slowly toward her.

"I'm a friend of your mom's," he said, as he walked.

"Um…" said Annie. How did he know who she was?

"You are?" Annie said hesitantly, backing away. He was getting too close.

"From high school. In fact, she was my girlfriend."

"Okay," Annie said, backing away another small step as the man moved another step closer.

"You look like her, you know? Pretty."

Annie said nothing, staring at the cement between her feet.

"I paid you a compliment," the man said.

"Thank you," she said, softly.

He continued to come toward her, and she continued to inch backward, until she was up against the couch. She could feel the fabric scratching against her jeans. She was trapped.

"Have a seat," said the man.

"It's okay," she said. "I should go."

He laughed shallowly, then coughed. "I don't think so. Not yet. Don't you want to tell me what you're doing in my basement?"

Annie sat. She tried to keep her fear in check, but her hands were trembling. "I'm really sorry. I guess sometimes kids hang out here, and last night I didn't have anywhere else to go, so I came here. I was going to leave this morning."

"You *guess* kids hang out here?"

"Well, yeah."

"Like you and your boyfriend?" He came two steps closer, and was now towering over her where she sat on the couch.

"Yes," she whispered. "But I swear, we didn't know anyone lived here. And we didn't hurt anything. We won't do it again."

He nodded.

"So why didn't you have anywhere to go?" he asked.

Annie looked at her lap.

"It's my basement. I can call the police, or you could just answer my questions."

"Okay, so it's just…I have a lot going on, and I didn't want to tell my mom about it. I mean, there's more, and some stuff happened…"

"And?"

"And, I don't really understand yet," she said, her eyes filling with tears.

"You don't understand what happened?" he asked.

"I really don't."

"But you're sad about it. Maybe mad."

"Both."

"I get that," said the man. "I'm Jason, by the way."

"Annie," she said, sniffing.

"I know."

"O-kaaaaay," she said. "That's creepy, by the way."

"Yeah," he said. "I'm working on that. The creepy thing."

Annie smiled, just slightly, in spite of herself.

"So do you live here?"

"No. It's my dad's old place. I'm fixing it up to sell. Lots of ghosts around here," he said, looking around.

Annie shivered and crossed her arms, hugging herself tightly . "Gross."

"Not bad ghosts. Good ghosts. Like memories, and happy times. Some things you just don't want to forget, even though you might have to let them go."

Annie nodded. "I get that."

"I'll bet you do."

"Do you have kids?" Annie asked.

"I do. Two girls. They live with their mom but I get to see them a lot. They're younger than you, but smart, you know? And cute. They like reading, you know, books and teen magazines and stuff."

Annie looked at him, curiously. "Books? Why are we talking about this?"

"You asked *me* about my kids. I'm just trying to keep you calm until your people arrive. You don't look like you're going to cry at the moment, so I'm doing something right."

"My people?"

"Your mom, your boyfriend, the police. I figure you called someone when you heard me."

"Broken phone," she said, holding up the evidence.

"You can use mine," he said, reaching into his pocket. She flinched, thinking maybe she'd been tricked—was he reaching for a gun, a knife, a gag?—but he pulled out his iPhone and handed it to her.

"Um--your mom is programmed in as a contact. It's one of the creepy things I need to get past."

"Yeah, so I'm going to call her and then delete her contact. But it works for now," said Annie.

She was dialing when Jason touched her for the first and only time, gently, on her other wrist.

She looked up, startled.

"I'm sorry about your dad. That's terrible."

"Thanks," she said, tearing up again. "It really sucks."

"Back the fuck away from her!"

They both jumped at the sound of the unexpected voice. Jason dropped his hand, and Annie jumped instinctively to her feet, shocked at the sight of her Uncle Kyle at the bottom of the steps. Behind him stood her mom, Tommy, and another woman, who looked familiar.

"I am one hundred percent not kidding," Kyle continued, evenly. "Don't you move a goddamn muscle. Meg, Sarah--take Annie outside, now. Tommy, call 911." Annie recognized Sarah's name, even in the midst of this chaos. Tommy's aunt. What was she doing here?

Everybody moved, except Meg. Sarah put her own coat around Annie and pushed her quickly up the stairs, ahead of everyone. Meg stared into the basement, frozen to her spot. Annie was stammering. "I'm fine. I'm really...I'm...he didn't...I'm... seriously, wait...it's okay..."

"Meg, you need to go. Now." Kyle spoke to her in a calm tone, without taking his eyes off the man, still by the window.

"Jason. Oh, my God, what have you done?"

"Meg," Kyle said slowly, "you know this guy?"

Meg continued. "Seriously, what were you thinking? She's a *child*. You have *daughters*. What kind of sicko are you?"

"It's my house," Jason said, confused. "I mean, it was my dad's house. That's why I'm here. Meg, please." He had both his hands up in front of his body as if to show—what?— innocence? "I came this morning to finish some cleaning out and found her here in the basement. That's it. I swear. She's upset, and I let her call you on my phone. Her phone was broken."

"This is your basement?" Meg asked, incredulously. "How in the world…"

Jason stood, hands still up. Meg moved to stand closer to him, facing him.

"It is. But...apparently it's become a bit of a..hangout...lately?"

Tommy stared at the floor.

"Jason, Annie never called me, not from any phone," Meg said.

"That's because this guy," he pointed at Kyle, "came into MY house and screamed at me before Annie finished dialing," said Jason.

Kyle was still glaring pointedly at Jason.

Meg nodded. "Okay, well, we have her now, so that's the important thing."

"She's upset, Meggie. She's worried about something big, a fight or something. She's really sad. But she seems like a good kid."

Meg nodded. "Okay. Jason, I don't know what happened last night, but—"

"Go figure it out."

She nodded again, grabbed Kyle by the hand and went upstairs.

Once on the lawn, she reached out for her daughter, who was wrapped in Sarah's arms. Annie ran to Meg and burrowed close, while Sarah walked to her SUV, parked on the street. Willie and Fred were waiting patiently in the third row seat; Willie had his headphones on and seemed unaware of the events that had unfolded.

"Anniegirl," Meg whispered. "My girl. It's okay. It's all going to be okay."

"I broke my phone," said Annie, finally breaking down and starting to sob.

"Silly baby. Phones don't matter." Meg hugged her tighter, rubbing her back.

"Mom, what's going on?" Annie said, her words muffled into her mother's shoulder. What's going to happen with Aunt Elise?"

"It's too much. Shhh. It's too much."

"No!" Annie pulled back. "Tell me!"

"Annie." Meg wiped her daughter's face with her gloved hand. "I don't know what's going on with Elise. We're going to have to figure that one out, okay?

A police siren interrupted their conversation, and they saw the cruiser turn the corner from the main road. It slowed to a stop, and the siren stopped wailing but the car's lights continued to swirl in the morning light, reflecting red circles on the snow-covered lawn.

Sarah went to greet the officers, and she directed them through the house. Hopefully, Sarah, Kyle and Jason would be able to explain to the responding officers why Tommy had called at Kyle's request, and why there would be no report filed.

Meg took Annie to Sarah's car to warm up and wait. They crawled into the middle seat, where Annie immediately slid tightly next to Meg, almost buried into her mom's coat.

"Will I have to talk to the police?" Annie asked.

"Maybe," Meg answered. "I'm not sure."

"Hey, Annie," said Willie, from the back.

"Hi, buddy," she answered.

Suddenly, Fred was peeking over the back of the middle seat as an offering of comfort. Annie took the panda and snuggled it tightly in her grip. "Thank you," she whispered.

"No problem."

From the car, they all watched as Kyle, Tommy, and Sarah came from the front door of the house and walked toward the car. Sarah got into the driver's seat, and Kyle opened the door on the passenger's side. Tommy came toward the back of the car and started to open a back door.

"No," Annie whispered, nearly inaudibly. "No. He can't come in."

"Annie—" Meg started.

"I can't see him. I can't talk to him. I don't want to." Annie was beginning to talk quickly and her breath was coming in short, shallow bursts.

"Annie, come back with me," Willie said. "There's room right here."

Annie turned to look at her baby brother in the back seat, who was patting the empty seat next to him. Thomas was still standing outside the SUV in the cold.

She less-than-gracefully maneuvered herself into the third row, where she tucked her knees up to her chest and turned her head to face the back of the vehicle. She used Fred as a make-shift pillow.

"Thanks again," she whispered to Willie.

He nodded. "It's okay."

Tommy opened the car door slowly and got in, not looking toward the back or saying a word.

Kyle spoke first. "The officer said we should wait here until he tells us it's okay to leave."

"Okay," said Meg.

"Annie, are you all right?" asked Sarah, looking into her rearview mirror.

Annie nodded.

"Who is that guy, Meg?" asked Kyle.

Meg sighed. "My high school boyfriend. I haven't seen him in years, and suddenly he's here in town, showing up at the bookstore, and now this? God, I don't even know what to think." She shook her head in disbelief. "Thank God you knew where to find her, Tommy."

"Yes, thank *God*, Tommy," Annie snapped from behind.

Tommy was looking at his lap, saying nothing.

"Annie," Meg said patiently. "I know how upset you are. We all are. But Tommy was the one who figured out where we might find you."

"Yeah, lucky. He's the one who took me to the basement weeks ago, Mom. He's the reason I knew about the basement, because he took me there to hook up. And the whole time he was messing around with me, he knew that his mom was playing this horrible joke on you. I mean, are you kidding me? How psycho is that?"

"I did not know. How could I have known?" Tommy whispered. "I knew she had sent one email, that's it. I tried to get her to stop. I tried." Meg heard his voice catch.

"One email. *One email*? That email was to me, and it changed everything. You're a fucking liar. I'm glad you found me today, I really am. Great job. But never talk to me again. Got it?"

"Got it," Tommy said quietly. "Loud and clear, Annabelle."

Annie started to cry. Kyle turned to look at Meg, who caught his eye and shook her head sadly. Annie saw the look the look they exchanged. Knowing her mom as well as she did, she could guess what her mom was feeling. At least, if it was anything close to what she herself felt. So many losses—Ben, Elise, and for her, now Tommy. Now her mom was going to be so worried about her. Annie burrowed into the corner of the back seat. Willie rubbed her awkwardly on the arm, which made her cry even more.

Kyle reached back to pat his son on the leg. "It's going to be okay," he said.

"Here they come."

They saw the officers leave the house with Jason, heading toward the squad car parked on the street.

"Oh, no!" cried Annie. "He didn't do anything to me!"

But then, as they watched, Jason shook hands with each policeman and exchange good-byes. He started to head back inside his house, but made a sudden turn toward the SUV, and approached the back window, knocking lightly. Meg lowered the window.

"Hey," he said, shoving his hands into his pockets.

"Hey," she answered.

"I just wanted you all to know I'm not going to bother you while I'm around. You don't have to worry about me."

"Jason, I…"

"I mean it. I think I gave everyone the wrong first impression, to say the least." Jason winced. "And then, today, of course."

"Today was not your fault," Meg said. "I'm sorry about anything I said, and about the kids, and just everything."

"It's okay."

"Okay."

"Take care, Meg.'

Meg nodded, and he walked away.

A policeman approached the driver's side window.

"Everybody doing all right in here?" he asked.

"Annie?" Sarah inquired, glancing again into the mirror.

"I'm fine," Annie said.

"We may need to get a statement from you today," said the officer. "Just to wrap up this whole thing. Why don't I let you go home and get cleaned up, and then I can swing by in about an hour if that's convenient?"

Meg nodded. "That's fine. Thank you, Officer."

He walked toward the squad car, lights still shining on the snow.

"Am I in trouble for trespassing?" asked Annie in a whisper.

"Only if Jason presses charges," said Kyle. "And that seems unlikely."

"Ready to go?" asked Sarah.

"More than ready," said Meg, looking back at her daughter, still curled up in a ball.

Sarah stopped at the Parker's house first, and dropped Kyle and Tommy off. It was heartbreaking for Meg to watch Annie ignore Tommy as he got out of the car, as he tried to catch her eye. Meg reached out to him for a quick hug. "It's going to be okay, kiddo," she whispered. "Give her some time."

She turned to Kyle. "Thank you," she said, "for everything."

"Meg…"

"I can't think about it right now. Tell Tommy I love him. I can't imagine what it was like carrying this around." Meg glanced at the door of their house, a door she had walked through thousands of time, without knocking, without waiting. With babies, kids, food, bearing news, gifts and wine. She'd come here in pajamas and in tears. Today, she couldn't bear to think of her best friend inside that door, existing in a state of mind that had allowed her to perpetrate a crime against Meg's own soul.

"Let me come over and help you handle the police," said Kyle. "I'll get Tommy situated and check on Elise."

Sarah called out of the window of her SUV. "Kyle, I can help Meg and Annie this afternoon, really." Kyle looked at his sister gratefully.

"Yes, that's even better. Meg, is that okay with you?"

Meg nodded, thinking that if Annie needed someone to talk with, someone who was not her mother, Dr. Sarah Parker was the right choice.

Back at home, Annie headed for the shower, and Willie, now with Fred back in his possession, went to his favorite spot on the couch and turned on the television.

Meg turned to Sarah in the kitchen. "Tea?"

"Please."

While the water was heating, Meg looked at her best friend's sister-in-law, and said, frankly, "So, Sarah, what the hell am I supposed to do?"

"Well, that depends on what the hell we're talking about," Sarah said, with a grim smile.

Meg poured steaming water into two mugs and brought them to the table. While the tea steeped, the women spoke.

"Annie. I guess Annie first, since the police could be showing up here any minute."

"Do we know what she's going to say?" asked Sarah.

"I'm not sure what they're going to want to know," said Meg. "Why she left? Why she was there? What Jason said or did? She says he did nothing—that they just talked and that he was nice. It's all so strange. What happens next?"

Sarah paused for a moment. "I guess it all depends on what Annie says, and what Jason said, right?"

Meg nodded. "I guess we'll just wait for that conversation to happen."

"And we'll be here for her, to listen and to help," Sarah said.

Meg smiled, "Yes, Doctor. We will."

"I can't help it. It's what I do," Sarah said, laughing, but then, she turned serious.   "Now, what about Elise?"

Even hearing her name filled Meg with a new sense of loneliness.

"What is there to say? Annabelle was in the room and heard it all." Meg shuddered. "Annie is crushed, it's why she didn't come home last night." Meg took a sip of her tea and her eyes filled with tears. "I've lost my best friend. And my husband."

"Something else is going on here, don't you think?" asked Sarah, looking out the window at the frozen lake.

Meg didn't answer, and didn't have to. There was a knock, and Sarah stood to meet the officer at the front door, with Meg trailing behind.

He introduced himself as Officer Mike and only stayed about forty-five minutes, thankfully. The two women flanked Annie at the table, her hair still damp from the shower, while she answered questions. She had gone to the house after midnight, upset. Jason Brinkman had shown up this morning, but seemed to know that she'd been there before, other kids too, and said it was his house.

"It think it had been his dad's home?" offered Meg.

"That seems to be the case," confirmed the officer. "Looks like his dad moved out a couple of years ago and into an assisted living place about four miles away. The kids have been sneaking in"—he looked at Annie —"which isn't a good idea, or a safe plan. Now this guy's trying to figure out what to do with the house."

Meg nodded.

"I'm sorry," whispered Annie.

"Did he hurt you?" asked Officer Mike.

"No, he actually just talked with me. It even kind of helped."

Meg shook her head. "Unbelievable."

"Here's the thing," said Officer Mike. "Mr. Brinkman has every right to press charges against Annie for trespassing, and actually against each of you for breaking and entering this morning."

"What?" cried Meg.

"But when we spoke to him," continued the officer, "he said absolutely not. He's just glad that Annabelle is safe and that he believes nothing good would come out of any further action."

"Thank God," said Sarah.

"No more trespassing on his property," said Officer Mike to Annie, "or any property, to be clear."

"I promise. I'm sorry."

"He said one more thing. He said to tell Annie that 'the contact is deleted and he's working on the creepy.'" Officer Mike looked at Annie.

"Sounds good," said Annie, smiling, just a tiny bit.

The two women in the room looked at Annie quizzically, but she simply shrugged.

"Please call me if you need anything." He handed Annie, Meg, and Sarah each a card. "I know you've been through a lot lately, Mrs. McAfee. I hope you can finally get some sort of peace."

He poked his head into the family room and called out to Willie.

"You okay in there, little dude?"

"I'm good."

"This is for you," he said, handing Willie a business card and a pretend police badge.   Willie smiled. "Thanks!"

"It's an important job, man-of-the-house. I know you can do it, but call me if you need me, okay?"

"Okay."

Meg walked him to the door, thanked him, and watched him leave.

"You okay?" she said to Annie.

"Kinda. Kinda not."

Sarah was taking it all in. "It's a lot, Annie. Do you want to talk?"

Annie looked sadder than Meg had seen her since the day they had received the worst news of their lives. "No. And I don't ever want to talk about them again."

Them. Meg felt her heart clench, but she said, "Okay. Not now, then, but later. Annie, I know it was a terrible night, but you didn't come home. You didn't come *home*. Do you have any idea how scared I was this morning? I can't lose you, Annie. You can't do that to me, or to Willie." She watched as the tears spilled over from Annie's sad eyes. "We are going to have to talk about Elise and Tommy at some point. But not now; now, a nap."

Annie walked to Meg and laid her head on her mother's shoulder, saying nothing.

"I know, baby," Meg soothed, petting her daughter's head. "You're okay. It's okay."

Annie turned and went upstairs.

Sarah looked at Meg. "So, should we talk about Elise?"

Elise
November 1, 2013

"Tommy, can you get the door, please?" Elise had asked. She was in Meg's kitchen, tidying the counters and loading the dishwasher when she heard the doorbell chime. Meg was occupied in the family room, and the last time Elise had checked, she was actually sitting down which was a very good sign. Elise's own eyes were tired, almost achy, from the crying, and being alone in the kitchen was a tiny respite from the sadness of the day.

When Tommy opened the door, a representative from the airline was standing stiffly on the porch. He was holding a large paper bag and a small plastic bag. Next to him was Uncle Ben's briefcase and a rolling suitcase.

"I'm sorry for your loss," said the driver, not much older than Tommy.

"Thanks?" said Tommy. "I mean, I guess?"

He took the large bag and the smaller envelope into the McAfee's kitchen and set it on the table. He didn't want to be touching any of these things, particularly. His mom was there, pulling something out of the oven, pouring a soda, taking the lid off a bottle of Advil.

"What's all that?" she asked, distractedly.

"Some things from the airline, I guess."

Elise paused and glanced up. She inhaled sharply, seeing all of Ben's personal things right there in the kitchen. She could almost picture him, standing among them, holding the suitcase handle, clutching the briefcase strap. "Hey guys!" he'd say, "looks like a party!"

"Tommy, Aunt Meg can't see that. It will kill her." She winced at her own choice of words. "Wheel that suitcase into the hall closet, at least for now. Here I'll take the other stuff." She put down the hot baking dish and grabbed the large brown bag and the briefcase. Elise carefully avoided the areas where people were still gathered, speaking softly among themselves, and entered the back master bedroom with the packages, which she stashed in Ben and Meg's closet, under the winter coats in the back. She would tell Meg later that his things were there, for whenever she was ready to see them. Elise looked at the small bag still in her hand. It held only Ben's phone, protected and transported in nothing more than a Zip-lock lunch baggie. Now, here in her palm was this thing of Ben's, something he had held so recently. The idea sent sharp darts of sadness spiraling into the myriad of feelings she was already trying to sort. Definitely not now, Elise thought, slipping the phone into the pocket of her apron, because if it hurt her, it would destroy Meg. In the moment, she was acting as Meg's best friend, her advocate, helping her get through the most difficult day, taking care of the tough tasks that Meg would have to face soon enough. Later, Elise would think back and wish that she had given Meg the packages immediately. Later, she would realize the belongings, including the phone, would have provided Meg with comfort, closeness, and closure. Later, Elise would wish that she had never seen the phone in the baggie and tried to help in so many ways. But later, it would all be far too late.

Sarah
December 8, 2013

Sarah was surprised at how calm Meg seemed during their conversation in the kitchen. Of course, she could be in shock. Sarah had seen it before; patients seemed fine, excessively calm, handling everything smoothly and evenly. Then came an emotional break. Meg had certainly been on a tumultuous ride, with one horrible event triggering the next. Sarah could only imagine that Meg would do anything she could to stop the cycle.

There wasn't much either of them could say about Elise.

"She came to see me a few weeks ago," Sarah told Meg. "It wasn't a clinical visit, so I'm not bound by oath. She claimed to be worried about you and the texts you were receiving from Ben. She wanted to make an appointment for you."

"For me. Huh. Well, it was an appointment, anyway."

Sarah nodded wryly, but wouldn't push.

So Meg continued. "She really does look out for me, and she has always, always been there for me. It's not surprising."

"Isn't it?" asked Sarah, in a probing tone. "Isn't it surprising, now that we know the truth?"

"It is," Meg agreed. "Of course. But I don't know what truth Elise believes."

Sarah nodded, listening. "She didn't know that Tommy had come to me, of course."

Meg looked up, startled. "Tommy came to you? When?"

"I'm sorry, Meg. That was information that I really couldn't share. Of course, now, it's all out there. I guess Annie told Tommy about the email she received, and he came to me wanting to know what to do. I told him to talk to Elise. He did, and Elise assured him it was one message, that it was over. Something about trying to comfort Annie, that she could understand this kind of loss."

Meg nodded. "Elise still feels the loss of her dad, I know that. But it doesn't explain any of this. Does it?" She looked at Sarah for confirmation.

"Of course it doesn't," said Sarah. "But any information we can get to put some sort of stability around this situation, helps, don't you think?"

Meg raised her eyebrows. "Well, stability is not on my short list of feelings this morning," said Meg, almost laughing. "But maybe it's time to try."

Elise
December 11, 2013

She couldn't get out of bed. She would not turn on the light. At some point Kyle had left her a water bottle, but she couldn't drink. She had cried for hours, or perhaps days, and now she was weak from the exhaustion of it all, drained from the sorrow of her own creation. Tommy had come in to check on her at least twice. She had heard him quietly call her name —"Mom?"—but she had stayed lying on her side, facing the other wall. How could she face her baby after what she had done, after the things he had screamed at her? Elise knew that even in his anger, he was worried about her, worried about the things he had yelled, the way they had left things, the fact that she was now in her bed, as unmoving as a corpse. She wanted to reassure her son, but she could not speak. So, she heard him leave both times, slowly closing the door behind him.

Kyle had not come to bed the last three evenings. She could hear him downstairs every now and again, so she knew he hadn't left her for good, yet.

Tommy was right; she had tormented Meg and her family. It hadn't been on purpose, none of this had ever been on purpose, but she had tortured them. It had never been with evil intent, but she had hurt her best friend and the children. Oh, my God, what had she done? Elise turned her face into the pillow and began to cry, again. Her supply of tears was obviously endless.

Under the soft sheet and heavy blanket, she could feel her bandaged feet. Who had... ? She couldn't remember. Then it came to her, slowly. Kyle, in the bathroom, over the bathtub. Holding her head while she convulsed with sobs. Dosing her with several Advil tablets for pain, and Benadryl so she would sleep. Elise had been sitting on the toilet with her feet over the tub. Kyle had rinsed them, making sure there were no shards of glass embedded in her skin. Every now and again he would shush her, like a baby. Elise remembered maybe saying Meg's name, and asking about Tommy.

"Tommy tried to chase after Annie," Kyle said. "But she left in her car. Tommy is here. He's fine."

"Annie," Elise had moaned. "Oh God, Annie." She had burst into sobs again.

Kyle had slathered her feet with Neosporin and wrapped them in first-aid gauze before slipping on a pair of her favorite fuzzy socks. He helped her limp to the bed sometime very late on Friday night. Then Kyle had left her alone. It was now sometime on Monday, Elise thought. Maybe late afternoon. Maybe not, she wasn't entirely certain.

She had to get up, if only to use the bathroom and maybe brush her teeth. She inched herself up to a seated position to begin the process of getting out of bed. There was a soft knock before the door opened a crack, letting in a strip of light from the hallway.

"Elise?" It was Sarah, peeking her head around the door.

Elise shook her head.

"It's okay. We don't have to talk. I just wanted to see if you needed me for anything."

"If I...? Me...?" The words brought Elise to a new level of emotion. She did not deserve to need anything.

She couldn't bring herself to speak, but as Sarah came in, she was sitting on the side of the bed, shaking her head back and forth. "I need nothing. I need... I need...I just need..."

"What? What do you need, Elise?"

"I can't."

"You can. Take your time."

Elise took in a big shuddering sigh.

"I need...Tommy and Kyle...and Meg. Annie and Willie...but..." She looked at Sarah, "I've lost everyone."

Sarah sat on the bed next to her, softly laying a hand on her shoulder

"I'm not so sure," said Sarah, quietly. "Kyle's downstairs taking care of dinner for Tommy. I know that Tommy has been up to check on you every couple of hours, bringing you fresh water bottles, seeing if you're awake. He's worried about things that were said."

Elise nodded.

"They don't seem like people you've lost forever. And Meg..." Sarah began.

Elise shook her head violently, as if she wanted to dislodge any thoughts or potential ideas pertaining to her best friend. Former best friend.

But Sarah continued. "Meg sent me here."

She watched as Elise's body took in the words. The idea that Meg still even cared at all rolled through her like a wave. Elise felt the words so fully that she had to lie back down on her bed and cry into her quilt with relief.

"She sent you? Why?"

"I don't think she can come herself quite yet, but she did want to make sure that you were all right." The thought of this sent another wave of emotion through Elise, and she tried to choke back tears again.

"I'm not really okay, it seems."

"Elise, can you tell me what happened?"

"I never meant to hurt her."

"I believe you," said Sarah, patting her hand.

"The phone. I had the phone from that very first day. The day after he died. Maybe two days. I was going to give it to her, and I forgot. And then, I just ... didn't."

"You forgot," Sarah said, questioningly.

"I did," Elise said, still prone on the bed, but rolling over to face Sarah directly. "At first I forgot. I meant to put it with the other stuff, or to give it right to her. I had it in my pocket. She was with family, she was so upset. Handing that to her...it would have been like... like a grenade. So I tucked everything away, but I wanted to help her. Not hurt her."

"I'm sure putting Ben's suitcase away was a good idea."

"It wasn't even really an idea. Tommy just rolled it into the hall closet and stored the other belongings in the bedroom." Elise gulped back a sob, remembering the day she'd sat with Meg, pouring over Ben's belongings on the closet floor.

"The texts, Elise. How did it start?"

"God. I didn't even think about that phone again until the day of the funeral when I put that same damn apron on, and there it was, still in the pocket. It had been hanging there in Meg's kitchen—anyone could have found it. Why didn't someone else find it? Anyway, I thought it was dead, but it was just powered down. When I turned it on, the text screen was the first thing that opened. There was a text from Ben that was written but not sent. It said "I'm here."

He probably texted her from the airport—he checked in with her all the time. My guess is that Ben got on the plane before the message went through. When I clicked on it, late that night after the service, I really was just looking to see what time and date it was written. I mean, it was the strangest, saddest thing to see those words written by him. Whatever I did, that damn text sent in the middle of the night.

Oh, my God. You have no idea—the panic I felt. I was a wreck all day and all night. And then nothing happened. God, I really thought I was in the clear. I could somehow get the phone back to her, and explain everything, and apologize. Then Meg texted back, just one word, but I know her, you know? I knew it probably kept her up all night, trying to figure out what was going on, and she was scared and upset, and I couldn't let her get nothing in return. That's what happened, that's really all. Sometimes days and days went by, because I hated myself for continuing and I would try to stop, but I loved her more than I cared about my own feelings. She wanted to hear from Ben, she carried that phone around, patting it, feeling it, worried about it.   Before she thought I knew about it, I could see her, checking it, holding it, rubbing it through her pocket. There was something about the messages that even seemed to be helping her to heal. I know, I know that in her heart Meg had to understand that someone was playing a nasty, sick joke. " Elise choked on the words. "She would never have suspected me. Not ever. Because it wasn't a joke. That's not the right word. And when I came to see you... '

"What?" said Sarah.

"Even you said it might be helping."

"That doesn't make it right."

"I know."

"Do you?"

Elise lay back on the pillow and tears rolled down from the corners of both eyes.

"I do. I think I do."

"What about the kids?" Sarah prompted.

"God," Elise sighed, and continued. "It was all stuff I found on Ben's phone. Willie had been texting him daily, right up to the day Ben died, and there was a text from Willie that Ben hadn't been able to answer. So, once I had sent Meg's text, I thought... I don't know what I thought. I thought it would make Willie feel better to get that last message. And Annie, well, there were no recent texts. So I sent an email a few weeks later. I just got this weird feeling that she was left out. I know that if I had been Annie, I would have been devastated."

"You mean losing your dad."

"Well, of course," Elise said. "But beyond that. If something strange was going on, like messages from... well, beyond or whatever...and everyone in the family was receiving them except me, I would be so sad and hurt. Even more sad than I already was, which would be almost impossible."

Sarah looked pointedly at Elise.

"But you knew these messages were not coming from Ben to Meg. Or to Willie. Annie was not being left out of anything real. You understand that, right? Nothing was happening that you were not in control of. Just you. You could have stopped any time."

"I know. I get it. But also, when Willie would text Ben--me--whatever--these sweet little messages about school or just his day. I mean, it was heartbreaking, Sarah. And in the end, he would text over and over sometimes, are you there, are you there, are you there Daddy? What was I supposed to do?"

"You were supposed to stop. Or perhaps never to have started."

"Sarah, all I can tell you is that I never, ever meant to hurt anyone. When I would write the messages, I would think of myself as a child, with no dad, and I would write the text with that in my mind. How would I feel if my dad could have spoken to me? That was all I had in my heart every time I texted."

"Or emailed."

"Yes. The one time I emailed Annie," sighed Elise. "I was worried about how much she would miss her Daddy. Like I do."

"Of course."

"And I didn't want Annie and Willie to feel that. It's horrible."

"And it all...snowballed," said Sarah.

"Yes," answered Elise. "That's exactly right. It snowballed. A big horrible awful snowball."

"Tommy found Ben's phone, right? That's when this all started to fall apart?"

Elise sighed.

"He was getting something from my nightstand. He found the phone, he saw the email. He couldn't understand, no matter how I tried to explain. But really, what could I say? So I told him I would stop. 'Stop what?' That's what he kept asking." Elise's voice grew soft. "He never knew about the texts. That's what caused everything to go so badly Friday night, after he learned about the texts. The fight, the screaming, Annie—oh God, poor Annie. It's all because of me."   Kyle had briefly told her about finding Annie in that basement. Elise had been horrified, though she had offered very little reaction.

Sarah listened quietly to the whole story, only asking questions to keep the information flowing.

"Thank you for telling me. I understand."

"You do?"

"I don't think you meant to hurt anyone. Unfortunately, I'm not the one who matters, but I am an exceptionally good judge. Now it's up to you."

Elise spoke slowly. "To tell Meg."

Sarah nodded, and continued, "…yes, to tell Meg and everyone involved. To tell them everything."

Elise nodded again. "You don't think I'm horrible?"

"Elise, I love you. I know you're not horrible, but while I think you did a horrible thing, I don't think you did it on purpose. I'm not going to lie to you--I never would-- it's not going to be easy. But I believe that the best intentions are hard to overlook, and I don't believe that you intended to hurt anyone, especially Meg. This might be your ticket out of this mess. And by "mess" I don't just mean this bedroom."

Elise sat up slowly and looked around the room.

"I'm a mess," she agreed. "This is a giant mess."

"You'll have to eventually move forward."

Elise gave a very slight nod.

"Even if it's just moving out of this room."

Another nod.

"She may not forgive you," continued Sarah. "You should be prepared for that. But she did send me, so that's a good sign."

"I've got nothing to lose, that's for damn sure," said Elise.

"Start with Tommy and Kyle," Sarah suggested. "Get your own house in order. First things first, take a shower. Eat something. You absolutely cannot deal with Meg and the kids until you are on solid ground."

Elise leaned in to give Sarah a hug. "Thank you," she whispered. "I love you."

"I love you, too. We'll work it out," said Sarah. "I'm here for you. And if she doesn't forgive you, well, that's the consequence for the choices you made in those moments. And Elise, I need you to understand that this all could have been fixed with one text, one call, one sentence to Meg, right at the start."

Elise looked at her.

"You could have told her that you sent that very first text by mistake, if that is, in fact, the truth."

"It is."

"Then this could have been fixed very easily. You need to acknowledge that to Meg. Because you chose differently."

Elise took a breath in. "Sarah? Is it possible that at the core of all this, I'm just a terrible person?"

"I don't think so," said Sarah. "I think you've missed your dad for a really long time. And I think you got caught up in something bigger than yourself. But until we're sure," she gave her sister-in-law a sidelong glance, "let's not take terrible off the table."

Meg
December 24, 2013

"Mom? Where are you? It's starting!"

"I'll be right there!" she called.

She should have anticipated it, but now that Christmas Eve was here, she wasn't doing quite as well as she'd hoped. Meg knew she was about to give her kids a nice Christmas; the gifts were wrapped, the stockings were stuffed, she and Willie had baked dozens of cookies, and Annie had helped her decorate the house.

"It's okay, right Mom?" Annie had said. "I know I'm not Dad, but I can help you."

"Honey, this is great," Meg had assured her. And it was true. Together, they hung fresh greenery on the front porch, tied with big, red bows. Annie found the Christmas lights, and wound them into the bushes along the front windows, and she had helped to hang the wreath on the door. By the time they were finished, Meg had to admit that it was even more beautiful than in past years. They had high-fived each other, and celebrated by taking a selfie on Annie's phone, the two of them, bundled in coats and hats in front of their festive porch.

The tree had been different story. Meg had taken the kids to the Christmas tree sale at the corner lot in town, just like always. No one said anything, but Meg could feel Ben's absence that night so acutely it was almost like seeing him among the trees; she imagined the kids felt the same. Instead of lingering among the pines, comparing and contrasting, they picked a tree quickly and paid the extra money to have the "elves" tie it to the top of Meg's car. The short ride home was quiet, with the occasional comment about a carol on the radio or holiday light display.

"One more night," she thought, sitting on her bed, gearing up to face Christmas Eve with her children, alone. "One more night, then Christmas, then we've made it through. And if we can make it through Christmas, we can make it through anything."

She missed him so much. She still reached for her phone out of habit, she still rubbed it with her thumb and held it in her hand. She still waited for texts, even though she knew the truth, she strangely missed the wonder of it all. The idea of what-if. And she missed Elise.

One more night. One more day. And then a new year. She really needed a new year.

She stood, resolutely, just as Willie burst through the door.

"Mom! 'Home Alone' is starting!"

"Oh, my gosh. Let's go," she said, holding out her hand.

"And you said you'd make us some popcorn."

"Yes, I did. But would you get out some of the cookies? The ones with extra frosting? I want some of those, too."

"Yes!" Willie bounded ahead of her, and Meg ventured out of the bedroom and into the family room. The lights were dimmed, the tree was glowing. Annie was sprawled on the couch under a blanket, playing on her phone, but she caught her mom's eye.

"Mom, you okay?"

"I'm okay. You okay?"

"I think so."

Willie joined them with a plateful of decorated cookies, and Meg promised the popcorn at the first commercial break. They snuggled on the couch, perhaps a little closer than usual, and let the silliness of the movie be the forefront for a couple of very welcome hours.

At bedtime, she tucked Willie in under the covers, making sure to give Fred a good-night pat.

"I'll see you on Christmas morning," she said, planting a kiss on his head.

"I'll see *you* on Christmas morning," he answered.

She peeked into Annie's room; she was on her bed, scrolling on her phone.

"Night, honey."

Annie looked up. "You sure you're okay?"

"Don't you worry about me. It's Christmas. It will be a great day."

Annie nodded. "Okay. Night."

Meg closed the door.

She walked down the darkened hallway, the ghosts of Christmases past following along.

The kids are toddlers, and she and Ben are waiting for them to fall asleep before pulling out the racetrack and tricycle that need to be fully assembled and displayed under the tree. The room is full of boxes and presents, and they are scrambling to find batteries and screwdrivers, trying to be quiet. She is coming down the back stairs, Ben is in the kitchen, waiting for her with a mimosa on Christmas morning. Annie is unwrapping her new camera, the winter she decides to become a photographer. It's Willie's third Christmas, all he wants is an inflatable beach ball and they can't find one anywhere, until Ben appears with one at the eleventh hour.

In the kitchen downstairs, she is snapped from her reverie. There is nothing to be assembled this year, no batteries required. She is alone in the room. Meg finds a bottle of champagne and puts it on the counter next to her juice glass for her Christmas morning Mimosa.

"Merry Christmas, Ben," she whispers, and turns out the light.

Meg
February 27, 2014

There are those magical stretches of time— a few days slip peacefully by, and snow flurries fall gently. Even the sunshine peeks through at surprising moments, lifting the veil of grey that might have otherwise settled.
Meg looked out the window and realized that, lately, she'd been able to find
a few more happy moments in each day. She reached for the phone in her
front pocket, pulling it out to check for messages. Nothing from Willie, one
from Annie saying she'd be about thirty minutes late after school--she was
going for a frozen yogurt with Lizzy. Meg smiled. Her new phone was
working very nicely. The truth was, they all needed—and wanted—new
contact information, and she definitely required virtually constant connection with both of her children.

The events of the last few months had shaken their family, shaken
their faith. They were slowly regrouping, but little things were holding them
back, and oddly, cell phones were one of them. Annie's phone had been
shattered and broken; for a teenage girl, that alone is a trauma, but she also
worried about losing any stored messages from her dad. Meg's phone still
stored all of the texts from Ben before his death, and from Elise, after. There
were reasons to both keep and discard the device, and Meg couldn't make
that decision very easily, so more often than not, she just didn't look at it.

Willie used to be constantly connected to his iPod, but now it was in a drawer.

Kyle had delivered Ben's phone to Meg a few weeks after the second worst day of Meg's life. When he had handed it to her, he had tears in his eyes.

"I don't even know what to say. I looked back through the texts, Meg. I want you to know that I saw them. I didn't mean to invade your privacy, but I wanted to see what she had done. I am so sorry."

"Kyle," she said, touching his hand. "You helped us whenever we needed you." Meg started to cry. "I miss her so much."

"I know you do. She misses you too."

"Is she okay?"

Kyle looked at Meg incredulously.

"I mean it, Kyle. Is she okay? Something must have gone really wrong for this to have happened."

"You're a good girl, Meg. She's okay. She's not great, but she's okay."

"Tell her we're okay. We're not great, but we're okay."

And then she held Ben's phone. While her first instinct had been to throw it away or destroy it, she found herself instead simply placing it on Ben's nightstand, connecting it to his charger where it had always been. Before.

One particularly sunny Saturday in February, Meg had called upstairs to her kids. "Get your coats and your phones and meet me in the garage in five."

"I don't have a phone," said Annie, hanging her head over the banister. She'd been using an old iPad to text until her phone contract was up for renewal.

"Me neither, Mom," called Willie.

"Bring what you've got," she called.

Willie and Annie showed up in the garage minutes later bundled in their coats, Willie with his iPod clutched in his mitten, Annie with her hands shoved into her pockets. Meg had her own phone in her hand.

"I'm sorry your phone is broken, Annie. It wasn't your fault. None of this was."

Annie nodded.

Without warning, Meg slammed her phone on the ground. The screen shattered, and pieces of the casing skittered across the garage floor and under the car.

"Oh my God, Mom!" Annie shrieked and brought her hands instinctively to her face. Meg noticed immediately that she was clutching a well-worn letter, or note of some kind, but said nothing.

"I'm sick of this phone that tricked me," said Meg, emphatically. "I'm tired of sad texts and this sad, old phone. Since Annie's phone broke, I think she should get a new phone. And look—my phone just broke!"

They laughed.

"What about you, Willie? Are you sick of that iPod with those fake messages?"

He looked hesitant. "I like my old messages from Dad."

"Remember, baby. They're not from Daddy. All of your real messages from Daddy are still on his phone. I checked and double-checked and they are all right there, so you can look at them whenever you want. The good texts, the good emails, and the good everything. But I'm sick of these old things with the tricky messages and the bad stuff." Meg kicked her phone with her toe.

Willie looked uncertain. "Will I get a new one?"

"Better smash it and find out."

He smiled. Willie slammed his iPod on the ground.

"New phones for everyone!"

"I'm getting a phone?" cried her ten-year old.

"Meg nodded, putting her arm around him, in the garage.

Annie hugged her from the side. "Thanks, Mom."

"You got it, kiddo."

They had tiptoed around the shards of broken phone in the garage and headed off on an impromptu field trip, which resulted in three new phones, three new numbers, lunch at the Cheesecake Factory, and selfies taken over giant desserts. Willie's Nestle's Crunch cheesecake was a huge hit; he ate the whole slice while Meg and Annie investigated the features on their new phones. Annie was teaching Meg about Instagram when they were interrupted.

"Hello Annie, Mrs. McAfee," a male voice said.

They looked up to see, that Mr. Garvin, Annie's Junior guidance counselor, and his family had stopped by their table. Meg smiled widely and moved to stand.

"Please," he said. "Don't get up! I just wanted to say hello."

Annie looked flustered.

"Hello, Mr. Garvin," said Meg, happily.

"Hi Mr. Garvin," said Annie, shyly.

"Hi!" said Willie, mouth full of cake.

Mr. Garvin laughed and introduced his wife and two daughters.

They had a few moments of conversation, and then Mr. Garvin leaned down and said something quietly in Annie's ear. She listened, smiled, then looked right at him and nodded. Goodbyes all around, and then the Garvin family continued on its way.

"What was that all about?" asked Meg.

"He said that he was glad that I looked happy, and he said I should still stop by if I ever need anything."

"Mm," said Meg. "Would you?"

"I will if I need to."

"Good."

Annie smiled. "He also said that my dessert looked way better than peanut butter crackers."

Every now and again came a day that restores your inner strength, and today was a day of restoration for Meg. After a long, wonderful afternoon with her two favorite people and an evening spent experimenting with silly apps on their phones, they played a few games of gin rummy around the kitchen table and laughed while they snacked on leftover Christmas candies and chips. No one was hungry for a real meal after such a giant lunch, and Meg was happy for a restful, casual Saturday night. Finally, Willie decided to excuse himself to the couch where he found "Toy Story 2" playing on one of the movie channels, and he was content to snuggle with Fred for the rest of the evening. Annie was still sitting at the table, fiddling with her phone, and Meg began gathering the cards.

"It was fun today," said Meg.

"I loved today, Mom."

Meg moved over and sat in the chair closer to her daughter. "So, what was the letter in your pocket. Is it okay for me to ask?"

Annie didn't say anything for a few beats. Then she reached into the pocket of the hooded sweatshirt she was wearing and pulled it out. Her name was scrawled on the envelope. *Annie.*

"Tommy?" asked Meg.

"Mm-hmm," mumbled Annie.

"What's it about? Do you want to talk about it?"

"Just what you'd think. He misses me, he loves me, he's sad, he's sorry. You know," Annie's eyes were filling.

"Annie." Meg reached out and grabbed her hand. "I do not know. This was new territory for all of us. I'm sure he does miss you, terribly. I do not doubt that he is sorry, that he is sad, and that he loves you. I miss him, and I love him."

Annie looked shocked to hear this.

"But I can't see him ever again," she said.

"Why?" asked Meg.

"Why?" said Annie, looking like Meg had just asked either the stupidest or easiest question in the world.

"Do you miss him? Do you love him?"

Annie didn't answer.

"If you are worried about me, don't be. This is not Tommy's fault. It is not your fault. Tommy was put in no-win situation between people that he loves very much. It's natural for him to want to protect his mom. But it doesn't mean he doesn't love you, or even that he doesn't love me. In fact, he tried to make it all stop. For us."

"For us?" Annie still sounded cynical.

"Just think about it."

Annie sighed. "Okay. I'll think about it. I'm heading up." Annie kissed Meg good night, and gave her an extra long hug.

"Annie."

Her daughter pulled back and looked at her. "What?"

"There is a reason that some women are older than others. We know things." Meg tapped her own forehead and winked.

Annie smiled. "Okay, Mom."

Meg smiled back.

"And Mom?"

"Hm?"

"Thank you for my new … phone."

Tommy
February 15, 2014

10:17 pm
Annie: *hey*

Tommy wasn't sure what he had done to deserve it, but he wasn't going to question it, either. She'd texted him! With any other girl, in any other lifetime, he'd have played the game, waited hours, made her wonder, picked his words carefully. But not in this lifetime, and not with this girl.

10:18 pm
Tommy: *annie i miss you so much <3*
Annie: *i have a new number*
Tommy: *i can see that*
Annie: *so i just wanted you to know*
Tommy: *annie can i see you*
Annie: *i'll see you tomorrow*

10:21 pm
Tommy: *pick me up for school*

Annie: *mooch*
Tommy: *see you in the driveway :)*
Annie: *see you in the driveway*

10:23 pm
Annie: *thomas*
Tommy: *hey* :)
Annie: *i miss you too <3*
Tommy: happy valentine's day yesterday.
Annie: you too yesterday xo

He set his alarm for five minutes earlier than usual, so he had time in the morning to gather some things from the hall closet.

"What are you hunting for in there?" called his mom from the kitchen.

"Just my ski stuff, in case my friends go later," he answered from inside the closet.

When Annie pulled into the driveway, he slid into his seat, kissed her on the cheek, and handed her the stack of postcards and letters.

"What's this?" she asked.

"I'm not sure it will mean anything," he said. "But maybe it will help."

Elise
October 2014

She could never have imagined a day when she would feel nervous, sitting in this booth, waiting for Meg. Elise had wanted to stop at the Crooked Nook to pick up a small gift—a bestseller, beautiful notecards—but she was afraid, not knowing what Kate or Piper might think or say. Instead, she swung by the florist and hand picked a spring bouquet, all blues and lavenders, tied with organza ribbons. Elise tried several times to write a note to accompany the flowers, but at this point, there was nothing left to be said. She ripped up the card and threw it away.

Far too soon after the events of winter, Elise had attempted to apologize.

December 20, 2013
Meg's Voicemail
Meg, it's me. I mean, it's Elise. You probably know that. God, I don't know what to say. What can I say? I am so, so sorry. I know you don't want to talk to me now. Maybe not ever, but I love you and I miss you and I never

meant to hurt you. Oh my God, I would never hurt you. I'm here when
you're ready. I hope you're okay. Please call me.

Elise left four or five voicemails a week on Meg's landline, all of
which went unanswered. Sarah had warned her that one possible repercus-
sion was Meg's complete rejection.

"But she did care enough to have you come check on me,
remember?" Elise's eyes were pleading with Sarah as they talked during a
"casual counseling session" (as Elise liked to call them) but Sarah constantly
reminded there that they were really just conversations.

"Elise, you're my family. You know I can't be your therapist," Sarah
would say as they sipped coffee at Starbucks.

"I know, I know. But you were there, so you know. I promise I'll get
a real therapist, too."

Sarah laughed. "Yes, by all means. Get a real therapist."

. Elise recalled how stunned she had been that Meg held any interest
in Elise's well-being; everything had just blown-up, and Elise was to blame.

"I remember," said Sarah. "But you need to realize that Meg hadn't
fully processed everything. She was still seeing you as her best friend. It's
hard to shut that off instantaneously."

"I am her best friend," Elise said.

"That's Meg's decision, not yours," Sarah said.

It was when she appeared on Meg's doorstep that she knew she'd
pushed too hard, gone too far. She'd been leaving her bedroom a bit more,
spending time in the family room, coffee in her kitchen. Kyle was still sleeping on the couch, but he hadn't said anything about leaving, and was driving
her to her appointments with his sister. Other than driving to Cleveland for
counseling, she hadn't really been outside. She had absolutely no reason to
think she should go to Meg's house. Sarah would have advised against it,
and Kyle would have locked her in the bedroom. Nothing was working,
though, and Elise thought that maybe, if she could look Meg in the eye, if
she could be brave and apologize for her terrible mistake, everything would

be better. "I should have called you after the very first text. I should have returned Ben's phone." Elise wanted Meg to hear the words from her mouth; she needed to speak the terrible truth and know that Meg could not delete, erase, or ignore the apology. After that, whatever Meg chose, Elise might be more able to accept.

She placed herself on Meg's doorstep, blood thundering in her veins, and rang the bell. The door was thrown open easily, obviously by someone not expecting … her.

It was Annie. Elise's eyes welled up.

"Annie … I …"

"Mom!" Annie screamed back into the house, a horrible, piercing scream. Then she whirled back to Elise, screeching. "What are you *doing* here? Oh my God, you seriously need to get out of here! Are you kidding me? " Annie was completely out of control. Her reaction forced Elise backward off the porch and onto the walkway, just as Meg appeared behind her daughter.

"Annie, what is it?" Meg looked frantic. Elise watched as Annie pointed, and Meg finally saw her.

"Annie, go inside." Meg stepped out and closed the door behind her. She stayed on the porch with her back against the front door.

"Now what? Now what did you do?"

"Meg, I only wanted … "

"You only wanted what, Elise?" Meg said, sadly.

"I came to apologize. I came to say that …"

"Elise! Enough. Please. You really have to stop." Meg turned to look back into the house. Annie was crying in the background. Elise could hear cartoons on the television. She wondered how Willie was doing.

"Meg, I miss you. I'm so sorry. What can I do?"

"Nothing."

"Nothing?"

"Nothing. Don't you see?" Meg opened her hands wide. "There is nothing."

"But … Sarah said you sent her to my house that day."

"I did."

"To check on me, to see if I was okay."

"Yes."

"So I thought … "

"You thought what? That it was all going to be fine? That we would be okay? God, Elise. I sent Sarah to make sure you weren't completely nuts. I sent Sarah to make sure you weren't going to hurt my family any more. I sent Sarah to protect myself."

Elise stared at her.

Meg turned and went inside and closed the door behind her, leaving Elise standing on the front walk.

At Sarah's advice, Elise took a break, but she didn't give up entirely. For a few months, she retreated and focused only on her own counseling and on Kyle and Tommy. Kyle moved back into their bedroom, and though he wasn't ready to be intimate, she was comforted by his presence in the bed. Tommy was slower to warm, but the fact that he was back together with Annie was certainly helping. Annie wouldn't come to their house; in fact, she wasn't allowed to come, even if she wanted to, which stung Elise.

She stopped leaving messages for Meg, and she stopped writing to her mother. And then, Elise began writing to Meg.

April 2, 2014

Dear Meg, I don't know how to start this letter except to say that I miss you so much, and I'm so sorry.

Today I had an appointment with Sarah. We talked a lot about everything, and I want you to know that while I can't take back what I did, even though I wish I could (God, I wish I could) I'm really trying to figure out what part of me would make me think that what I did was going to help you. I'm trying to figure out how I could ever make it up to you and your family. If this was a 12-step program, I would call it

"making amends." And if we were still friends, we would totally make fun of the idea of "making amends" even though that's totally inappropriate, I'm sure.

I think of you every day, and I hope you are okay. I know you are grieving and even though everything else may feel like a lie, my heart is still broken about Ben. And I only want you and Annie and Will to be okay. All of that is real. And I miss you.

Love, Elise

April 15, 2014

Dear Meg, Today at grief group (can you believe I'm finally going to grief group for my dad?) we talked about forgiveness. I have to forgive my mom for leaving —supposedly, it's holding me back. Time to let go. I thought you'd be interested, because you're one of the only people who knows all about her.

I hope everything is good with Annie's college application process. Tommy keeps her information kind of private, which I understand. I just can't believe that we've reached this stage. I miss you.

Love, Elise

April 24

Dear Meg,

I was wondering about something. Did you ever open Ben's suitcase? I'm probably overstepping, and I'm sorry, but I just happened to think about it, and remembered that we never pulled it out of the hall closet that day. If you did, I hope it wasn't too difficult for you. And I also hope that anything I did along the way hasn't made your healing even more difficult as you move forward, now knowing everything.

Even with all the terrible things that I did, I will never forget those moments that we spent going through Ben's things. It was kind of a sacred experience, wasn't it? I just want you to know that I have that memory safe, and I didn't just toss it away. It's important to me. Miss you.

Love, Elise

April 28, 2013

Dear Meg,

I'm sorry if my last letter was too much. I had an appointment with Sarah today. It's going pretty well. I only wish I had been in counseling long before this ever happened. Well, Sarah says this isn't counseling. She's looking into a therapist that will be a great fit for me. That sounds good, but also hard, but I suppose I'm due for some hard stuff.

I'm not sure I'm up for a long note today, but I just want you to know this: Please forgive me. I should have called you after the very first text. I should have returned Ben's phone. I'm sorry. Miss you.

Love, Elise.

The letters continued. She started by writing weekly, but sometimes Elise dropped a note in the mailbox twice a week, or even more, if she found something particularly interesting to share, or felt the need to express a specific apology that she felt she'd forgotten. Sometimes the notes were short, sometimes inordinately long. There were deep confessions and brief updates. Occasionally, Elise sent beautiful postcards. She sent a note on Memorial Day, and on the Fourth of July, and sometimes she simply said hello. In every note, she wrote that she was sorry. Around Halloween,,she even dared to reference an inside joke, add a bit of humor. In passing moments, it felt like a friendship, then Elise would remember.

Seven months, forty-four cards, notes, and letters.

And then came the day that she had been working toward. Elise came out of her therapist's office one morning, pulled her phone from her purse to check her texts, and saw her reward:

November 7, 2014
Meg: Missed Call & Voicemail

It was a brief message. "I'm ready to see you. Can you meet me for lunch?"

Now here she was, waiting for Meg with a lump the size of a peach pit in her throat.

Elise rearranged her jacket on the seat next to her, shifted the flowers yet again, and reached into her purse to find her lip balm.

The waitress came by. "Can I put a drink order in for you?"

Elise hesitated. "I'll have a diet Coke, please. Oh, and I'm expecting a friend."

"No problem. I'll be back in a sec."

She heard the swish of the door and looked up as Meg came in, wearing her favorite green windbreaker and carrying her pale blue tote. Elise could see that Meg had stuffed an extra sweatshirt into her bag, as usual, and an umbrella. Her blonde hair had been tossed by the windy day, and her cheeks were pink. Instead of the usual big smiles they'd once traded, the sisterly hugs and kisses, Meg made eye contact from the door, then simply approached the booth slowly before sliding in across from Elise.

"Hi," Elise said.

"Hi," Meg answered.

They stared at each other. The months had felt like years to Elise, but she could only guess how Meg had experienced the same stretch of time.

The waitress brought a diet Coke to the table and placed it in front of Elise.

"Can I get you a drink, hon?" she said to Meg.

"A diet Coke, please."

As she hurried off, Elise said, "I was going to order you one, but I just wasn't sure if I should...."

"I still love diet Coke," Meg said.

"Sorry."

"Not a big deal."

"Right."

"Are these for me?" asked Meg, glancing at the wrapped flowers.

"They are. They looked like you. And your house."

"They're perfect. Thank you."

"You're welcome."

Meg sat back against the booth with a big sigh. "Elise, I..."

Just then the waitress came by to take their lunch order. Elise saw that Meg's eyes had filled with tears, and Meg shook her head, indicating that couldn't speak. Elise should handle it.

"We'd like two turkey clubs, please, on wheat. No ham, extra avocado. One order of fries, one onion rings." She looked at Meg. "Right?"

Meg could only nod.

Elise handed the menus to the waitress. "Thank you so much."

It was becoming obvious to Elise that Meg was overwhelmed, maybe by being in their favorite place, being so close, the beautiful flowers, the same lunch. Meg's tears were dangerously close to spilling, and she sat still as a statue in the booth, yet she appeared as if she could bolt at any second.

"Meg, it's okay."

Meg shook her head, apparently still unable to do more than just that.

"I need you to know that I understand that we can't be what we were," said Elise, slowly and quietly, starting the conversation.

Meg's tears fell, as she began to speak. "I didn't know we were going to lose what we were."

Elise nodded. "I get that. I'm sorry."

"I needed you."

"I know."

"I lost you."

"I know."

"I lost Ben and then I lost you."

"I'm so sorry."

"And my kids? They lost you. They trusted you."

"Oh Meg, I know." Now Elise's tears were threatening. "There is nothing I can say. I would never hurt them. I would never hurt you. I thought I was helping." Elise covered her mouth with her hand, shaking her head. "I thought I was helping. I saw the texts were making you feel...I don't know, better? Connected? Even excited? And I guess I didn't want that to stop for you."

"But the kids?" asked Meg.

Elise shook her head. "It was a horrible decision to bring them into it. I wanted them to feel connected, probably in a way I never..."

Elise trailed off.

"What?" prodded Meg.

"I'm working on figuring out a lot. But it doesn't excuse any of it. I know that. And I'm sorry."

Meg sighed. "I don't know what to do. I don't know how to move past it."

"Maybe we don't move past it," said Elise. "Maybe you can't be my friend any more." Elise's eyes filled anew. "But I hope you'll forgive me someday.

"But I want that part of my life back," said Meg. "Everything else has changed. I want something back. And I don't know how to get there."

"Me neither," Elise said.

"Thank you for the letters," Meg said.

"You read them?" Elise said, with a tiny smile.

"I did. All of them. I was glad to hear about your therapy. It helped me decide about today. And I did open the suitcase, by the way. It was just clothes, but it was good to have them, you know?" Meg paused. "They smelled like Ben."

Elise nodded. "I worried about the suitcase later. I worried about a lot, later."

"I'll bet."

The waitress came by with their lunch, plates of sandwiches, Meg's drink, and lots of fried goodies.

For a moment, they nibbled in silence, considering.

"I brought something to show you," said Meg.

Elise looked up, questioning.

Meg reached into the tote on the seat beside her and pulled out the stack of postcards and letters, now tied up with a pretty pink ribbon.

"Are those the letters from me?"

"No. These are … these are the letters you wrote to your mother. And the postcards from your dad."

Elise looked confused. "But, where did you … why?"

"Tommy. He found them in your closet. He showed them to Annie, and then to me."

Elise was staring at the very familiar, yet out-of-context, bundle of cards in Meg's hands, which so unexpectedly had appeared at the lunch table like an uninvited guest. The envelopes had been opened.

"I'm sorry we read your letters, but Tommy thought maybe it would help us to see some sort of reason behind your actions. Not an excuse, but a reason. Those were his words, you know. He's a bright kid." Meg smiled.

"Tommy said that?"

"He did," said Meg. "He said he could feel all of the love between you and your dad in these postcards. And he saw how you wrote to your mom, all the letters she never answered." Elise flinched. "It helped him understand you a little bit better, so he thought it might help us."

"Did it?"

"It did." Meg handed the packet of correspondence to Elise. "I think this might be what you were trying to explain before about Annie and Will. And making a connection for them."

Elise caressed the edges of the cards. "Thank you," she said, looking at her friend.

"You're welcome," said Meg.

"It's good to see your face," said Elise.

"Yours too," said Meg.

"I'm sorry."

"I know."

"Are you okay?" asked Elise.

"I'm doing better. I have sad days, but I have some good days, too."

Elise nodded. "I'm glad. You must miss him so much. Meg, I know I have no right to say this, but I really miss Ben. We all do, so much."

"I believe you."

Elise looked physically relieved. "I just wanted you to know."

"Are you okay, Elise?" Meg asked.

"I'm getting there. This, I mean, today? It's helping."

Meg nodded in silent understanding.

The women sat facing each other in the booth, contemplating what was next.

Elise squirted a puddle of ketchup for the remaining fries, and Meg took a long swig of the diet Coke.

The jingle of the restaurant door caused them both to look.

"Mom! It was Annie, with Lizzie. Both had backpacks slung on their slight shoulders. Annie looked happy, and Elise was glad to see her smiling face. As Annie approached the booth, she saw Elise, and froze.

"Mom?" Annie looked from one woman to the other, confused.

"It's all right, Annie," Meg said, "we're having lunch."

"Lunch."

"We are, too, right Annie?" Lizzie said, putting her arm around her best friend, squeezing. "Hi, Mrs. McAfee. Hey, Mrs. Parker. We're just grabbing a burger on senior lunch period."

"That sounds fun," Elise said.

"Do you want to join us?" Meg asked, beginning to scoot over in the booth.

Lizzie glanced at Annie before answering.

"Um, I think we'll just grab a seat at the counter if that's okay. We won't be here long."

Meg pulled out a twenty-dollar bill. "Here, girls. Lunch on me."

Annie bent down to give her mom a hug. Meg whispered something, and hugged her daughter tightly.

"Thanks, Mrs. McAfee," said Lizzie, as the girls turned toward the lunch counter.

"Bye, girls. Have a good day," said Elise

Annie turned back, with a small wave. "You have a good day, too, Aunt Elise."

The teenagers locked arms, and Elise looked at Meg incredulously.

"What did you say to her?"

"I reminded her that I'm the older woman who's been through some stuff."

Elise nodded, not quite understanding the comment, but feeling grateful for every small kindness.

The afternoon had teetered between how it had once been, and what might lie ahead, but his particular moment was bursting with potential.

EPILOGUE
November 2014

She turned out the light at the bottom of the back staircase and walked toward her bedroom, picking up shoes, tidying piles of books and papers, and fluffing throw pillows along the way. Her cookbooks and magazines were spread on the counter—she loved pulling out her fall recipes in anticipation of Thanksgiving. Meg glanced out the window toward the lake — a few lights bounced on the snow. Hopefully, it would snow even more before the holiday.

In her bathroom, she washed her face and put on her coziest pajamas. Meg was aware that it had been a long while since she had felt peaceful in her own space, and she was suddenly most aware of her bare feet on the ceramic tiles she and Ben had picked out so carefully. Cold, her feet were cold, but she felt something else. Solid. Her feet felt solid on the floor.

As she padded past the shower, she saw her bathrobe hanging on the hook, its pocket seeming stretched and empty. She would buy a new robe.

Meg closed the bedroom drapes and crawled into the center of the bed, pulling the covers up to her chin. Her new phone was on her nightstand, charging. She had carefully set the "do not disturb" feature, so she could no longer receive calls or texts during the night. Anyone who might truly need her was either sleeping in a bedroom upstairs or could call her on the landline.

She rolled onto her side and saw Ben's phone, charging on his nightstand.

"Ben," she whispered.

She knew that she had grieving left to do, that Elise had essentially stolen that time, putting Meg's grief on hold by allowing her to cling to a fantasy. Still, in reflection, Meg felt she had been given an accidental gift. The chance to ease into her sorrow. The very idea that maybe, just maybe, her reality wasn't what it had seemed, had allowed Meg to slowly wade into her new life without Ben, and for that, she was oddly thankful. No matter what Elise's intention, Meg had more strength than before and felt prepared to face any unexpected aftershocks.

She reached back to her own side of the bed and took her phone off the charging cord. There, in the dark, Meg slowly and deliberately scrolled to his name.

The text screen popped up in the dark, she typed two words.

Meg pressed SEND and turned to watch Ben's phone. She heard a chime, saw the light. She put her phone back on the nightstand, curled up in her favorite position, patted Ben's pillow, and closed her eyes.

Made in the USA
Middletown, DE
23 December 2018